TOTALLY DEVOTED

⌒⌒⌒⌒

BY

E. M. BANNOCK

E. M. Bannock

ISBN: 1490919708

ISBN 13: 9781490919706

Library of Congress Control Number: 2013912508

CreateSpace Independent Publishing Platform

North Charleston, South Carolina

To Keith and Annette,
My Wil and Maddy

CHAPTER ONE

"Return your tray tables and seat backs to their upright and locked position..."

Marie had heard the flight attendant's announcement so many times before she knew it by heart. How many times had she seen this scene repeated? She looked out the window. The names of the cities were different, but they always came into view the same way.

She could see tiny cars, with tiny lights, playing follow-the-leader along a narrow highway. The cars were so small they looked like ants with headlights. Miniature cities, with their toy-like houses and wee, glowing streetlights, grew larger and brighter with every minute as the plane continued its gradual decent to the runway.

She opened her appointment calendar one more time to review her schedule for the upcoming week. A bold, black "April 1998" in large print dominated the top of the page. She couldn't believe it was 1998 already. It seemed as though the last ten years were just a fuzzy, tiring blur.

No wonder she was sick of her project-management job. She wondered how many more flights she would have to take. How many more times would she have to endure the torture of business travel—crying babies, smelly passengers in the seats next to her, plastic dinner trays with plastic food, people that wouldn't shut up, and hours wasted in airports? How many more prayers of thanks would she have to pray when the giant bird finally touched down safely?

"One of these days...one of these days," she thought to herself, "I won't ever have to fly again unless I want to."

Life had not been easy for Marie Trousdale, not ever. She was the eldest girl in a family of five girls. There was a five-year difference between her and daughter number two. Her four little sisters had been born within a year or two of each other. Her mother and father had done their best, but life had always been a struggle. Her mother was never what you would call healthy. It had been up to Marie to care for both her mother and her little sisters. Her parents were very "old-world," which meant that the oldest daughter did most of the housework. She couldn't wait to graduate from high school and go off to college. She struggled through one year of college while working part time as a receptionist at a busy medical clinic. That was where she met Charles.

He was a young, attractive, ambitious doctor just out of medical school. Charles had been at the clinic for about six months before Marie started there. His dreamy blue eyes, handsome face, soft smile, and shy nature had made him the mysterious heart throb of many women he came in contact with. The nurses and clerical staff were constantly competing for his attention, though none of them succeeded. His demeanor was always unattached and aloof.

On Marie's second day, she and Charles arrived at the clinic at the same time. They had parked at different ends of the parking lot but arrived at the staff entry door at the same time. Marie was mentally going over her new job duties in her head and, as was her custom, looking down at the ground while she walked. Charles was deep in thought about a new patient he had seen the day before who had an ailment he could not diagnose, and it bothered him. Neither one was paying attention when they put their hands on the doorknob at the same time. She felt a flush of embarrassment and a surprising comfort in the warmth and softness of his hand as it encircled hers. He hesitated and didn't remove his hand before she looked up.

Immediately, she was lost in the vastness of his hypnotic eyes. "Why do the guys always get the long eyelashes?" she thought as an inviting and slightly seductive smile came across his face. He looked down at her, making no effort to remove his hand; in fact, she felt his grip tighten slightly. She had been introduced to Dr. Charles Trousdale yesterday, as part of her first-day initiation at the clinic. She, too, had been taken by his looks when she saw him from afar. But at their introduction, he had seemed disinterested and distracted, glancing up only briefly from the file he was reading as she was rushed down the hall to the next doctor's office.

"Marie, right?" he said, bringing her out of her trance. He made no effort to remove his hand from hers.

"He remembered my name!" She flushed red at the thought and smiled up at him. "Dr. Trousdale, isn't it?" she said, hoping he couldn't see her heart beating wildly through her blouse.

"Charles, please," he said. "I'm sorry. I guess I was preoccupied. I didn't see you coming."

"It's OK," she said, looking up. "I should have been watching where I was going." Inside, she was still mesmerized by his eyes and hoping he didn't notice that she was turning into jelly. She could feel the heat of her blush growing.

"Allow me," he said as he gently removed her hand from the doorknob and opened the door for her.

They kept bumping into each other all day, and at the end of the day, Charles convinced her that it was a sign that they should have dinner together and get to know each other better. Marie thought the "accidental meetings" weren't so accidental, but she was drawn to him as she had never been drawn to anyone before. Was it his good looks, his comforting voice, or those eyes? She could lose herself in them forever; they were deep, clear, mysterious, and sexy. The other women in the office had said that he never showed interest in going out with anyone from the clinic before, so Marie felt relatively sure his invitation was sincere and she would be safe with him. She accepted his invitation.

That night they had an elegant dinner at an upscale, riverfront restaurant in downtown Detroit. Charles picked her up in a late-model Grand Prix. Not too prestigious, but then again, he was just starting out. He was quiet; she was shy. But there was something—something unspoken yet special. She felt very at ease with him, and he seemed comfortable with her. Every time their eyes met, there was a sizzling, sensuous connection. Every time they touched, Marie felt an unexpected but exciting electricity charge through her. She felt a longing, a need for this man whom she barely knew. She knew enough. She knew she loved him.

They had only kissed that first night, but it was magical to Marie. He had walked her to the door of her apartment. She had paused for a moment, not wanting the evening to end, enjoying just being in his company.

"I had a nice time," he said, looking deep into her eyes. "I like you. I like being around you. I'd like to spend more time with you."

"Me, too," was the only thing she could say, not believing what this gorgeous man was saying to her. She wanted to tell him how he made her skin tingle, her heart race, and her body ache, but she didn't want to appear too bold with a man she just met.

He put his arm around her and pulled her close to him. She went willingly and lifted her head up to meet the kiss she hoped was coming. His lips were firm on hers as he encompassed her mouth, sucking in her sweetness, tasting her longing. She met his eager mouth and felt his ardor. Charles suddenly pulled away and stared at her.

"I think I better go," he said, perspiration beginning to glisten on his forehead. She smiled inwardly. "Let's do this again, Marie," he said as he adjusted his coat. And it began.

The night he proposed, he confessed that he felt the connection the first night as well. He knew from the moment his hand touched hers at the door, from that first look into her eyes, that he needed her, desired her, and loved her. He explained that he had never spent much time thinking about a girlfriend while concentrating on becoming a doctor. He was no virgin. He had his share of high-school sweethearts and college escapades but nothing serious. That was how he had wanted it. As a rule, he never dated co-workers. But she was different. Something inside him had changed, and he knew he was in love. She was the one, and now was the time.

They were married six months after their first date. Charles took a job in northern California, where they moved. Three months after that, she was pregnant. Their beautiful son, Andy, was born nine months later. Charles could support them all on his salary. So, after Andy's birth, she dropped out of school, quit working, and became a full-time wife and mother. Those were happy times. They were the only happy times she could remember now, watching her young son grow and loving and being loved by Charles. She felt truly blessed.

And then, in a blink of an eye, it all ended. Charles had enjoyed his Saturday-morning outings with little Andy. It gave him a chance to have "Daddy time" with his son and gave Marie a chance to relax. Sometimes the boys would go to the park. Sometimes they would go to the beach. But they always stopped for ice cream on the way home. That was Andy's favorite part. Marie's precious little boy would always be sticky and covered with chocolate when they returned, and he would be grinning a sweet, little chocolate smile from ear to ear.

One Saturday, two weeks after Andy's third birthday, everything changed forever. Andy and Charles didn't come home. They would never come home again. No one knew why the driver of the other car was so drunk at one o'clock in the afternoon. No one could ask him, because he died, too. The doctors said that Charles and Andy never knew what hit them. Their car was crushed beyond recognition when the drunk driver hit their car on the driver's side and smashed it into the side of the mountain. But Marie knew what hit them. She lived with the memory of having to identify their bodies that bright, sunny California afternoon. It still pained her to think of it, like a hot sword searing through her heart, whenever she pictured Andy's poor little body, all black, burned, and twisted. Then there was her beautiful, noble Charles, all bloody and torn. His handsome face was cut to shreds from broken glass. This was the man she had planned to raise a family with, the man she promised to have and to hold, until death do us part, the man who had become her world, her life.

Charles had some life insurance but not enough for her to live on for the rest of her life. She knew she would have to invest the insurance money and get a job if she wanted to retire at an early age. Hell, if she ever wanted to retire at all. So she sold their house and bought a small duplex. She got a menial job and went to night school. Being so busy kept her mind off thoughts of Charles and Andy. The rent from the other half of the duplex was enough to cover the mortgage. She was lucky enough to find good tenants. In a few years, she was able to graduate and get a real job.

A real job—that was a laugh. Is that what you called it when you traveled three weeks out of every month? When you woke up in the middle of the night and forgot where you were? Or worse, when you woke up at home and thought you were at a hotel. At least she worked independently and didn't have to deal with office politics or have the boss breathing down her neck every second of the day. She was a project manager for a large consulting firm. A college professor had recommended her for the job. It wasn't a hard job. She was good at it. But sometimes the travel just got to be too much.

Oh, there were perks. There were the frequent-flyer miles that were piling up. She could go anywhere for free. What a thought! Her idea of a vacation was staying home. Every once in a while, her travel took her to Detroit, her hometown. She had lived in California now for over ten years, so she didn't get much of a chance to see her family. Whenever she visited east coast clients, she always managed to spend the weekend at her sister's house, her favorite sister, Madelyn.

This was one of those trips. Detroit stretched out beyond the horizon as the plane got closer and closer to the ground, a myriad of twinkling lights. It was dusk, but she could still see the Detroit River and the downtown area. She saw the Ambassador Bridge as it stretched across the river, joining Detroit and Windsor, Canada. She could see the Ford Rouge plant on the Rouge River. Her grandfather had worked there years ago making cars, like most men in the early 1900s. Many of her relatives still worked in the auto industry in one form or another. It was Detroit, the Motor City.

It was past eight when she pulled the rental car into her sister's suburban driveway with the mailbox that read "McBain." The motion-sensing lights announced her arrival. Within minutes, she was hugging her sister and was grateful for her brother-in-law, Jake, who was hauling her heavy suitcase out of the car and into the guest bedroom.

"You look beat," her sister Madelyn observed. "You hungry? I made one of your favorites, Shepherd Pie."

"Do I really look that bad?" Marie quipped, adjusting her hair. "And, yes, I'm starving for some real food. But first, where's that baby?"

Just then, three-year-old Justin raced around the corner of the living room. "Auntie Ree, Auntie Ree," he squealed as he leaped up into her arms and planted a sweet, little kiss on her cheek.

Marie squeezed him tightly as flashes of Andy raced through her mind. "You're growing like a weed, my boy," she said as she tickled his little tummy. "Who's your favorite auntie?"

"Auntie Ree," he announced loudly between laughs.

"That's right. And don't forget it," she said, gently putting the boy down. He immediately took off running and disappeared around the same corner he'd come from.

Dinner was a simple but delicious affair, a tasty garden salad, steamed Swiss chard, and vegetarian Shepherd Pie.

"So, what's new around Motown?" Marie asked as they sat around the table.

"Well," Madelyn said solemnly as she exchanged glances with her husband. "I might as well tell you now, since you're going to find out sooner or later." She paused for a moment. Marie's face grew serious, expecting the worst. "Naomi is pregnant. We found out at bowling last Saturday. Tommy was buying everyone beer and toasting the occasion. And, get this, his toast was, 'No more damn girls.'"

"Well," Marie said, "I'm not surprised. We knew it would happen sooner or later. That fucking bastard! What does he mean 'no more damn girls'? Katie and Tommie are the most beautiful girls anyone could ever want. Shelly is probably turning in her grave right now. What is he going to name it if it's a boy? He can't very well name him Thomas. That would be cute, wouldn't it?" Changing her voice into a mock masculine imitation, she said, "And these are my children, Katie, Tommie, and Tommy."

Everyone laughed.

Then they all fell silent as if on cue. Marie was thinking about their deceased sister, Shelly. She could tell by the expression on Madelyn's face that she was thinking about her, too. It had been barely two years since Shelly died of breast cancer. She had fought a brave but brief fight against the terrible disease. Although no one had expected her to pull through, her death was a terrible blow to the family. Their mother had fallen into a deep depression that still surrounded her like a heavy blanket.

Six months before Shelly was told she had cancer, she had found out that her husband, Tommy, was having an affair with Naomi, a woman from work. When Shelly confronted Tommy, he swore he would break it off with her. Shelly gave him a chance, but she later found out that he never did. She had spoken to Marie and Madelyn about it several times. Shelly had decided to divorce Tommy, but before she could start the proceedings, she found out about the cancer and never went through with it.

Shelly went through all the terrible, painful cancer treatments without success for fifteen months before the monstrous disease claimed its victory. Madelyn was with her through it all. It was Madelyn who had taken her for the chemotherapy treatments and to the hundreds of doctor's appointments. Tommy was always too busy. Madelyn had taken Shelly to the hospital every time she had a setback. It was Madelyn, not Tommy, who took her to the hospital the day before she died. It had taken three calls to Tommy that day to finally convince him that Shelly was going to die this time and if he ever wanted to see her alive again, he had better gather the girls and get to the hospital immediately. The bastard was never there for her, and Madelyn and Marie hated him for it.

It was barely four months after Shelly's death when Naomi moved in with Tommy and the girls. It was a slap in the face that Marie couldn't take sitting down. She had written a letter to Tommy and Naomi telling them that Shelly was not stupid and neither were her sisters. In the letter, she told them that Shelly was going to divorce Tommy before she knew about the cancer. The family knew all about Naomi and Tommy's affair, and it insulted them to be lied to.

Before the letter, Tommy had always denied that Naomi was the other woman. The letter also said that she knew Tommy was trying to keep the girls away from Shelly's family and that he was not being fair to the girls or the family. The family had nothing but love for the little girls and would never hurt them or tell them the truth. She told Tommy and Naomi that what they did in their lives was something they had to live with, and she was not judging them. She just wanted the lies to end and wished them luck and happiness. Talk about lies…What she really wanted to say was "Burn in hell, you assholes!" But she didn't.

Ever since she wrote the letter, Marie had been banished from visiting her nieces at their home. The only time she saw them was when Madelyn was able to snatch them away for a weekend when Marie was scheduled to be in Detroit. And this was only after months of planning and obtaining the proper approvals from Thomas (as Naomi called him) and Naomi.

Marie broke the silence that shrouded the table. "So, what do the girls think about this?"

"Tommie is happy about it. Katie hates the idea of another baby in the house," her sister said.

"All right," Marie laughed. "Shelly would be proud of her. She never wanted Tommy to marry that bitch anyway. Katie knows that Naomi is not her real mother and isn't looking for a replacement. Maybe subconsciously, Shelly implanted a deep-rooted hate for the woman in Katie."

"I wouldn't be surprised," replied Madelyn. "Katie is one of us."

"Well, like I've said, we just need to keep cool about the situation. One day, when the girls are older, they are going to want to know about their real mother, and we need to be there for them," Marie said.

Madelyn almost choked on her food. "You're a fine one to talk about keeping your cool! Who wrote the scathing letter calling them liars?"

"Well," Marie said, blushing slightly. "I just couldn't stand it anymore. I knew how hard it was for you to see those two together, knowing the truth and having him lie to your face."

"I've got to hand it to you, Marie," Jake chimed in. "At least you had the balls to do something about it. You know, ever since you sent the letter, it *has* been easier for us to see the girls."

"There, you see?" Marie said. "Then it did some good."

"Not for you," said Madelyn. "Tommy won't even let you in his house. You know, I heard that Naomi comes from a Mafia family. You better watch your back; she might put a contract out on you."

"She wouldn't dare. They frown on home wreckers. Besides, I have my own connections. And, as your big sister, I willingly sacrificed my house privileges to help the family get access to the girls,"

Marie told them. "Who cares anyway? The less I see of that bastard and his tramp, the better. The only thing I want is to see the girls."

"You know," Madelyn said. "He told me that he was going to tell the girls about his affair with Naomi when they got older."

"Oh yeah? What version? His?" Marie was getting hot now. "I can just imagine how sugarcoated that will be. He'll make it sound like Shelly was the bitch and forced him into the arms of another woman."

"Settle down now," Madelyn said soothingly. "It's like you said. We need to be there for the girls, so we can tell them the real story after Tommy tells them his fairy tale. Enough about that. What about you? You look like you could use a vacation, really." The concern on Madelyn's face was genuine.

Marie shrugged her shoulders. "I don't know. This traveling thing is really starting to get to me. Don't get me wrong; I love being able to come and see you two and being here to see Justin grow. It's just...well, you know...tiring."

"So," her sister replied. "What are you going to do about it?"

"I don't know. What can I do? I've got to eat."

"Don't you still have that property in Oregon that Charles inherited?" Madelyn asked. "Why don't you take some time off and go there? You and Charles used to love Oregon."

"Yeah, but it's raw land. There's nothing on it," she protested. "I'd have to camp, and I haven't done that since Charles died."

"Well," her sister said. "Just a thought."

"You ought to consider what your sister is saying," Jake said. "She *is* right. You need to rest up. We're only telling you because we love you, and we're concerned. You haven't allowed yourself to live a normal life since the accident. And besides that, this job is killing you. Find a man; spend a lustful week in the woods. Get laid. It'll do you good."

"Jake!" Madelyn scolded. "Don't be so crude!"

"It's OK, Maddy. I know you're both right," Marie said. "And I love you both, too. I'll think about it...about the camping that is."

And she did. That night she thought about the last time she was on the Oregon property. It was Andy's second summer. They had camped out for two weeks. It was as if the rest of the world did not exist. Charles had inherited the land when his grandmother died, and Marie inherited it when Charles died. She had thought about selling it after the funeral but just couldn't. It had too much of Charles on it. He had loved that land so much. She had loved it from the first time Charles took her there, right after they moved to California. What was not to love? It had green trees, running creeks, wildlife, and privacy. They had planned to build a small home on it and retire there someday.

The property was 150 secluded, wooded acres of southern Oregon's finest land. Two crystal clear creeks ran through it. Sometimes Charles would catch fish early in the morning, and Marie would fry them up for breakfast. They woke with the sun and spent the days hiking, exploring, or just lazing around the campsite without a care in the world. At night, the sky was ablaze with stars. When the moon was full, they didn't even need a flashlight to see. It was so bright. But that was long ago. It seemed like another lifetime now, a life full of laughter and love.

"I could never love another man like I love Charles," she said to herself as she lay in the bed in her sister's spare bedroom. "There is no other man like Charles and never will be. No one could ever set my body on fire and consume me in love and passion like him. And I could never have another gift as precious as my sweet Andy."

She felt cheated. Was her life always going to be like this? Would she always feel the crushing pain of lost love? Could she ever love again? She felt like she had aged a lifetime. Would she ever feel happiness again? Would she ever again feel the touch of a man who lusted after her? Would she ever feel the comfort of a home to call her own and find a beloved to grow old and gray with? What was she going to do with the rest of her life? She thought of this all too often these days. She yawned and realized that she was tired and didn't want to think about it now. She tried to clear her mind, to no avail.

Tears welled up in her eyes as she dwelled on her lonely life. Memories of Charles and Andy continued to rush through her sleepy head. It had been ten years, but the hurt was as fresh and painful as if it had happened yesterday. Finally, fatigue overtook her, and she faded into a restless sleep.

CHAPTER TWO

—⚍—

MARIE HAD ONLY BEEN GONE FOR EIGHT DAYS, but the mail practically filled a grocery bag. Almost all of it was junk mail. Cindy, the girl who rented the other half of the duplex, was gracious enough to collect the mail and water the plants whenever Marie traveled.

Marie had just showered and rid herself of what she called the "road dirt." After wrapping herself up in an oversized robe and slipping into her blue fuzzy slippers, she fixed herself a soothing mug of hot herbal tea in her favorite giant Pendleton mug. Resting the mug on the table next to her, she began to sort through the mail.

"Junk, junk, junk, bill, junk, junk," she said as she tossed the junk mail, unopened, into the trash, and began a pile of bills to be paid later.

"This looks important," she said as if speaking to an imaginary friend. The envelope looked legal, thick, and sterile. The return address was city hall. Upon opening it, she couldn't believe her eyes. The city had rezoned the block her little duplex was on and was in the process of buying all the residential properties to be "upgraded" to a commercial development. They were going to build a shopping center where her house was.

Just what she needed...when did all of this happen? They couldn't just kick her out, could they? She read on. Apparently there had been several council meetings to discuss the development. Maybe if she was ever home long enough to read the local paper or watch the local news, she would have known. She seemed to remember getting something in the mail about this about a year ago. At the time, she had thought it was junk mail and had thrown it away without a second glance. "Well, what's done is done now," she thought. "Time to develop plan *B*."

Cindy took the news well when Marie broke it to her the next day. She told Marie that she had been planning to move in with her boyfriend anyway, so it would work out fine for her. She would stay until the end, of course, so Marie wouldn't be stuck without a tenant. She wasn't in that big a hurry to move. She said she wanted to enjoy her independence a little longer. And, of course, she *had* been watching the local news and reading the local paper, so it wasn't a surprise to her at all.

According to the letter from city hall, Marie would be paid fair market value for the duplex and had six months to move. She did some quick math in her head and realized that she had until the beginning of November. Where would she go? What could she do? Well, at least she could live anywhere with the job she had. Maybe it was time to move to Oregon. For the last ten years, she had gone nowhere and done nothing but work, and her bank account was quite substantial. She was sure she had enough to build a small cabin on the property. It would be a peaceful weekend reprieve after her hectic workweek. She was on the road three weeks out of every month anyway. It was worth a shot.

She decided to take two weeks off and fly to Oregon. If she wanted to get a house built in six months, she would have to line up a contractor—and quick. It was time to cash in some of those frequent flyer miles.

Oregon was as beautiful as ever. It was a forty-five-minute drive to Grants Pass from the airport in Medford, but Marie didn't mind. The trees and mountains seemed to welcome her. She felt a sense of serenity that she hadn't felt in years. It felt good. This was going to be a good move.

Memories of good times with Charles came flooding back. Funny, they didn't make her sad. They made her feel safe and warm. Was it fate that brought her back here? Was Charles watching over her and guiding her here?

After checking into the hotel and unpacking, she made some inquiries at the front desk and got the name of a contractor that everyone said she could trust. They said he was kind of a loner and a bit strange, but he built good homes, and he was reasonably priced. It all sounded good until she found out where he conducted most of his business transactions, the Wonder Bur. The locals called it the Blur. Marie was surprised the place was still around. She remembered it as a little hole-in-the-wall bar where the drinks were stiff and cheap. It was the locals' bar. There wasn't much ambiance, so it held no attraction for tourists.

She took a deep breath of fresh air before opening the door to the Blur and walking inside. It was just as she remembered it, small, dark, smoky, and loud. Twangy county music blared out of a jukebox. The smell of beer and cigarettes always disgusted her, but she figured what the heck; she needed to line up a contractor. It was just the initial meeting and shouldn't take long.

From the description she was given by the hotel desk clerk, she figured she wouldn't have much trouble finding the guy—grungy black cowboy hat, well-worn cowboy boots, scruffy beard, jean jacket, and Levi's, sitting at the corner table. She was right. He wasn't hard to spot. It was Monday night, and there were only a handful of people in the place. There he was, sitting at his regular corner table, with his back to the wall, his chair up on two legs, and his feet propped up and crossed on the chair next to him. There was a glass of beer and a half-empty pitcher in front of him. She wondered how many pitchers he had drained before this one. The desk clerk said he had a lot of funny habits. The clerk said the guy always sat with his back to the wall, so no one could get the jump on him. He probably watched too many John Wayne movies.

"Mr. Townsend?" she asked as she held out her hand in friendship.

He peeked up at her from under the rim of his hat, turning his head slightly. "Who wants to know?" he grumbled in a low tone.

He made no motion to shake her hand, so she put it down, a little embarrassed and perturbed at his attitude. "Great," she thought. "If this dude is a drunk, this is going to be a short conversation."

She gave it one more try. "Mr. Townsend, my name is Marie Trousdale. I own some property out toward Selma and was wondering if I could contract you to build a small cabin up there for me."

"Selma, huh? That's a long drive from here. It'll cost you extra for traveling time," he muttered.

"What's with this guy?" she thought. "Doesn't he want the work?" She spoke to him again. "Well, I'd like to talk to you about it, if that's OK?"

"Suit yourself," he said as he pulled his legs down from the chair and kicked it out for her with his boot. "Wanna beer?"

"No, thank you. I don't drink beer," she said as she sat down.

"Humph," he said, sounding displeased. "You from California, I suppose."

"Well, yes, but…"

"Figured." He paused for a minute as he gave her the once-over. Marie did the same and noticed that although the room was dimly lit, she could see that he was younger than she had imagined.

"Girl, you stick out like a sore thumb round here," he observed.

She looked down at her clothes. In her world, they were considered business casual, a silk blouse and scarf, tailored khaki slacks, and low-heeled pumps. Glancing around the room, she noticed that the proper attire consisted of flannel shirts, jeans, and cowboy hats and boots, whether you were male or female.

She had heard enough. "This guy is a jerk," she thought. It was dark, and Marie wished she could get a better look at this guy. He seemed awfully critical of her; maybe she could return the favor. It was time to set the ground rules.

"Look," she said sternly. "I didn't come here to get insulted. Do you want to build my house or not?"

"Feisty, too," he said with a laugh. "Don't get your knickers in a knot. I'll build your house. Where's your husband? Or do you wear the pants in the family?"

"He's dead!" She said it so loudly she surprised herself. The bar became quiet. The few people in there all turned and stared at her.

The contractor almost flew out of his chair as he stood up, and it came down with a thud. "Hey, I'm sorry," he said in a low tone. "Didn't mean to get personal. Just don't usually deal with the missus."

"Now I've got his attention," she thought smugly. "Well, I'm afraid if you build my house, you'll have to deal with me," she said with force.

He pushed his hat back. For the first time, she was able to see his face clearly. He was probably in his late thirties, about her age. He was taller than she expected, too. She had to look up to see his now dimly lit face. He actually was kind of handsome, in a rugged, mountain man kind of way. Nice build, slender hips, broad shoulders, he must work out. Then she thought better of that; he didn't look like the gym type. It must just be the hard work. She could barely see his mystifying, dark, piercing eyes, but she detected sadness in them. "I wonder what cruel joke life has played on this guy to make him so cynical," she thought.

"Fair enough," he said. He reseated himself next to her. "Now just what did you have in mind, little lady?"

"That's better," she thought. "Well, Mr. Townsend—"

"Wil," he interrupted.

"Pardon?"

"Wil, my name is Wil. Makes me nervous when people call me Mr. Townsend. Makes me think I'm in trouble."

"Oh, OK," she continued. "Wil, what I want is just a small two-bedroom cabin, nothing fancy, very rustic. Maybe a barn for a couple of horses."

"I see. And what do you intend to do up there in Selma all by yourself, Mrs. Trousdale, once I build you your little two-bedroom cabin?" he said with a slightly sarcastic tone. "Ain't good for a woman to live alone that far from town."

"Marie," she said.

"What?"

"My name is Marie. Makes me feel old when people call me missus."

"Touché," he said with a crooked smile.

Marie detected a twinkle in his eyes and couldn't help but notice how his face softened when he smiled. She wondered why he didn't do it more often.

"OK…Marie, what are you? Some kind of rich widow lady? Building out there ain't cheap," he continued.

"Not at all," she explained. "My husband died ten years ago in a car accident. I work, and I've saved up some money since then. The property was his. He inherited it from his grandmother years ago. Just how expensive do you figure it will be?"

"That depends on a lot of things," he said. "Got power out there?"

"No."

"Got a well dug yet?"

"No."

"Got a septic tank?"

"No."

He looked up at her with squinting eyes. "Then call me when you do."

She was losing her patience with this guy, handsome or not. "Look Mr....Wil, the city just decided they want to put a shopping center where my house is. I have six months to get another place to live. I travel with my job three weeks out of four. I'm only here for two weeks. I need someone who can do everything for me. I was hoping it would be you. You come highly recommended. I guess I was wrong. I'm sorry I wasted your time. I wish I could say it was a pleasure meeting you."

She had gotten up and turned to walk toward the door when she felt his strong grip on her arm. She was surprised at his strength.

"Hold on there, ma'am," he said apologetically. "I didn't say I couldn't do it. Just wanted to find out where you were at, that's all. Sit down; let's talk."

She hesitated for a moment, looking down at his hand, which still gripped her arm. He let go. "Please," he added.

They talked for two hours about house plans, permits, timetables, and money. She was pleased to find out that she had more than enough money to build the cabin and barn. Wil convinced her that she should build small living quarters in the barn, in case she wanted to hire a man to help her tend to the place, especially if she intended to buy horses and continue to travel.

Marie felt invigorated after their talk. It was close to midnight, and she had been up since five o'clock that morning, but she didn't feel tired at all. They had decided to hook up in the morning and drive out to the property. She could barely sleep that night; she was so excited. She hadn't felt this alive in years. "Thank you, Charles," she whispered as she finally drifted off to sleep.

The morning blossomed with sunshine and dewy moistness. Marie woke up feeling refreshed and revitalized. On her way to the restaurant to meet Wil, she stopped at a grocery store and loaded up on water, juice, and some snacks to sustain them until they could get back to town.

When she got to the tiny cafe, Wil was already seated at a corner table in the back. He motioned her to come in and sit down. As she got closer, their eyes met. She found she couldn't look away. He really was a good-looking guy. He still had the five-o'clock-shadow thing going on, but it made him look even more appealing in a rugged sort of way. She wondered what he would look like without his cowboy hat and shirt. Did he have a hairy chest? A strange feeling came over her as she caught herself thinking such lewd thoughts about a man she knew nothing about and was just about to hire.

"Want some breakfast?" he asked, as a pink-clad waitress set down a plate in front of him.

Marie looked down at it, hashbrowns, bacon, and sunny-side-up eggs floating in grease, accompanied by two pieces of white-bread toast with several globs of butter.

She looked at the plate as if it were a plate full of death. "Just tea, please," she said to the waitress.

"How's your cholesterol?" she asked him.

He tilted his head to the side and looked up. He raised one eyebrow and looked her straight in the eye. "What's that?" he asked with a half smile. Not waiting for an answer, he continued to munch on a piece of bacon. "Ah-h. Breakfast of champions," he said after he swallowed and washed it down with a sip of black coffee that looked as thick as mud.

The waitress came back with a little silver teapot filled with hot water, a cup, and two tea bags, Lipton's, and put them on the table in front of Marie.

"Excuse me; do you have any herbal tea?" Marie asked before the waitress could get away.

The waitress and Wil exchanged glances. She looked at Marie over the edge of her horn-rimmed glasses and said, "Sure, honey. Be back in a sec."

Wil looked straight at Marie and said, "Remember what I said last night about sticking out like a sore thumb? If you're gonna live round here, you better try to blend in."

Marie looked right back at him and said, "I'm a vegetarian, and I don't drink caffeine. They better get used to it."

"Well," he said, rolling his eyes. "I can see we ain't gonna be sharing too many tables for two around here."

She detected a smile creeping around the edges of his mouth and a softening in his deep, hypnotic eyes. The strange, tingling sensation she got from his look took her by surprise. She was finding herself attracted to this guy, in a crude sort of way. She caught herself and wondered, "What am I thinking?"

They decided to take Wil's truck to the property. One look at the little rental car that Marie was driving had convinced him that the truck was the better choice. It didn't take much to convince Marie. Silently, she thought it would have been comical to see him squeeze into the little import.

He opened the passenger-side door of his truck for her to get in. She looked in and wondered where she was supposed to sit. The truck was littered with rolls of house plans, tools, old work clothes, cans, discarded potato-chip bags, and other things that Marie couldn't even identify. "Sorry," Wil said when he noticed that she hesitated to get in. He quickly swiped the seat with his arm and threw everything from the front seat to the back, opening up a space for her to sit.

The drive out to the property was peaceful, and it took about forty minutes to get to the cutoff. On the way, they talked about some of the preliminaries that had to be done before they could break ground, permits and such. One thing she had to say for this guy, he knew his stuff. He paid great attention to detail and was very organized.

She noticed that while he had no hesitation in asking her personal questions about her life, he avoided the subject of his life. She wondered if he had some deep, dark secret that he was hiding. Maybe he was on the witness-protection plan. Maybe he was hiding out. Maybe he just didn't like talking about whatever it was that had happened in his life up to this point.

The road into the property was overgrown. Marie was glad now that they had decided to take the truck. Her little car would never have made it past the entrance. There were huge ruts in the road from the years of nonuse and heavy rains. The branches from the trees that lined the road along the way had merged to cover both sides. Wil had to get out and move fallen trees that were blocking the road a couple of times. It had been ten years since anyone had driven on the road, and it showed.

The road twisted and turned around the side of a tree-covered hill. Ferns and underbrush scraped on the side of the truck as it moved slowly up to the peak. The view from the top of the rise was breathtaking. Marie had forgotten just how beautiful and secluded the property was.

Slowly, the truck found its way down to the larger of two creeks that rambled through the property. The bridge looked sturdy, but Wil drove across cautiously. Marie was pleasantly surprised to see that the bridge across the creek was still solid.

Finally, they reached a large clearing and got out of the truck. Marie got out and breathed in the fresh, crisp Oregon air. It was beautiful. She was going to enjoy living here. It was so quiet, so peaceful, so pristine.

"Where do you want the house?" Wil's words broke the spell and brought her back to reality.

"Well, I hadn't really thought about it," she said. "It's been ten years since I've been here, and I've never really thought about living here until recently. I want to be able to hear the creek when the windows are open. Where would you suggest?"

Wil went into a long monologue about how far away from the creek the septic tank had to be and how far away the well should be from the septic tank and so on. Most of it was over her head. She just nodded in agreement as if she understood everything he said. She found herself staring at his face. As good-looking as he was, surely he didn't have trouble getting women. One look with those seductive eyes and women would be lined up at his door. She wouldn't mind being at the head of that line. "I've got to stop thinking like this," she thought as she forced herself to stay on task.

She decided to put the house facing south to get as much sun as possible. Wil had planned out where the septic tank and well should be located. They picked out a spot for the house that would give her everything she wanted, sun and the creek, and met with his restrictions for the septic tank and well. When the discussion turned to how to bring power to the house, they hit a stumbling block.

Bringing in power from the road would be outrageously expensive. But Wil thought that it was the way to go. Marie disagreed and said she wanted alternate power. She didn't like the idea of ugly power poles spoiling the landscape, and going underground would be almost as expensive as using alternate power. The discussion got so heated at one point that Marie was sure Wil was going to take a swing at her. She could see the tiny veins in his forehead and neck popping out and filling with blood as they started to pulsate, turning his face red. Instead, he just turned around and walked toward the creek. She heard him say, "Fucking California fruitcake," under his breath as he walked away.

She decided to let him cool down a little. Then it hit her; why not put a turbine in the big creek? Between that and solar power, she should have all the power she needed.

After what she considered an appropriate cool-down period, she walked over to Wil. She quietly, but forcefully, told him that the power would come from the creek and the sun. He agreed under the condition that she would also have a natural-gas boiler. A compromise was reached.

The rest of the morning went smoother as they paced off the building area and put rocks on the ground to mark out where the house and barn would be located. After the work was done, Marie persuaded Wil to walk the property with her. She ran to the truck to grab some of the snacks and drinks that she had picked up that morning.

Wil followed her to the truck and saw her grabbing the trail mix and juice. "What are you going to do with that? Feed the birds?" he asked.

She turned toward him. "I thought you might want a snack."

"Not that stuff," he replied, retrieving some beef jerky and his handgun out of the glove box.

"What do you need that for?" she asked in startled amazement. Was he going to shoot her and dump her body in the woods?

He looked at her in disbelief. "You really got a lot to learn, lady," he said. "Ever heard of bears and snakes? Around here you never know when you might run into one of 'em. If you are serious about living on this property, I suggest you pick yourself up a little protection in town."

"I don't know the first thing about guns," she replied.

"Lord, help me," he prayed, shaking his head and turning his eyes heavenward. "I'll pick one out for you if you want."

"I would really appreciate it. Thank you," she said. "Will you teach me how to use it, too?"

"It would be my pleasure, ma'am," he said, touching the tip of his cowboy hat in mock reverence. Then he added, "I'd never forgive myself if you went and shot off one of your little toes."

They both started to laugh. "He really is a sweetheart under all that roughness," she thought. This felt good. Maybe it wouldn't be so bad working with this guy after all.

It was past two o'clock before they headed back to town. The ride back was quiet. Marie was so exhausted from the excitement and the long walk that she fell asleep almost as soon as they hit the highway. She woke up as they were pulling into the parking lot of the restaurant where she had left the rental car.

"So," she said, turning to Wil after the truck stopped next to her car. "Will you build my house?"

"Just like that?" he asked. "You know that alternate energy stuff is going to cost you more."

"That's OK," she replied. "I trust you. You look like you know what you're doing and I know you won't take advantage of me."

"You sure about that?" he asked. He looked at her with one raised eyebrow and that twisted, smirky smile that took her breath away.

She looked deep into his dark brown eyes and said, "I'm sure."

For the first time since she had met him, he looked like he didn't know what to say. She got out of the truck, unlocked the door of the rental, got in, and started it up. She rolled down the window and called out to him. "Let's meet here tomorrow morning, same time. We can discuss the details." Then she drove off.

Wil sat in the truck without moving. He caught himself smiling. What was it about her? What made her so different? What was this feeling he got when he was with her? He thought about it for a while. She did have a nice body, a real woman's body, not like one of those anorexic gold diggers that were always giving him the eye. And she did have great titties. Yes, indeed, nice titties. "Not bad lookin' for a city gal, cute ass, too. I could hit that real easy," he thought. Then he stopped himself, started up the truck, and went home.

CHAPTER THREE

ON THE WAY BACK TO THE HOTEL, MARIE decided to buy some more appropriate clothes. She really wasn't prepared for the outdoor ruggedness of the area. The running shoes she'd worn walking the property were pretty much ruined. She really needed to get a pair of boots. She found a boot shop and purchased a comfortable pair of Ropers that she hoped would pass even Wil's inspection. A quick trip through Main Street convinced her that her best shot for clothes would be the local Walmart. She had no trouble finding it. The Walmart Supercenter was the largest building in the area and, judging by the number of cars in the parking lot, the most popular. She picked out a couple of flannel shirts and a couple pairs of jeans and tried on a cowboy hat, but it just didn't feel right. She found a ball cap that would suffice. It had an embroidered horse head on the front. Perfect. She almost felt like a local.

By the time she was finished shopping, it was dinnertime. The night before, she just had a salad at the hotel restaurant. Tonight she needed something a little more substantial. "Must be that mountain air," she thought. She decided to go for a safe bet and find a Chinese restaurant. She could usually find some vegetarian fare there. After driving around for about ten minutes without finding one, she resorted to looking in the phone book. There were a handful of Chinese restaurants in Grants Pass, and one was close to her hotel. It was hidden away on a side street just two blocks away.

The food was not exactly authentic but palatable. "This place would never make it in California," she thought, although the service was excellent. Why wouldn't it be? She was one of only five people in the whole place. She wondered how they managed to stay in business.

While eating, she thought about her property and what it would be like to wake up to the sound of the creek and the smell of the forest every morning—every morning she wasn't traveling that is. She had to do something about that.

The thought of returning to her project management job was depressing her. She was good at her job, she knew that. But lately the job held no joy for her. The stress level had risen since the company had been bought out. Her old boss had been transferred and her new boss was an idiot. After seeing the Oregon property, she felt that it might be time to look for something different. There had to be something she could do that didn't involve travel, something she could do from home. A job in Grants Pass would involve almost two hours of travel a day. And she was sure it wouldn't pay much. She thought long and hard for a while but came up with nothing. She decided to file that one away for a while. The first order of business was getting the house built and moving to Oregon.

Good Lord! Moving! How was she going to do that? She had sold most of her furniture when she moved into the little duplex. Whatever didn't fit in the duplex had been stored away in a rented storage unit for the last ten years. Besides Cindy, she really didn't have any friends in California. And she would feel awkward asking Cindy and her boyfriend to help her move to Oregon. There really wasn't enough stuff to hire a moving company. Did she dare ask Wil for a suggestion? Why not? What would be the worst he could do? Call her a fruitcake again? Most likely he knew everyone in town. Surely he knew someone she could trust with all of her worldly possessions.

The next morning, she walked into the little cafe dressed in her new flannel shirt, jeans, boots, and cap. There he was, at the same table as yesterday. "Boy, this guy is a creature of habit," she thought. Wil saw her and studied her new look. She couldn't help but smile when she saw what she interpreted as a pleased expression on his face.

He had already been served and was eating the same thing as yesterday. Except today it was sausage instead of bacon.

"What do you think?" she asked as she sat down.

"You're learning," he said dryly, trying hard to conceal a smile. "Next thing you know, we'll be sharing a hamburger."

"Don't get your hopes up on that one," she replied with a grin as she seated herself across from him.

"At least you don't look like a California fruitcake anymore," he said.

"I think I've just been paid a compliment," she said cheerfully.

He just kept on eating, expressionlessly. He was a hard guy to read.

The waitress came over to the table with a menu. She did a double take when she saw Marie in her new duds. "Herbal tea again, miss?" she asked.

"Yes, please," answered Marie as she did a quick pass over the menu. "And I'll have the fruit plate, too."

Wil just shook his head and continued to eat.

"So," Marie said, "what do we do today? Do I have to sign any papers? Leave you a deposit?"

"What for?" he said. "Ain't my word good enough? Yesterday you said you trusted me."

She looked surprised. "I just think—"

"Don't think," he interrupted. "It just confuses things. I know what you want. Just leave me your address and a phone number, and I'll call you when I need you or your money."

"What's with this guy?" she thought to herself. "What is he afraid of?" Just when she thought she was getting through, he closed her out. Should she ask his advice about moving? She decided to wait until he finished eating. Maybe he was one of those guys who needed food before talk.

The waitress brought the herbal tea and fruit plate and set them down in front of Marie. They ate in silence.

Finally, Marie spoke. "Wil, listen, I was wondering if you knew anyone who might be willing to drive a truck full of my belongings up here from California once the house is done. I don't have much. I'd pay them, of course."

"Yep," he said, without looking up from his plate.

"Pardon me?" she asked.

"You asked if I knew someone. Well, I do," he said.

"What is with you today?" she asked critically. "Did they close the Blur early last night?"

He put his fork down and looked her hard in the eyes. "You're paying me to build a house, not to be your damn friend and make chitchat," he said brusquely.

Marie looked stunned. She thought they had made a connection yesterday. She must have been wrong. "Well, I didn't think people had to be paid to be friends," she retorted, obviously upset.

He could see the hurt in her eyes, and it made him feel uneasy. Why? She was just some dame who wanted to live in the country. Why did she have this affect on him? Why did he feel like he needed to apologize? He didn't like this feeling. It made him feel weak, and he hated that.

"Don't go crying on me now," he said with obvious concern. "My son will be able to help you move when the time comes. Just didn't think we needed to get into the details now."

Her eyes widened in wonder at this sneak peek into his personal life. "You have a son? Are you married?" she inquired.

"No."

"Oh, divorced then?"

He took a deep breath. She could tell this was not an easy subject for him to speak of.

"You think you're the only one whose other half has died?" he said impatiently. The look on his face told a story Marie didn't want to hear.

She blushed. "Oh, Wil! I'm sorry; I'm so sorry. It's just that trying to get anything out of you is like pulling teeth. Maybe if you would drop this tough-guy act once in a while, you might find that some people are caring and sensitive. It might help if—"

"Look," he cut her off. "I don't need your help. It happened a long time ago. I got over it. You don't know the whole story. It was no great loss."

She decided to let it drop. Obviously, she had touched a raw nerve, and he didn't want to talk about it.

The rest of the morning was spent at the county building obtaining the necessary permits for the construction of Marie's new home. Wil knew his way around there and was familiar with the staff. He had no trouble getting what he needed. Surprisingly, he also seemed to be well liked. He charmed the building clerks. One was downright flirtatious with him. The inspectors were friendly and on a first-name basis with him. But then again, he wasn't as gruff and short with the clerks and inspectors as he was with Marie.

She wondered why he singled her out for special treatment, or if that was just the way he was with women on the outside. Something must have happened between him and his wife. Whatever it was must have left a really bad taste in his mouth. She was sure he was able to satisfy his sexual urges whenever the need arose. After all, Medford was a relatively big city and less than an hour from Grants Pass, if that was where he lived, and he really wasn't that bad looking. But she was just as sure that he was a man who had never found a life partner. He had never experienced the type of love that she and Charles had shared, that special electricity between two beings that glowed inside and bonded two souls for eternity.

He had a son. That meant that he thought he felt something close to love at one time. If his son was old enough to drive that meant that whatever it was that Wil experienced, if only briefly, had happened a long, long time ago and was most likely a forgotten memory by now.

He had raised his son. At least he was able to experience that. She almost envied him for it. He had been able to watch his son grow from a newborn infant to a young man. "How wonderful," she thought. She wondered what Andy would have looked like when he was of driving age. She was sure he would have been handsome and popular. He looked so much like Charles as a baby that she knew he would look just like him when he grew up.

Charles was the most handsome man she had ever seen, and he was kind. That was what had drawn her to him in the first place. Almost immediately, she'd found out that his inner person was as handsome and kind as he was on the outside.

For the first time since she got to Oregon, she became sad. She was sad for the life she was cheated out of. Things were so different now than they should have been.

The sound of rustling papers brought her back to the present. She could hear Wil thanking the clerk and inspector. He was gathering up the paperwork and heading toward her.

He announced that they were finished and that all the paperwork was in order. She had her permits. In a few minutes, they were heading out the door.

"When can we break ground?" she asked when they got into the truck.

"Soon as I can get the road fixed," he replied. "We gotta reinforce the bridge if we want to get a concrete truck in there."

Suddenly, the sadness she had felt in the county building came back. She felt the need to be alone. She turned to Wil and said, "So, what do you need from me?"

"Not a thing," he replied. He already had her name, address, phone number, cell-phone number, and e-mail address (not that he would ever touch a computer).

They rode the rest of the way to the restaurant parking lot in silence. Wil pulled the truck into the spot next to her rental.

"OK then," she said, turning to him. "I'll be waiting for your call. I'll be in town until the end of next week. You know where I'm staying, and you have my other numbers. Maybe I'll see you around town sometime."

"Right," he said as she got out in a hurry.

Wil watched the little car drive away. Suddenly, he wanted to think of a reason to call her, to be around her. She was weird, but he kind of liked her. She was pretty, his kind of pretty—not all made-up and phony. Sure, she needed a few lessons on living out in the country. But he was sure she could learn and probably would like it. He could even put up with the vegetarian nonsense. Why didn't he say something to her? He laughed at himself. She would never look twice at a guy like him. He had only been with women he picked up in bars for so long that he wondered if he would even know what to do with a real lady.

He was not expecting to feel the sadness of separation that he was experiencing now. It caught him by surprise. It made him feel uncomfortable. He hadn't felt like this since Maggie left. Maggie… he hadn't thought about her in so long. She was his first and only love, the mother of his only child, his son. She was also the woman (though she was really just a girl at the time) who ripped his heart out. He had been hurt so badly by her that until he met Marie, he thought he had no heart left.

He remembered the first time he saw Maggie. It was his first day of sixth grade. She and her family had just moved to Grants Pass. He was tall, gangly, and awkward. She was small, graceful, and beautiful. She stole his heart away that first day so long ago. They had become boyfriend and girlfriend that fall, on Halloween. Wil sneaked a kiss from her behind her daddy's barn that night after they had been trick-or-treating.

They went steady all through middle school. He believed he was in love with Maggie. But she couldn't help being a tease. She was so beautiful that she had all the boys after her, a fact that she knew and played on. But she was happy enough with him as her protector. After sixth grade, Wil had matured rapidly. He was very athletic and strong. He was easily one of the most handsome boys in school. He wasn't always a good boy either; she liked that. He would get into fights with the other boys from time to time. But he always managed to come out on top. Maggie enjoyed being his girl. But she never really wanted to settle down. She always said she wanted to leave Grants Pass. Wil never wanted to leave. He loved the country. He felt as comfortable in the mountains and rivers as most people felt in town. It wasn't uncommon for him to take camping trips alone in the mountains for weeks. He was a natural hunter and fisherman.

Maggie's desire to leave Grants Pass became immaterial the day she found out she was pregnant. They were both only sixteen.

Abortion was out of the question. Maggie wanted to give the baby up for adoption, but Wil would not hear of it. He begged her to marry him. He promised that he would always take care of her and the baby. She finally relented, and they were married four months before Duke, as in John Wayne, was born.

Maggie moved in with Wil and his mother. Her parents were disgraced by her and had disowned her when they found out she was pregnant. Wil's father had died of lung cancer the year before, thanks to a four-pack-a-day cigarette habit. It was because of his death that Wil never picked up the nasty habit. He was already starting to help out with the household bills to supplement the insurance money that his mom was living on. As soon as he turned seventeen, he got his GED and a full-time job. That was when he started building houses.

Everything seemed to be working out. Maggie finished out the tenth grade in June. Duke was born on the Fourth of July. Maggie was very attentive to Duke. She breast-fed him and did all the things that a good mother should do. Wil's mother tried not to interfere but was always there with an encouraging word or a help-ing hand whenever needed.

When Duke was nine months old, Maggie decided she didn't want to be a wife and mother anymore. She had met a man from Los Angeles who said she was so pretty she could be a movie star. Wil couldn't believe his ears when she told him she was leaving with the man in the morning. He was going to be her agent. He knew a lot of studio people and was certain she would be famous.

He asked her how she could leave him after what they had been through together. He loved her. How could she leave Duke?

She told him she never really loved him. She just liked the prestige of being Wil Townsend's girl. She thought Duke was cute, but she was tired of being a mommy. Wil felt like a knife had been thrust into his heart.

He pleaded with her to stay. He cried and begged to no avail. Maggie was crying, too. But she kept packing her bag. When she was finished, she walked out the door, without turning back and without saying good-bye to her son. He never saw her again. She never called, and he never tried to reach her.

Wil had felt his heart turn cold that night. He was hurt so badly; no one should be able to do that to another person. What kind of woman could leave her infant son? He vowed that night to never fall in love or take the risk of being hurt like this again. He couldn't survive it.

The only ones who could ever reach him again were his mother and, of course, Duke. Duke was his reason for living. Wil's mom helped out with Duke's rearing. She watched him when Wil was at school or working, but Wil spent every free moment with the boy. He didn't date again until Duke was in high school. And even then, it was rare. It consisted mainly of the occasional night in Medford, the only big city around. It was big enough for a guy to pick up some lovely stranger and pleasure himself discreetly. Medford was far enough away from Grants Pass that he didn't have to worry about running into the dame in some local store or restaurant.

Five years after Maggie left, Wil got a phone call from her mother. Maggie was dead. It seemed that Maggie had made it as a star all right, a porn star. Apparently she lied about her age and made a few low-budget movies. She hung around with Hollywood sleaze, the drug-and-alcohol crowd. She had gotten very drunk one night and died choking on her own vomit. Maggie's mom thought he should know.

Wil had tucked those memories away long ago. Now they were all coming back fresh. Was this a red flag on this California woman? Funny, his first love left him for California. Now this one was leaving California for him. For him? What was he thinking? She didn't love him. Hell, he wasn't even sure if she liked him. She probably cared as much for him as she would a stray dog.

Besides, who said anything about love? He didn't love her either. Or did he? He did feel alive when she was there, younger even. He even looked forward to her criticism about his eating habits. She had a cute way of squinting her eyes and twitching her nose up when she was puzzled about something. And she was puzzled a lot. She may be city smart, but the girl didn't know anything about living in the country. Then there was that curvaceous body.

She had been hurt by love, too, in a different way but hurt just the same. Her loss was quick, without warning, and complete. Did she at least have a child that helped to lessen the blow? He wondered. She never said anything about kids. Wil didn't know how he could have lived if Maggie had taken Duke.

Maybe he should call her and ask her out for a drink or something. He thought about it for a while. What would he do if she said no? Better not to ask than to get rejected. He let it pass. It was time to go home.

CHAPTER FOUR

—ɯ—

Back at the hotel, Marie couldn't shake her uneasy feeling. She ordered a salad from room service and watched TV until it arrived. Then she took a hot bath and curled up in bed. It was only three o'clock in the afternoon. She was depressed but didn't know why. Was it something about being *here*, where past memories were created with Charles? Now she was creating happy, new memories without him. She was going to start a new life with land she wouldn't have if it weren't for him.

She also felt anxious because, she hated to admit it, she was feeling herself strangely attracted to Wil. He was so different from Charles, rough in all the places that Charles wasn't, both in looks and actions. Charles was kind, sweet, and patient. Wil was rough, sometimes rude, and certainly on a short fuse. Charles had soft, handsome features. Wil had a rugged, weathered...what was that look? He looked western, like a mountain man. He looked like he could wrestle a bear. But he was handsome in his own way, almost sexy. Really, sexy? Is that what you'd call it? He did awaken a feeling down inside her that she had forgotten about, a desire to be touched and kissed and a hunger for passion, for sex. She surprised herself, and her face blushed. She hadn't thought about sex for a long time. She felt strangely safe with Wil, as if she could trust him with her life, and that made her feel good.

Even with his short temper and apparent aloofness, she instinctively knew he had deep feelings, and somewhere, hidden in that tough-guy exterior, was the heart of a kind, sensitive man. It would take the right woman to bring it out. Could she be that woman? It presented a formidable challenge. She couldn't shake the amorous feelings she was having for him. The thought of being romantically attracted to him gave her goose bumps and made her giggle. What would it be like to lie next to him in bed? She wondered how he made love. Would he be gentle? Would he be rough and ride her like a rodeo cowboy rides a buckin' bronc? Such thoughts!

Like a splash of cold water in her face, a sudden soberness came over her. She began to feel guilty about thinking of another man in that way, almost as if she were betraying Charles. In the ten years since he had passed, she had never even looked twice at another man. She and Charles had spent less than five years of their lives with each other, yet she felt as if it were the only life she would ever have.

It *had* been a decade since his death, and she had mourned him for all of it. Would he mind it so much if she did get romantically involved with another man? How would she know if he did? Would he appear in a dream? He had only appeared once before, right after the accident. He had looked handsome as ever. He was smiling, and Andy was in his arms. Her baby boy was happy and beautiful. Charles told Marie that they were OK and at peace. He told her not to worry about them. It was their time. He told her that she couldn't stop living. She had a lot more to do. He said it was OK to cry for now, but she needed to pick a day, and from that day on, she couldn't cry anymore. She would know when that day was. He made her promise she would do it. She did; they kissed. She was holding them both so close. Andy kissed her and said, "I love you, Mommy." Then it was over. She'd woken up and realized that she was alone in an empty bed.

She had never broken a promise that she made to Charles. She wanted to do exactly what he said. But she had never been able to pick a day. Every time she tried, something would remind her of that horrible day of the accident, and she would break down. But she had learned to deal with the reality of it all. Charles and Andy were never coming back. She knew that. Still, she loved them both so deeply; she always would. But she could not make love to a memory. It had been a while since she had thought about the feel of a man's arms around her, kissing her gently, caressing her body, and the passion and heat of sex. She could not picture herself with any other man except Charles. No other man seemed to have the qualities that she was looking for until she met Wil.

She laughed to herself. And exactly what qualities did Wil possess that were on her list? Let's see, there was his crude behavior, his wardrobe, his drinking, and the way he made fun of her eating habits and dress? None of those qualities were on her list. Yet she could not stop thinking about him.

Then her thoughts turned to a side of him that seemed protected and unapproachable. He had a soft side. She could tell. He had a son, so he knew unconditional love. He could be kind. He must have loved the boy's mother at one time. Then there was that electric feeling she got when she was around him. The glances between them that said more than words could express. She felt comfortable with him. Although he never said it, she could tell that he felt comfortable with her, too. He could be cranky, but she thought that it was just a protection mechanism. "Why won't you let me in, Wil?" she thought to herself.

Could she ever break through that tough, peripheral, emotional armor that he always wore? He hardly ever let his guard down. There were only a few times that she could think of when there was a hint of smile, a softening of the eyes, and a glimpse into the other Wil Townsend, the one who existed before he had been hurt by love. He had always been quick to catch himself and shut the door.

Everyone, including her family, told her she should get married again. What was it that her brother-in-law Jake had suggested? "Find a man; spend a lustful week in the woods. Get laid?" Well, this trip might not end up with her getting laid, but surely it was OK to think romantic thoughts.

She shook her head. What was she thinking? Wil didn't seem like the kind of guy who was looking for a mate, certainly not a "California Fruitcake."

She needed a diversion. She was here for a while. She might as well do something to enjoy herself. She had always wanted to explore the mountains around her property. The few times she had ever been there before, she was either pregnant or had little Andy to tend to. She grabbed the phone book out of the nightstand and opened it to guide services. She found one that had a modest ad claiming to have experienced guides and offering horseback pack trips for day or overnight trips at a reasonable rate. They supplied all the equipment, horses, and food. Siskiyou Nature Adventures sounded perfect.

She dialed the number. She could tell the voice that answered was a young man. He was very knowledgeable and polite. After discussing the types of trips available, she decided to take a three-day trip, leaving the day after next.

She needed the time to get warmer clothes and rain gear. The daytime was warm, but it still got chilly after the sun went down. And you could never tell when it might rain.

It just so happened that the young man was scheduled to take another couple of visitors on a one-week trip. His father was going to accompany them and was planning on returning by the third day anyway. He had another job and couldn't be away that long. If she didn't mind, she could go up with the group and come back with his dad. The boy claimed that his father was the experienced one. He practically lived in the woods. She would be very safe with him. She agreed, and they set the time and the meeting place. Before she hung up, she asked him what his name was.

"Duke, ma'am," he said, adding, "Like John Wayne."

"Good Lord," she thought to herself. "Are they all John Wayne crazy up here?" She thanked him and hung up. She was feeling better now. She needed to talk to her sister and tell her the good news about the house. Marie had told no one about her plans. She was excited now and wanted to share her happiness.

Jake answered the phone.

"Jake, it's Marie."

"Marie! Good to hear from you. Where are you?" he asked.

"I'm in Oregon," she replied then added, "Get Maddy on the line. I have something I want to tell you both."

"OK, hold on." He put his hand over the receiver and called out to his wife. Marie could hear the click when Madelyn picked up the extension.

"Hello, Marie? Are you all right?" Madelyn asked in a frantic tone.

"Yes," Marie answered. "I'm fine. In fact, I'm finer than I have been in a long time."

"Don't tell me?" Jake broke in. "You got laid!"

"Jake!" Madelyn admonished.

Marie started to laugh. "No, it's nothing like that." Thoughts of Wil ran through her mind. "I wanted to tell you that I've decided to build a house on the Oregon property and move up here."

"All right!" Jake said, obviously approving.

Madelyn fell into her mothering role and started asking a thousand questions—why now; are you feeling OK; are you sure you can afford it; and, the always popular but comical, are you pregnant?

Marie explained about the city's plan to put a shopping center where her little duplex sat. She told them about Wil but only in the context of him as the builder, being extra careful not to let the discussion turn to any attraction she might feel for him. She wasn't sure herself what her feelings for him were and didn't want to give Madelyn and Jake any hope at all that she might have found a man. Just the thought of him made the hairs on the back of neck perk up. She felt a tingly sensation in her breasts that made her blush. Thank goodness Jake and Madelyn couldn't see her. What was happening to her? Why did this man have this affect on her? She had to stop thinking about him! She shook her head to clear her mind.

"Get back to reality. Think!" she told herself. She ended by telling them about the three-day, horseback camping trip she was planning to take in the mountains.

Madelyn got worried. "You don't know how to ride a horse. Are you crazy?" she said.

Marie assured her that she would be in good hands. She was going with experienced guides. Jake was all in favor of it.

All in all, Madelyn and Jake seemed genuinely happy for her. Jake hung up when the two women started to discuss drapery and furnishings for the cabin. He couldn't help but throw in a final farewell that included his wish for Marie's sexual fulfillment.

The sisters chatted for nearly an hour. Justin got on the phone at one point and proudly recited a silly rhyme for his favorite aunt, who was duly impressed. Before saying good-bye, Marie let Madelyn know that she would be in town again in six weeks. After Marie hung up, she was glad she had decided to call. Talking to her sister always cheered her up.

Madelyn had told her she thought this was a good move. Although she was Marie's younger sister, Madelyn's approval meant a lot to her. They had always been close.

Marie decided to grab a bite to eat in town and catch a movie. She would still be in bed by ten. Tomorrow she would shop for the camping trip and thought she might check out some solar and turbine-engine companies on the Internet. She was glad she had brought her laptop. If she put inquiries in tomorrow, she would surely have responses by the time she returned from her trip, if not sooner. Then she could give Wil the information. He had told her that there were no local companies that supplied alternate power.

She found an Italian restaurant that fixed a passable eggplant parmesan. She was surprised to discover that Grants Pass had a multi-theater movie house. *The Horse Whisperer* was starting within minutes. She wanted to run out and buy a horse when the movie was over. The movie ended at nine thirty. She was in bed by ten. She loved being on schedule. Maybe that was why she was such a good project manager.

The next day was spent making Internet inquiries and follow-up phone calls and shopping and trying to find another restaurant that could feed a vegetarian in a meat-and-potatoes town.

She had trouble getting to sleep that night. She was actually excited and anxious about the adventure trip. She was excited because she loved the land and could hardly believe she was about to really explore and experience it like she had wanted to since the first time she had seen it. She was anxious because she knew it would be like nothing she had ever done before. It would be wild and uninhabited. There was an element of danger. Hadn't Wil said there were bears and snakes? She hoped her hired guides would be prepared with "a little protection," as he called it.

Suddenly Madelyn's concerns came back to haunt her. Could she handle it? Was she competent enough? She knew nothing about the wilderness, a fact that Wil had pointed out to her several times already. She had been horseback riding before. But they were always trail rides with friends on slow, pokey nags that couldn't go fast if they were being chased by a pack of wolves. And those scanty equestrian experiences were over ten years ago and never for three whole days.

She shook her head in a sobering realization. It seemed like everything she had done in life had been done over ten years ago. Had the last ten years been wasted? She'd made no new friends, no new relationships. She hadn't even really taken any vacations. She never took chances, never did anything fun. She had just existed, living on from day to day, taking one day at a time until they added up to ten years. She did go back to college after Charles and Andy died. She got a degree in Business Administration. That was how she had gotten the project management job. Well, it was time to change all that. Tomorrow would be the beginning of the new and improved Marie Trousdale. It was what Charles would want; she was sure. Charles, the burning sadness of his absence hit her once again. "I miss you, my love," she said into her pillow as tears edged her eyes.

After a while, sadness, fatigue, and clean, county air finally got the better of her, and she drifted off to sleep.

She opened her eyes, and she was back in her house in California, the house she had shared with Charles and Andy. She was in her bed, and Charles was lying next to her, holding her in his arms. The look on his face was very serious, but she could still see the unending love in his eyes. She could feel it in his warm embrace. She didn't feel sad; she felt happy. Charles looked her squarely in the eye and said, "Marie, I want you to know that it's OK to be happy."

"Charles, I love you. I miss you," she moaned. She closed her eyes, feeling the warmth of his arms around her. When she opened them again, she was alone in her hotel room in Grants Pass. She looked at the clock. It was two in the morning. She turned her head into her pillow and cried herself to sleep.

CHAPTER FIVE

—ɯɯ—

MARIE AWOKE WITH ANXIOUS ANTICIPATION OF THE COMING days'
adventures. She spent extra time in the shower, knowing that this
would be the last real shower she would have for three days. She
wasn't quite sure what to expect on her adventure, so she treated
herself to a restaurant breakfast instead of her usual piece of fruit.
She had told Duke that she was a vegetarian.

"Here are some important veggie-cooking rules," she had
informed him. "Please don't mix the vegetarian pot with the same
spoon you just stirred the beef stew with. Know that broth of any
kind that originates from an animal is not vegetarian. A ham sandwich is not instantly made vegetarian simply by peeling out the
slices of meat."

Her sister Madelyn had a crude but effective little anecdote for
this one. When an unsuspecting host would suggest this to Marie,
Madelyn, the ever-protective sister, would look whoever it was in
the eye, with a straight face, and say, "Well, let's find something you

don't want to eat…say shit for example. Would you eat a ham and shit sandwich simply because I scraped the shit off?" This would always cause Marie to go hysterical and the offender to gag in disgust. Marie spared Duke the story.

"And the final and most important rule is," she continued. "Infraction of any of the rules previously mentioned would not only make me mad but also make me violently ill."

Duke had assured her he would follow her rules. He'd let out a sigh of relief when he found out that she ate fish. He guaranteed her there would be plenty on the trail. The main trail followed a creek into the mountains. This time of year there were usually plenty of trout in the stream.

It was funny how she never even conceived of meat as food anymore, while some people thought of meat as the only food. She had turned vegetarian in her first year of college. She was a vegetarian when she met Charles and would always be one. It was just the way she was.

She finished her oatmeal, paid the bill, and walked out to her car. The drive to the meeting point was about thirty minutes out of town. It was in the same direction as her property and easy to find. She parked the car and got out. She was ready for Mother Nature; she hoped. She was wearing one of her new flannel shirts, jeans, boots, sunglasses, and her trusty ball cap. With the exception of her new backpack, she looked the same as she had the other day when she tried to impress Wil with her new attire at the restaurant. Besides a change of clothes and toiletries, she had thought it wise to pack some granola bars, trail mix, fruit, herbal tea bags, and instant vegetarian soup mix, just in case.

There were two other vehicles at the spot when she arrived. One was obviously a rental; it probably belonged to the other tourists. The other was a well-used pickup truck that was hooked up to a large horse trailer. She could smell the horses as soon as she stepped out of the car. The smell didn't bother her. She rather liked it. "Good thing," she thought to herself. She would probably smell like them herself by the end of the trip.

She saw three people standing about a hundred yards off, near a small barn. Two of them wore ball caps (the tourists), and one, a young man, was wearing a cowboy hat (he had to be Duke). They were in various stages of preparation. She saw horses, five of them, all saddled and oblivious to the commotion the humans next to them were making. There were also three mules, wearing packs. A pair of black labs, who barked playfully at each other and ran around the horses, completed the group.

As she approached, the young man in the cowboy hat stopped what he was doing and came toward her with his hand out. "Howdy, ma'am," he said with smile. "You must be Marie."

"And you must be Duke," she responded, taking his hand and looking into his eyes. He had a firm handshake and a confident air to his manner. He seemed a friendly, likable young man. He looked like someone she should know, but she couldn't quite place him. She shrugged it off when Duke spoke to her.

"We're just about ready to go," he said. "My dad will be here any minute. He had some things to get laid out for his other job, the one I told you about."

Marie nodded in acknowledgment.

"Well, let's get you acquainted with your horse. Done much riding?" he asked as they walked to over to a beautiful bay gelding. Duke said his name was Rex.

Marie went through her brief equestrian experiences with Duke. He assured her that Rex was a ladies' horse and would be very gentle with her. He helped her swing into the saddle and told her to walk the horse around a little. She did and quickly found that Duke was right. Rex was very gentle. He responded well to the reins, stopping at the right moment, turning left or right as commanded by the signals from the reins. She felt comfortable in the saddle.

She dismounted and they all turned to see a pickup approaching. It left a trail of dust on the road. "Heads up, everyone," Duke ordered. "Here's Dad."

There was something strangely familiar about the truck. Marie felt the blood drain from her face as the realization hit. The truck engine shut off, and the door swung open. Out came a tall man wearing a grungy black cowboy hat, with shaggy brown hair sticking out under it, well-worn cowboy boots, a jean jacket, and Levi's. It was Wil.

Marie had to strain to contain her surprise. Of course! It made perfect sense. The clues were all there; he was at home in the woods and had another job and had a son named Duke. She should have known when she shook hands with the boy; he had his father's mystifying, deep brown eyes. She wondered what Wil's reaction would be when he realized she was going to be on the journey. And what would he do when he realized that it would be just the two of them for the last half of the trip?

She tried to stay in the background. How long could she hide?—as it turned out, not long. Wil was tending to his horse while Duke was making the introductions. Wil nodded in polite acknowledgement without turning back when Duke introduced Tim and Theresa Miller, the other couple. When Duke said, "Marie Trousdale," Wil's head jerked up so fast his hat nearly fell off. Duke hesitated for moment, thinking Wil had seen a snake or something equally deadly.

Wil swung around, and in an instant, Marie found herself face-to-face with him. "What are you doing here?" he inquired harshly.

"Surprise!" Marie replied, trying to smile. "I'm here for the adventure."

Duke had never seen his dad react like this before, and it took him by surprise. "You two know each other?" he asked.

"Yes," Marie replied confidently.

"No," his father said emphatically at the same time. "Well, not exactly. Well, yes…I guess you could say we do."

Marie was totally amazed that the subject of their friendship had this big lug of a guy so tongue-tied. By the smile on Duke's face, he was obviously enjoying this.

Marie was the first to speak. "I guess I'm the 'other job' your father is working on."

"Oh, really?" Duke said quizzically.

"I'm building her a house out in Selma," Wil added before Duke could read anything into it. He shot Duke a glance that said, "Let it drop."

"Well then," Duke said. "I guess you guys will be just fine coming back together tomorrow afternoon."

The realization struck Wil like a bolt of lightning. "Now wait just a damn minute..."

"Yes, that will be just fine," Marie broke in. She glanced at Wil. He looked so uncomfortable you would have thought he'd just sat on a prickly pear. She leaned over and whispered, "I won't bite," just loud enough for him to hear.

He grunted something under his breath. Could this really be happening? If he had known it was her he would be escorting home, he would have made some excuse and cancelled out on the trip. Then he thought about it. Would it be so bad? She was a pretty, little thing, and she sure was feisty. It might be fun after all. He was finally admitting to himself that he liked her. She was different, smart, maybe too smart. Ever since he met her that first night at the Wonder Bur, he had been thinking about her more and more often and sometimes in not such a gentlemanly way. What was it about her? He kind of laughed and resigned himself to his predicament. He shrugged it off and resumed the final checks on his horse.

Marie noticed the puzzled but amused look on Duke's face as he watched his father. Together, they loaded up the horses. It was just a short drive to the trailhead. Marie, Theresa, and Tim rode with Duke. Wil went alone.

Wil barely spoke as they unloaded the horses and began their journey. He took point, and Marie rode behind him, followed by the Millers. Duke took the rear position. They rode all day, stopping only long enough to let the horses drink water from the creek. Everyone took the opportunity to answer the call of nature when this occurred, and Marie silently blessed the horses for being thirsty. They stopped briefly for lunch, which was served brown-bag style. Marie's lunch consisted of a tuna sandwich and a candy bar. Everyone else's sandwich contained a hearty helping of animal meat.

Marie and the Millers were in constant awe of Oregon's never-ceasing beauty. The forests were thriving with wildlife. The creeks were crystal clear. The Townsends took it all in stride. Along the way, Duke brought their attention to native flora and fauna. It was springtime, and the dogwoods were blooming abundantly. There was a fresh, clean scent that filled the air. On occasion during the ride, Duke would give an interesting historical fact of the area or point out wildlife in the distance. It was breathtaking, the beauty, the peace, and the quiet. It was as if the rest of the world didn't exist. Marie didn't know if Wil was ordinarily this quiet, but other than shouting out a few directions along the way, he stayed pretty quiet and in the background, letting his son take control of the little adventure party.

As the sun began to set low in the horizon, the party reached an old log cabin that was tucked away behind a grove of Douglas fir trees. It was where they were to spend the first night. It had been an old homesteader's cabin, they were told. It belonged to the government now. There was no electricity or running water, of course, but it served as a good shelter from the elements for weary travelers.

They tied the horses and mules to the railings of a log fence that went all around the cabin, with the exception of about a twenty-five-foot opening in the front. Once they had unpacked the animals, they quickly set up camp. Duke started to prepare dinner. Marie noticed that Wil had grabbed a fishing pole and slipped off toward the creek. She decided to follow him. They hadn't been alone all day, and she wanted to explain that it was pure coincidence that brought them together again. She wanted to assure him that she was not a stalker.

By the time she was close enough to see him, he had already cast a line into the creek and was slowly reeling it in. She held back and watched the master at work. His movements were so fluid and graceful. It was like a dance; each motion was timed with delicate precision. The movements looked so natural for him. "He truly is in his element," she thought to herself.

After about three or four casts, she could tell he had one on the line. He gave the line an anchoring tug and began to reel in the catch. She approached him from behind just as he was lifting the fish out with a net.

"Nice fish," she said.

"Glad you like it," he said dryly. "It's your dinner."

"Wow, really?" she said in surprise. "I thought you just liked fishing."

"I do," he said. "Duke told me there was a fish eater on the trip. I should have put two and two together." He gently took the hook out of the fish's mouth. She watched as he grabbed a stick and struck the struggling fish with a sharp blow to the head. The fish lay quietly in his hands.

"If you'd known I was going to be on this trip, would you still have come?" she asked, hoping he would lift his head so she could look in his eyes when he answered.

"Don't know," he answered as he pulled out a pocketknife and began to gut and clean the fish, keeping his head down.

She watched for a moment. "Why don't you like me?" she asked to his surprise.

"Never said I didn't like you," he said, continuing his task with single-minded concentration. "Damn, why don't she let it drop?" he thought to himself.

"But you don't act like you do," she said.

"You're just different," he said. "Takes some gettin' used to; that's all."

"Different good or different bad?" she asked.

Wil stopped what he was doing. He looked her up and down with that cold, icy stare. He tilted his head back, squinted his eyes, lifted one eyebrow, and said, "Both. Now leave it be. You ask too many questions." He wiped the blade of the knife on his pants, closed it, put it back in his pocket, and headed up the creek bank. Marie trailed behind, not quite sure what to think of his answer.

But he did like her. Every time he looked at her, he liked her even more. He was even starting to think about what she would look like naked in his bed. He felt a stirring in his pants. "No," he thought. "Not now, not a fucking boner." He quickly thought of something else, and by the time he reached the camping party, he was no longer aroused.

Wil handed Duke the fish and went off to tend to the horses.

Marie was surprised to see that Wil chose not to sleep in the cabin that night with the rest of the party and set up his bedroll outside. He preferred the company of horses and mules to that of humans. That was what Duke told her when he saw her concerned look. "Just as well," she thought. "He probably snores."

Wil excused himself right after dinner clean up to turn in for the night. The little group, minus Wil, stayed up awhile, chitchatting in the cabin about the beautiful things they had seen during the day's ride. The Millers explained that they were vacationing and had taken the adventure trip on the recommendation of a neighbor who had done the trip the year before.

Everyone was curious to know why Marie was traveling alone. Duke was especially interested in the home Wil was building for her outside of Selma. Without going into too much detail, she told them about the death of her beloved Charles and her precious son, Andy. She told them about her job and her plans to live on the Selma property after Wil built her house.

Duke was familiar with the area and said he had always wondered who owned the beautiful chunk of property that no one ever visited. He said he was glad she was going to be a neighbor. That made her feel good. She liked the young man. He was kind and polite and handsome, too. Wil was so lucky to have such an extraordinary son. "See he is capable of kindness," she thought. "Duke couldn't have turned out this good if he didn't have the love of a good father."

By the time the Millers and Marie woke the next morning, Duke and Wil had already saddled the horses and had the mules partially packed. Breakfast consisted of bacon and eggs, just eggs for Marie. Duke was careful to cook her eggs in a clean frying pan and used a separate spatula to flip her eggs so as not to "contaminate" them with bacon grease. Although the coffee smelled delicious, Marie chose to have herbal tea. Funny, she often thought, how something that smelled so good could taste so vile. She never did care for the taste of coffee, even before she cut caffeine out of her diet.

Breakfast was eaten in a hurry and cleaned up just as fast. Within an hour of waking, they were in their saddles, heading up the mountain. Marie noticed that Wil looked at her more intently than he had the previous day. And she couldn't help but notice that his looks were a little different, not quite so harsh. Had Duke told him the details about Charles and Andy? Did that soften his cold heart a degree or two? She wondered. He knew that her husband had died. Did the fact that she had also lost her son make that big of a difference? Wil wasn't what she would call friendly to her per se, but he did offer to help her pack up and even gave her a boost into the saddle.

The morning's ride took them through some of the most beautiful terrain Marie had ever seen in her life. The vastness and beauty of the forest made her feel like an intruder in a virgin land. She couldn't help but wonder how the Indians must have felt before white men came. To have all of this, to live in harmony with it all—it must have been glorious.

Around noon, they stopped by a secluded mountain lake and had lunch. This time Marie had a cheese sandwich and a candy bar. After lunch, Duke and Wil went about dividing up the provisions and equipment. From here, they would go their separate ways. Duke would take two of the pack mules with him. He would take the Millers on up the mountain to the high camp, where they would spend a few days fishing and photo hunting. Wil would take Marie back down the way they had come.

Lunch was finished, and equipment was put away. Everyone mounted up. Duke and the Millers headed north. Wil and Marie headed south. "Now the real adventure starts," Marie thought to herself. She could tell by the pained expression on Wil's face that he was not looking forward to the next day and a half.

They rode for two hours in silence. Marie missed Duke's trail-side commentaries on nature and the history of the land. Finally, she decided to break the ice.

"Wil," she called out.

"Yeah," he answered, without turning around.

"You still alive up there?"

"Yeah."

"Why don't you talk to me?"

"Got nothing to say. Came through here this morning. Nothing new since then."

"I see."

More silence.

"I like Duke."

"So do I."

"You did a fine job raising him."

More silence.

"I believe the appropriate response is 'Thank you.'"

More silence.

"Wil, did Duke tell you anything about me this morning?"

"Like what?"

"Like about my son."

"Said you had one."

"Yes, I did. And I loved him very much." She was getting choked up thinking about Andy. "He died in the car accident with my husband. He was only three years old."

"Sorry," was all he said.

She could feel the tears starting to fall. She felt so alone.

Wil turned around and saw her wiping tears away with her sleeve. What had he done? Why was he being so hard on this poor woman? She didn't plan this trip to be with him. Poor thing had lost her husband *and* son. He thought about what it would have been like if Maggie had taken Duke with her when she left, how meaningless his life would have been and the empty hole it would have left.

He turned his horse around and rode up next to her side. He pulled a bandanna out of his pocket and handed it to her. "No need to cry," he said softly.

His words were spoken with so much compassion that they took her by surprise. This simple, kind gesture by this ogre opened the floodgates of her tears. She began to sob uncontrollably. Wil got off his horse and quickly tied it and the mule to the nearest tree. He ran over to Marie and grabbed her off her horse. He gently cradled her in his arms, stroked her hair tenderly, and told her that it would be all right.

It had been a long time since Marie had been held in the arms of a man. His strong embrace warmed her like a safe and secure blanket. She believed him. It would be all right. She didn't know how or when. But she knew in her heart that one day, it would be. She was so close to him that she could smell his manliness. It was a mixture of pine and sweat and horses. It was a fragrance both new and exciting to her. He was surprisingly gentle as he pushed her hair away from her tearstained face. After a few minutes, she stopped crying. Wil held her face in his hand and turned it up to his.

"Feel better?" he asked tenderly.

"Yes, thank you," she replied meekly. "I'm sorry. I'm not usually so emotional around strangers."

"No," he said sincerely. "I'm the one that's sorry. I've been ridin' you pretty hard."

She looked deep into his eyes. "He really means it," she thought. For a moment, she lost herself in his intense gaze. They were so close that she could feel his heart beating in his chest. She felt the urge to kiss his lips. She wondered if he could feel the electricity of the moment. She hoped he could. She closed her eyes and waited.

Wil's heart was pounding in his chest. He looked down at her tiny face, so fragile, so beautiful, so full of pain. He was not used to this feeling. It had been a long time since a woman had touched his heart and set the fire in his gut aflame. He felt the stirring in his groin again but hoped she didn't. Her lips looked so soft and inviting. He wanted to kiss them so badly it hurt. He wanted to kiss her all over and tell her he would take away the pain. What would she do if he kissed her? Would she kiss him back? Or would she scream and run off? He'd better not chance it. What could become of it? What would a high-class dame like her want with a country lowlife like him?

The anticipation was killing her. "Kiss me, Wil," she was thinking, hoping he could read her mind. She gently parted her lips.

"We better get back on the trail if we want to make it to the cabin before nightfall," he said, breaking the spell.

Marie regained her composure. "You're right," she said and pulled herself away from him. What was she thinking? He didn't feel the same way about her. He was just as distant as ever. But what was that she had felt growing beneath his jeans as he embraced her? If he wanted to kiss her, he would have, right? And if he didn't... well, maybe it was just a fold in the material. She breathed a sigh of relief that she had not made a complete and total fool of herself by kissing him.

They rode in silence the rest of the afternoon, each silently thinking, "What if?"

CHAPTER SIX

—⁓—

As they rode toward the cabin, Marie felt a deep sadness inside. She was confused by her feelings for Wil. What kind of magnetic force did he have that drew her so strongly to him? It certainly wasn't his charm. He was harsh, unsophisticated, and, at times, bad mannered. He had never disrespected her, but, then again, he never really complimented her on anything. He seemed so unapproachable. What had happened to him to build such a thick, impenetrable wall around his emotions? At times she could feel it breaking away, ever so slightly. But just when she thought she could see over it, the wall was put back up, each time stronger and higher than before.

She had not pursued a man for quite some time and didn't know what to do next. How could she let Wil know what her feelings were? It wasn't totally out of the question that he could be attracted to her. Her body was still pretty good. Getting him to notice her romantically would be a challenge. She watched a lot of movies; certainly she could figure it out. But, on the other hand, did she want to devote the kind of energy it would take to fulfill her desire for him? She wasn't sure.

But the strong sexual attraction she felt for him was growing by the day, and it was undeniable. Just thinking about the possibility of having sex with him gave her a tingly feeling. She hadn't felt that in a long time either. Since Charles, no man had turned her head. For a while, she had thought no man ever could. Now, each time she was with Wil, she felt a stronger draw, even when he was critical of her. She often found herself staring at him. Could he feel her staring at his back at this very moment as they rode the mountain trail together? She could feel herself getting all tingly and flushed. Thank goodness he couldn't see her.

She started to fantasize about what it would be like to kiss him, to make love to him, and to feel his arms around her in the night, protecting her from all of life's evil and pain. What would his manhood be like? How would it feel in her hands? She looked up and saw him in the saddle and admired his cowboy stature. He was built to ride a horse. It looked so natural. What was he thinking up there? Was he feeling the current of emotions she was feeling? Why was he ignoring her?

She felt protected with him. Intuitively she just knew he wouldn't hurt her emotionally either. Surely he was a man of honorable intentions. He was not the kind to toy with a woman's affections. If he gave of himself, it would be sincere and true.

Wil kept running through the past event over and over again in his mind, like a motion picture. He was holding her in his arms, her heart beating against his chest. It would have been so easy to just bend over and kiss those soft lips. She looked so tempting. Her eyes were closed. His heart ached to see those tearstained cheeks, those petal-soft, perfect cheeks. He could smell her fragrance. She had been on the trail for over a day, and still he could smell traces of the perfume she wore. What was it? He had never smelled anything quite like it before. It smelled something like flowers in the springtime but very subtle, like wild roses. The aroma suited her. He had remembered it after their first meeting. He could close his eyes and imagine her and the way she looked and smelled. He could imagine those soft, full breasts naked and heaving as he ravaged her. He had caught himself in just such a daydream more times than he cared to admit since they met. Each time it ended with a giant erection and no one but himself to remedy the situation.

He tried to concentrate on the trail ahead, but his mind kept drifting back to thoughts of her. He wanted to take her, right there on the trail. He wanted her so badly it hurt. He hadn't felt such sexual excitement in years. Even now, just thinking about how her body felt so close to his, her lips so inviting, and breathing in her intoxicating scent, he felt the heat in his crotch. His manhood was beginning to rise, making it hard to stay comfortably seated in the saddle. He felt himself silently praying that she wouldn't ask any questions requiring more than a one-word response. In his present condition, it would be impossible to twist his body around in the saddle to face her.

Finally, they reached the cabin. They had made good time. There was still plenty of daylight left. Wil quickly tied the horses and mule and began setting up camp. He shouted out orders for

Marie, which she quickly carried out without complaint. They unpacked the mule together. Tingling electricity passed between them each time their hands chanced to touch. Marie brushed down the horses as Wil took off their saddles and prepared their feed. After putting the horses in a small corral, they quickly got the cabin organized. Marie smiled quietly to herself when she noticed that Wil was setting up his bedroll in the cabin and not out with the horses as he had done the previous night.

They spent a half hour collecting wood. There was already a pile of cut wood next to the cabin, but Wil said he never liked to use it unless he had to. They had enough to keep the cabin fireplace going all night. Wil gave Marie instructions on the correct way to start a fire. Before long, the fire was crackling and glowing. Everything looked to be in its place.

They worked well together. Their movements were synchronized and efficient. They were more comfortable with each other now. She could tell that he was pleased with her performance. He didn't complain once the whole afternoon. He was like a different person, casual and seeming happy. He even smiled at her more than a few times. She liked it when he smiled. It softened his face and took some of the sadness out. Now that she had a chance to really see him in his element, she realized that he was quite handsome. He was even sexy in an erotic, rugged sort of way.

Wil looked at Marie standing next to him. She was smiling. The light from the fire gave her face a shimmering, golden glow. She looked like an angel. He began to feel the heat. Was it from the fire in the fireplace or the fire of his desires? It felt as if there was no air in the room. He was having trouble breathing. His groin started throbbing, and he could feel himself getting hard. "Oh, shit," he thought to himself. He couldn't let her see his excitement now. The room started closing in on him. He had to do something. He had to get out of there and fast. He looked around and grabbed his fishing rod.

"Sun's going down. Better catch dinner if we want to eat," he said as he headed for the door.

"Mind if I join you?" she called back.

"Oh, shit. Not now," he thought, feeling his pants tighten against his erection, but he said, "Suit yourself."

He opened the door of the cabin and felt relief as the cool evening air hit him in the face. "Grab the net," he yelled behind his back as he headed out the door, soaking up the blast of chilly air as it blew into his face. It was revitalizing. His head cleared, and he regained his composure.

They walked down to the creek without speaking. Wil threw a line in as soon as he reached the bank. He reeled it in and cast it out again in a single dance-like movement. Marie just watched from a distance in awe. She couldn't get over how natural he looked doing this. He made it look so easy and effortless. She found herself smiling as she watched. It excited her, and she felt the stirring again. She was beginning to lust after him. She couldn't help herself. Something had awoken in her, and it was beyond her control.

He glanced over and saw her smiling at him. Involuntarily, he smiled back.

"Wow," she thought, "he smiled at me." All was right in the world. Just then, he got a hit. It had to be a big one, because he had to steady himself before he began to slowly reel in the catch.

Marie squealed in delight and ran down to the bank with the net in her hand. The fish was a real fighter. Wil worked the line, letting it go out awhile then reeling it in. After several minutes of this, the fish was getting close. Wil instructed her on the proper procedure for netting the fish. She ran to the bank downstream of him and got in ready position with the net outstretched. It was a brook trout, a large brook trout. It was big enough for both of them.

Wil reeled the fish close to the bank and told Marie to net it. She obediently scooped up the fish, just as he had instructed. The fish, showing no signs of fatigue after the struggle, wriggled with great strength. Marie had to use both hands to keep the net steady. In the midst of the struggle, she felt herself slipping on the rocks of the creek bank. In an instant, she was sitting in the creek, soaked from head to toe. She triumphantly noticed that she still had a firm grip on the squirming, netted fish. It made her start laughing at herself and at what must have been quite a sight.

To her delight, she could hear Wil laughing as he approached her from the back. She felt his strong hands grasp under her arms and lift her out of the creek in a single motion. He grabbed the net and looked at her. She looked almost childlike when she laughed. He held the fish up in acknowledgment and salute to her. For a moment they both stood there, laughing together, the current between the two almost visible.

Marie sneezed, and Wil suddenly got serious. "We better get you inside, next to the fire, and out of those wet clothes," he said as he grabbed her by the shoulders and headed her toward the door. "I'll clean the fish while you change," he added.

She changed quickly. The creek water had been ice-cold. The sun was practically down, and the night air was downright chilly. The fire inside was roaring, and the heat felt good. She laid out her wet clothes over some chairs and put them close to the fireplace. She was warming her hands over the fire when she heard a knock on the door.

The door opened a crack. "You decent?" Wil called out.

"Why don't you come in and judge for yourself?" she answered mischievously. It was a bold statement, seeing as how she wasn't even sure if he wanted to see her decent or not. But somehow this afternoon had changed things. He seemed to be opening up and becoming more relaxed, so different than the grumpy, unkempt man who she met at the Wonder Blur.

"OK," he answered. "I gave you fair warning." Suddenly the door swung open, and he came charging in, waving the rather large, gutted fish in his hands.

She squealed in delight, and she could see that her glee was reflected on his face. As their eyes met, time stopped as the fire of passion burned within them, an unspoken desire that was becoming all consuming.

There it was again. He couldn't look at her without feeling desire. He fantasized about what it would be like to lay her down and explore every part of that womanly body. He could feel his own body heat rising. When he felt the familiar twinge in his groin, he decided to stop it before it got out of control.

Deliberately breaking the mood, but still smiling, he said, "Let's cook this old boy up. After all the trouble he's caused, he deserves to be eaten."

Marie smiled back at him. "Sounds good to me. I'm starving." She was a little sorry he had spoiled the moment but quickly thought it was probably best. "What am I doing?" she thought. "This is *so* inappropriate." Or was it? Did she detect a glimpse of longing in his eyes, too? Could it be that he desired her as much as she desired him? "Oh, please, make it so," she silently prayed.

Wil got the camp stove lit, and Marie assembled the needed utensils and seasonings. He took over cooking the fish. Marie prepared instant rice and canned corn. She set the table and poured them both a glass of water. They made a good team. A couple of times she looked over at him, only to catch him staring at her. Their eyes would meet for a quick, electrifying moment. She would smile shyly and look away. Each time, she could feel her face flush red. More than that, she felt a rush of excitement all the way to her toes.

Wil announced that dinner was ready as he lifted the frying pan off the camp stove and headed toward the table. Marie walked over to the counter to retrieve the rice and corn she was keeping warm. Wil lit the camp lantern. It gave off a soft, romantic glow and made the room sparkle.

She put the rice and corn on the table and sat down across from him. She looked at her plate. The fish was expertly cooked and served and looked tasty. Across the table sat a smiling Wil. Marie lifted her plastic water glass in a toast and said, "Thank you." She looked deep in his eyes. She could lose herself in those dark pools if she didn't watch it. Then, without warning, she could feel her own eyes filling with tears of happiness.

Even in the dim light, she could tell he was blushing. "Hey," he said shyly. "I didn't do much. You're the one who fell on her butt in the creek. I'm just being nice to you so you don't sue me for negligence."

"Is that so?" she replied with a chuckle. "You're not off the hook yet. I'm starting to feel a slight pain in my back."

"Uh-oh," he joked. "You mean I gotta be nice to you the whole night?"

"'Fraid so," she said. "Don't worry; just keep doing what you're doing. I like this side of you."

He got serious. "I should be thanking you," he confessed. "I've actually had fun tonight. I haven't had fun in a long time."

"I could tell," she said sympathetically. "I don't mean to get personal, but I get the feeling that some cruel woman broke your heart and you haven't forgiven womankind since then."

"You're partially right," he said. "It was Duke's mother, in case you were wondering. But that was a long time ago, and I don't want to talk about it now. But I have forgiven 'womankind,' as you put it. I just hadn't found a woman I could have fun with…"

He paused for a minute and thought about what he had just said. "Fun," the word sounded strange. It had been a long time. What he wanted to say was that he desired her, more than he had desired anyone in a long, long time. He wanted to rip her clothes off of her and take her right there in front of the fireplace. He wanted to tell her that he had been fighting his feelings and yearning the whole afternoon. Instead, he gazed into her eyes and completed his sentence. "…until now."

She was shocked at the compliment he had just paid her. Even in the dim light, he could see her face blush. He smiled and said,

"Marie Trousdale, you're all right." He lifted his water glass and toasted her.

"Why, Mr. Townsend," she said coyly. "I do believe that is the nicest thing you have ever said to me. Thank you." She lifted her glass and touched his gently. The glasses made a dull thud as plastic met plastic. At the sound, they both laughed. "Success," she thought, smiling inside. "He likes me."

By now the evening sky was pitch black. Crickets and other creatures of the night were singing a melodic, nocturnal serenade outside the cabin. Inside, the room flickered with a warm, golden glow from the fireplace and lantern. It was magical. It was romantic. Both Wil and Marie could feel it. They couldn't help it. They were two lonely souls whose search for a true love was over. But neither one knew how to tell the other.

Together, they cleaned up the dinner dishes and repacked the supplies and utensils. Each accidental touch set the spark of electricity flowing between them as their bodies came in contact. They would exchange glances momentarily. His look made the hair on the back of her neck stand up and sent chills up her spine. She wondered if her touch had the same affect on him.

It did. He still couldn't put his finger on what made this woman different. But she could get the fire burning in him just with a look. Every time he was close to her, he could feel his manhood rise. He hoped she hadn't noticed how he had to turn in order to conceal the visible hardness of his penis through his pants. How was he going to sleep in the same room with this woman? Normally when he felt this urge, he could always retreat to the privacy of his bedroom and relieve himself. This time that was out of the question.

Besides, he wanted her. He wanted to experience the full pleasure of her body in the act of lovemaking.

Wil had felt sexual desire for other women since Maggie, but this time it was more than sex. He wanted more. He wanted to be part of her life, to find out what she liked and didn't like. He liked being around her. So what if she didn't eat meat or drink coffee—didn't they say opposites attract? If she could put up with his habits, he would be willing to put up with her little eating oddities. No one was perfect. There was no question that her body was perfect. Those big titties, that round ass, her body was driving him wild.

They found themselves sitting together on the couch in front of a roaring fire. The conversation turned to Marie's new house and how wonderful it would be to live on the creek. They were feeling comfortable with each other. Suddenly, a crackling sound came from the fire, and a hot ash propelled through the air toward Marie. She jumped toward Wil to get out of the way. He instinctively stretched out his arms to catch her. She fell right into them.

He looked down at her. She looked up impishly. His heart was racing. She just stayed there, looking up at him. "She's not moving," he thought. "Could she want me to kiss her? What the hell," he thought and pressed his lips down to hers. She reached her arms around his neck and kissed him back. Their kiss was soft and tender but full of passion. His lips pressed hard against hers, and he explored her mouth with his tongue. She circled his tongue with hers and sucked on it gently. He tasted salty and manly. She tasted sweet and smelled of flowers. Their souls were blending into one. The connection was made. He gently caressed her back with his hand, letting it slip down to her buttocks, squeezing it gently in his hands. She felt weak and energized at the same time. It was exhilarating. She felt alive. She pushed her breasts into his chest.

Suddenly, he pulled away. "I'm sorry," he apologized, looking away. "I didn't mean to do that."

"Don't apologize," she scolded, still feeling the heat of his kiss. "I wanted that just as much as you did."

"Well," he said shyly. "I don't want to make you feel uncomfortable. I don't think we should let this get any further. Besides, I don't want you to think I do this with all the women I take on the trail."

"Really, Wil, don't be silly," she said. "It's OK." She could tell he was embarrassed and didn't want to push it. "I think we just got caught up in the moment. Heck, here we are in a very romantic situation, candlelight dinner, fireplace…Besides, how could you resist me?" She smiled coyly, trying to defuse the sudden tension in the room but secretly hoping it wasn't just a one-time thing.

She wanted to say, "Don't stop there; take me." But she didn't.

Wil was breaking out in a sweat. He felt those sexual stirrings again and needed some air. Excusing himself, he walked out the door.

She could feel his tension. Just a moment before, they were kissing. Had she read him wrong? She thought he was enjoying it, the next thing she knew, he was walking out the door. But they had kissed, hadn't they? It was everything she had thought it would be. His lips were strong but tender. His embrace was gentle but firm. He had pulled her close to him. Her body had rubbed against his. She could still feel his hands on her, squeezing and caressing her backside. She had felt his hardness growing. She'd wanted to reach down and grab it. Why couldn't that moment have lasted just a little longer? What made him stop? Did he change his mind? Maybe he was right, at least for now. But they did kiss. She would always remember it. He was interested.

It was late. Not knowing how long Wil was going to be out, she slipped into her bedroll and tried to sleep.

Wil walked toward the creek. The cool night air felt good. He started to think about what just happened. He'd kissed her, and she'd kissed him back. She was willing. She didn't bolt. She said she wanted it, too. And what did he do? He apologized and told her he didn't want it to go any further. Stupid, stupid, stupid. He felt like a grade-school punk. What was wrong with him? Why was he always so self-conscious of himself with her? John Wayne never had this problem with women.

Well, what was done was done. He'd better get back in there before she started to think he was a bigger jerk than she already did. He headed back to the cabin. He checked the horses and mule one last time before he went back inside for the night.

Once inside, he could see that she had turned in. "I guess she's sleeping," he thought to himself. He put more wood on the fire and put out the lantern. Then he silently slipped into his sleeping bag.

"Good night," he heard from across the room as he settled in.

"Good night," he answered.

"I meant what I said," she softly spoke.

"About what?" he asked.

"About it being OK. I wanted to kiss you, too," she said. "But it's OK if we don't do any more. Still friends?"

"Still friends," he answered. "Now get to sleep. We got a full day of riding to do tomorrow."

She smiled and closed her eyes. He closed his, but all he could see was her face in his mind's eye. All he could feel was her body next to his as he held her close. He could feel all that and his manhood growing again. "Damn, just what I needed," he thought. "Now how am I gonna to get to sleep?"

CHAPTER SEVEN

—∿—

SOMEHOW, WIL MANAGED TO FALL ASLEEP, BUT HE had a fitful night. Thoughts of Marie kept flooding his mind—her face, her smell, her feel. Something strange was happening to him. He didn't understand it, but he knew one thing; he was falling for this crazy, California dame.

Marie lay on her cot, wide awake, reflecting on what had happened that day. She felt as if she was coming out of a fog. Life seemed to have a meaning again, a purpose. Her body tingled when she thought about the kiss with Wil. What an unexpected joy. He stirred erotic feelings in her and made her feel alive. How hungry she was for his touch. How safe she felt with him, her protector. She lay there staring at him, almost willing him to turn around. But it didn't happen. She fell asleep wanting more.

Wil woke just before sunrise. He always loved the sunrise. This was what he called the best part of the day; each sunrise was a miracle of nature. Observing the daily event had become a personal ritual. There was always something lacking if he missed it.

Spending the whole day with Marie would be both pleasurable and painful. But he was looking forward to it. He was in a good mood and wanted to know more about this widow from California.

The morning air was chilly and fresh. The sun was just about ready to make an appearance. A rain-cloud–lined horizon was ablaze with color. The red, orange, and lavender tones were so vibrant they made the sky look as though it was made of fire. He took a deep breath in and tasted the air. Rain…it would be there soon. Wil said a silent prayer of thanks for the privilege of witnessing Mother Nature's great beauty. He wasn't a churchgoer, but he believed in an all-powerful being and felt its presence in nature. The little morning prayer of thanks was his own way of communicating with the Great Spirit. It was a custom he was taught by his grandmother when he was a boy.

After relieving himself by a tree, he stopped to feed the horses and the mule. The animals were frisky and ready to go, almost as if they could smell the rain in the air and wanted to get home. He spent a few extra minutes stroking them and talking softly in their ears. By now the sun had fully risen and bathed everything with a bright glow. The color of the clouds had begun to fade to white and gray, and the sky behind them began to turn a dazzling blue.

"You can feel it, too; can't you, boys?" he said to the horses, observing the dark clouds low in the horizon. He headed back toward the cabin.

Approaching the cabin, he could see movement inside. Marie was up. He liked that; he could never stand a woman who liked to sleep in. They were always lazy. Maggie liked to sleep in—should have been a clue. "Oh hell," he said out loud to himself. "Water under the bridge."

Marie greeted him cheerfully as he entered the cabin. "What a beautiful morning," she said.

"Yes, it is," he responded. "We better eat quick and get back on the trail. Looks like we're in for a shower or two later this afternoon."

"How do you know that?" she asked. "You been watching the Weather Channel when I wasn't looking?"

"It's my job to know that, Dopey," he answered. "I can't afford to take no tourists out if a huge weather system is about to move in. I check it out before each trip. The weatherman was wrong this time. Any fool can see we're in for a storm. Besides, the sky is red this morning."

"What's that got to do with it?" she asked.

"You must live a sheltered life, little lady," he said. "Don't tell me you never heard of 'Red sky at night, sailor's delight. Red sky in the morning, sailor's warning.'"

"Actually, no," she responded.

He just shook his head in disbelief.

"What about Duke and the other people?" she asked.

"Duke knows what to do. Don't worry about them," he responded.

"You know," she said, "I've noticed something about you. You are a detail man. You have all the bases covered. Makes me glad I chose you to build my house."

"One does what one can," he replied humbly. "Besides, like I said, it's my job."

"It's just that I like that about you," she said. "I'm safe with you. I know you would never steer me wrong. I trust you."

He blushed slightly. "Now, let's not get carried away. You make me sound like a damn hero. I'm just a regular guy."

She looked at him lovingly. "You're more than that, Wil. Don't ever forget it." Thoughts of last night's kiss entered her head. She wondered if that would ever happen again. She hoped so, more than anything. She liked the feel of his touch and wanted him to touch her all over. She wanted to get lost in his touch.

"Hey," he said, feeling self-conscious and uncomfortable at her comments and not knowing what to read into them. "Let's get a move on."

Breakfast was a simple affair. There was little time to waste. The breeze was more brisk today than the day before and was coming from the opposite direction, a sure sign of changing weather. They got packed up and loaded the mule together. Wil saddled up the horses while Marie straightened out the cabin. They were on the trail in less than an hour.

The distant sky looked threatening. The weather system was moving in fast and it was bringing more than light showers. He decided that they should take the shortcut. It was an unmarked trail and a lot more treacherous than the two-track path they had taken up. The trail they had taken up was actually an old logging road. There were so many ruts and fallen trees in it now, from the years of rain and no maintenance, that no one used it anymore, except by horseback. But compared to the trail he was about to take her on, it was a freeway. He had never taken anyone besides Duke on it before. Some of the passes were steep and narrow. But

Marie had done very well on Rex. He was a trained trail horse and very surefooted, and he had been on the trail before. The shortcut would cut three hours or more off the trip. The storm would be there before long. He wanted to play it safe.

They snacked on the trail, so they wouldn't have to stop for lunch. Marie nibbled on the trail mix she had brought, and Wil chewed on some beef jerky. The only time they stopped was when Marie could hold it no longer and just had to get off and pee. She noticed that Wil always took advantage of these situations, too. She figured he had to go just as badly as she did but didn't want to admit it. Macho pride, she figured, a strange thing.

Wil was right. The ride down was not easy, but Marie did fine. She didn't complain, not even once. She looked mighty scared sometimes though, especially on the parts of the trail that were no wider than two or three feet and had a hundred-foot drop on one side and a hundred-foot slope up on the other side. These were game trails that the deer and other wildlife used to get up and down the mountains.

It started to drizzle just as they spotted the cars and trucks in the parking lot at the starting point. By the time they got the horses and mule in the barn, it was starting to pour. Wil took the saddles and packs off. Marie helped brush the animals down before they turned them loose in the corral.

By now the rain was coming down in sheets. It sounding like popcorn as it hit the metal roof. Wil told Marie that the rain should ease up in a bit and if she didn't want to get drenched, she could wait in the barn with him until it did if she wanted to. To his delight, she agreed. Wil found a couple of buckets, turned them upside down, and offered Marie a seat.

"Wow, that was a close one," she said, grateful to be off the horse and in a dry spot. "Whose place is this anyway?"

"Mine," Wil said.

"You live here?" she asked, pointing to the little house at the end of the trail.

"No, I rent it out," he answered. "I use the barn and keep some of the trail animals and equipment here. Duke and I keep our horses at our house. We live a couple miles down the road."

"You and Duke live together?" she asked.

"Always have," he said with paternal fondness. "We work together, too."

She thought of Andy. "That's nice," she said. "I always wondered what my boy would have grown up to be. You're lucky to have Duke. He's a fine young man. You should be very proud of him."

"I am," he said with pride, "more than you know."

She took the chance that he was open for a touchy conversation. "What happened to his mother?" she asked.

Wil paled, and a pained expression came across his face. He tilted his head back, squinted his eyes, and rubbed his stubbly chin between his thumb and forefinger. He had a distant look on his face, like he was watching a bad movie in his mind. "It's a long story," he said.

"Well, unless I'm mistaken"—she gestured to the pouring rain—"I think we've got a little time."

And like the endless rush of rain flowing from the barn toward the ditch, he opened up to her. He told her the whole sorry tale of falling in love, getting Maggie pregnant, getting married, having Duke, and being abandoned by Maggie. He ended with the phone call from Maggie's mother and the news of her death.

He said it without emotion. It was almost as if he was describing someone else's life. His story filled Marie with such sorrow. How could a mother desert her own child? How could she throw away such a precious gift? And poor Wil…to have lived through that pain. No wonder he was so afraid to love again. She wanted to reach out to him and comfort him. She wanted to tell him that she would never hurt him, if he would only give her the chance. Instead, she just sat there, stunned in amazement. The only thing she could say was, "I'm sorry."

"Don't be sorry," he said. "You didn't do it. Besides, I know life hasn't been all that good to you either."

"No," she said, "you're right. When Charles and Andy died, I felt like I died, too. I've just been existing for the past ten years. My job has kept me busy, too busy."

Wil was sympathetic as she gave him the details of her short but beautiful life with Charles and Andy. She was able to get through it without crying this time. His heart went out to her. He had been hurt by a woman. She had been hurt by a terrible twist of fate. He had Duke. She had no one.

She told him about her job, how burned out she was getting, and that she was thinking of looking for something new, especially once her house was finished. She didn't ever want to leave it. She was falling in love with Oregon, and with him, but she didn't tell him that part.

By the time she finished her tale, the rain cleared, and it was time to go. Wil helped Marie put her things in her car. Saying good-bye was awkward. They were like two kids after a school dance. She thanked him for the wonderful adventure. He closed the car door for her. She started it up and rolled down the window. "I'd like to talk to you about the house before I leave, if that's OK," she said.

"Sure," he said, feeling hopeful. "Maybe we can have dinner together or something." Did he really say that? He couldn't believe it.

"I'd like that," she said, smiling. "How about tomorrow?" She wondered if she was pushing her luck.

"I'll pick you up at six," he said, grinning, with his face beaming and his heart soaring.

"Six it is. See ya then," she replied and drove off.

He just stood there, watching her little car disappear down the road. He was feeling pretty good about himself. They were having dinner tomorrow. Was this a date? No, this was business. She said she wanted to talk about the house. Who was she kidding? She was interested, and so was he. A huge smile came across his face. He thought back to the night before and their first kiss. He relished the memory of her soft lips, how sweet she tasted, how round and perfect her ass felt when he grabbed it, and how her breasts felt as she pressed herself to him. He wondered how her breasts would feel in his hands. He wanted to bury his head in those ample boobs of hers. His groin twitched. He looked down at the growing bulge in his jeans. "Calm down," he said to his pants. "I'm working on it."

CHAPTER EIGHT

—ⱲⱲ—

MARIE HAD THOROUGHLY ENJOYED THE PAST THREE DAYS'
adventure in the Oregon mountains, but the hot stream of water
hitting her back from the hotel shower felt like heaven. Her body
ached from the hours in the saddle and the physical work she
had done but was not accustomed to. Today had been especially
grueling. The shortcut had been treacherous. She was terrified of
falling off the side of a cliff most of the time. But she trusted Wil
and knew he would be watching out for her. Even though he had
his hands full with his own horse, and the mule to boot, it had
been fun.

She had managed to get a sneak peek at the other side of him,
the side she could love. That was the best part. She understood him
now and why he seemed so standoffish. Poor guy, he'd barely had
time to grow up himself before he became a father. She still could
not imagine a mother leaving her baby son. Well, obviously, Duke's
mother was unstable. Look at how she ended up. Marie felt little

sympathy for her. Maggie had made her life choice. It just turned out to be the wrong one.

As she stood in the shower, letting the water soothe her aching body, she thought of how it felt to be held by Wil. She closed her eyes and relived the moment that their lips met. She fantasized about what could have happened had he not backed off. How romantic it would have been to make love in the cabin in front of the fireplace. Then she thought about their pending dinner date. Could anything come of that? She smiled, thinking, "Yes, something could come of that."

She was pleased with her new self. She had a different attitude. Life had taken on a new meaning. She couldn't help but smile, thinking about that crazy mountain man. What was happening to her? It was as if she had been reborn.

She finished her shower and called down for room service. Her stomach was calling for food, but the recent days' events were catching up to her, and she didn't feel like leaving her room. About the time she finished dressing, room service was knocking at her door.

Her meal was eaten in a hurry. Tonight she had pasta primavera. She was quickly running out of things she could order on the limited hotel menu. She was tired, sore, and wanted to sleep. A real bed, it was bliss. As soon as her head hit the pillow, she fell asleep.

The next morning, she felt well rested. She spent the morning at the park on the Rogue River, just a short walk from the hotel. She read a book she had brought with her. Around lunchtime, she cruised around town and found a little sandwich shop on *G* Street that served avocado sandwiches.

After lunch she returned to her room and thought hard about quitting her project management job. Try as she might she couldn't think of anything that she could do that would give her the flexibility and income of her current position. She needed a fresh perspective and decided to call her sister Madelyn.

"Hello, Maddy? It's Marie," she said into the phone.

"Marie? Are you in Oregon? I thought you were going on an adventure trip?" Her sister sounded surprised and excited to hear from her. "Yes, I'm in Oregon. The adventure trip ended yesterday. It was wonderful. I'll tell you about it later. I want to pick your brain a little about something if you have a minute." Today Marie didn't want to chit-chat. She was on a mission.

Madelyn could tell she was serious. "I'm all ears, sis."

"You know, I've been a project manager for almost ten years now and at first it was great. I loved the travel, the challenge, and the people I met. But lately, it's lost its sparkle. The new owners' of the company are incompetent a-holes and they have taken all of the fun out of my job. My stress level is at an all time high and frankly, now that I'm going to move to Oregon, I want to start something new."

"That's great," Maddy said enthusiastically. "What it is?"

"I don't know," Marie answered. "That's why I'm calling you? Any thoughts?"

They batted around a few ideas like secretary, bookkeeper or store clerk. They both decided that being tied down to a nine-to-five office job wasn't a step up.

'Well, what do you *like* to do?" Maddy asked.

Marie thought for a while, "I like to go shopping."

Both women laughed out loud.

Then Maddy had an idea. "Do you ever make up stories anymore?" she asked.

"Stories?" Marie was puzzled. "What do you mean, like the bedtime stories I used to make up for you girls at night?" One of Marie's chores growing up was to put her younger sisters to bed. Some nights she would read to them, but sometimes she would make up stories about talking cats or roosters that went to school. They were fantastic tales of make believe, and magical adventure.

"Those were good," Madelyn answered, "But I was thinking about the stories you wrote in high school."

Marie was puzzled for moment. Then she remembered the X-rated sex stories she had written for her high school friends. It had started as a joke but the more her friends read them the more popular they became.

"How do you know about those?' she asked with surprise.

Madelyn confessed that she had found them in a box when she was helping her and Charles pack for their move to California. She had read a few when she found them in the box but they were way too erotic for her taste.

"Just a thought," Madelyn went on. "They don't do a thing for me, but that kind of stuff sells. I bet if you brushed them off and freshened them up you might be able to put a book together and get it published. That way you can stay at home and still make a living. Have you still got them?"

Marie thought for a moment. "I think so. I think I've got them in a box in the attic."

Madelyn was excited now. "Well dig them out. They could be your ticket to paradise."

"You really think they were that good? You think people would want to read that trash?" Marie asked.

"Trash?!" Madelyn exclaimed. "I never told you but those stories were still being talked about when I was in high school. I heard that some original copies were still being circulated around but it was all hush-hush. The teachers all knew about them, too, and were always on the look-out for them. Some of the football players offered me money once to get you to write more."

"You have got to be kidding!" Marie was in shock. "Why didn't you ever tell me about this?"

"I was too embarrassed," her sister. "Besides you were already with Charles and I just didn't think you were into it anymore"

"Well," Marie said cautiously, "I suppose it's worth a try. I'd have to revise them and write more stories."

Madelyn agreed and added, "Just think of how juicy they will be now that you've had years of sexual experience."

Both women laughed out loud. Madelyn knew that Marie had not had a man in ten years.

Talking with Madelyn had lifted Marie's spirit. It was a crazy idea, but it just might work. She had her laptop with her. She turned it on and opened a new document. Happy fingers started tapping away at the keys, weaving a story of erotic adventure and sexual lust. She still had it. It had been years since she had written one of her stories. She was surprised how easily the words came to her.

She had called her collection *Dirty Stories of a Rich Girl*. They were a collection of short stories about the sexual exploits of a wealthy girl from Beverly Hills. They contained very explicit sexual descriptions of the character having sex with different men, and the occasional woman—the pool man, the carpenter, a stranger in a dressing room, or guys she picked up at posh parties. The stories were a big hit with both the guys and the girls in high school. She had never been serious about writing before. The stories were just written for fun. She'd stopped writing them before she met Charles, and she had forgotten all about them until Madelyn reminded her. Charles had never even read them. They were not his style, and she had thought it best not to ever mention them.

She figured she had about fifteen or twenty hidden in the attic. She would need about thirty to make a good book. They would have to be rewritten to make them gel as a book and to give the book continuity. But that wouldn't be hard. Marie was tingling with excitement as the stories unfolded before her. That afternoon, she churned out two new tales.

They had the usual effect of making her sexually aroused. She thought about her upcoming date with Wil. Could this be her lucky day? She would have to work on it to make it so. He was definitely interested, but he seemed reluctant to expand their relationship to becoming sexual. She was out of practice, but she pledged to herself that she would get him in bed this very night, if it was the last thing she did. She needed it. She longed for it. Was she feeling sexual because of the stories, or was it Wil?

She thought about him, his captivating face; she wanted to run her fingers through his hair. She loved the way he looked at her with those piercing brown eyes, and she loved his well-shaped body, those arms with their strong embrace, and the way he swaggered when he walked. Sure, he had a little middle-age thing going, a little graying at the temples in his sideburns and his salt-and-pepper, stubby beard, but he was still in great shape. She thought about his straight, slick brown hair under the cowboy hat, which he seldom took off. She wanted to muss it up and let it fall onto his face. Then she thought about the kiss. If the rest of his sexual repertoire was as good as his kissing…She could feel her pulse quickening and her breath shortening. She closed her eyes and imagined what it would be like. She could feel herself tingling and getting wet down there.

She glanced at the clock radio on the nightstand. It was quarter after five. Wil would be there in less than an hour. She quickly saved and closed the document and began to prepare for her date.

When she took the trip to Oregon, she hadn't planned on a seduction and didn't really pack for it. Luckily, she had packed a silk blouse and a black crepe skirt. The blouse was a deep royal blue and was tailored to accentuate her curves. The skirt was straight and came to the top of her knees. She left the top two buttons of the blouse undone, exposing some cleavage, and wore a plain gold chain around her neck. The sparkle of the chain would be sure to draw his attention to her ample breasts.

For extra allure, she added a dab of perfume at the top of each breast. She laughed at herself as she applied the aromatic liquid. In the last ten years, she had tried hard to dress in a manner that would not bring attention to her bosom. There were plenty of times that she had caught clients and co-workers staring at her chest. Now she was doing the complete opposite, trying to emphasize her natural-born voluptuousness. She looked at herself in the mirror. Her large breasts had always been her best feature. They were big enough to be noticed but not so big as to make her look top-heavy.

"Not bad," she said out loud to herself, "for a woman who has been out of circulation for ten years." She was grateful she had kept up with her yoga and treadmill workouts.

She had been wearing her long, wavy brown hair braided in back to keep it out of the way in this rugged environment. Tonight her hair was loose and flowing. It added an extra element of sensuality to her appearance.

At six o'clock on the nose, there was a knock at the door. She took a deep breath and opened it. She hardly recognized Wil. He was wearing a dark tweed sport coat with a black collared shirt underneath, unbuttoned enough for her to see a few curly chest hairs peeking out. The sight unexpectedly made her weak in the knees. She quickly shook it off. His jeans were clean and his cowboy boots looked as though someone had spent some time cleaning and polishing them. He wasn't wearing his cowboy hat, and his shiny dark brown hair was slicked back. A few stray strands dangled in front of his clean-shaven face, making him look even sexier. His hair was long enough to hang in the collar of his shirt in the back. It begged for her to reach out and run her hands through it. She struggled to fight back the impulse.

They both stood speechless, staring at each other for a moment. Wil was taken aback by the vision of loveliness before him. She looked gorgeous. He loved the fact that she didn't have to wear a lot of makeup to look pretty. "She did something to her hair," he thought. "It's down. Looks sexy, nice legs, too. And look at those

titties." When he found his voice, all he could say was, "You look…
great."

"Thanks," she said. "You clean up pretty good yourself." She
had heard that in a western movie somewhere and figured the
phrase fit. It did, and he laughed. She loved the sound of his laughter. The softness came back to his face. He looked relaxed. It made
her smile.

"Now don't we just look like a couple of city folks out on the
town? Ready to go?" he asked.

"Oh, sure," she replied, grabbing her purse.

When they got to his truck, she noticed that it was missing
the thick layer of dirt and dust that had previously adorned it.
It sparkled like the setting sun. He opened the door for her and
helped her in.

"Thank you, sir," she said at this unexpected act of chivalry.

He walked around and got into the driver's seat and started
up the truck. "I know you eat seafood, so I thought we would go
to Medford. There ain't a seafood restaurant worth a damn in this
town. Hope you don't mind a little ride."

"I don't mind at all," she responded. "It's a nice evening for
a drive." She couldn't help but notice that the car had been spit
shined inside as well. Gone were the clipboards, empty cans, tools,
and odd pieces of paper that had occupied the cab on the previous
ride. The seats and floor had been vacuumed clean.

"The truck looks nice," she said, pausing a moment, then continuing. "Not as good as you but nice."

"Thanks," he replied shyly. "I like your hair down. It looks…"
He struggled to find the right word.

"Sexy," she said boldly.

He did a double take. "Well, yeah, but I don't want you to get the wrong idea."

"Oh, don't worry," she said coyly. "I've got the right idea."

Wil was feeling slightly uncomfortable and self-conscious. She looked downright hot. He wanted to jump her right there. He could feel the ache in his groin. "Damn, but she's got nice tits," he thought to himself. His desire for her was reaching a fever pitch. He tried to clear his mind of these arousing thoughts. But, by God, she looked sexy. All the feelings he had for her before were raised to new heights. This was a real woman, curved in all the right places. She didn't need a bunch of makeup to make her look good. She was what you would call a natural beauty. He wondered what it would be like to hold her naked body against his. He was feeling that heat in his gut again and could feel his manhood rising. Thank goodness he was sitting.

They made pleasant conversation en route to Medford, talking about the weather and current events. The sun was setting, and the sky was putting on a color show of exceptional quality.

The restaurant he had selected was a quaint, little place on a creek, off the beaten path. They were seated in a booth next to the window, so they could see the lighted creek and the adjoining flower garden. It was quite romantic. Wil ordered a Dewar's on the rocks; Marie had a Chardonnay. He was surprised to see that she had ordered alcohol.

She could see he was puzzled. "I said I don't drink beer; I didn't say I didn't drink," she said, answering a question that was not asked.

"Well, all right," he thought to himself. "There's hope for this gal yet."

They perused the menu. He looked up at her and asked, "Would it bother you if I ordered a steak?"

"Just as long as it doesn't bleed too much," she replied with a smile.

He shook his head and smiled. "It won't bleed too much," he promised.

The waiter brought their drinks and asked if they were ready to order. Marie ordered broiled steelhead with lemon-dill sauce. Wil decided on a rib-eye, medium rare. She ordered a salad; he asked for soup. The waiter took their menus and walked away.

She looked around the restaurant. It was cozy. She looked at Wil. He was staring at her, and it made her feel a little uncomfortable and glad at the same time. She had to break the tension. "Who would have thought we'd be sitting here having dinner together like this?" she said.

"Yeah," he said. "I just hope I don't run into anyone I know dressed like this. I got an image you know."

"Don't worry," she chided. "Your secret is safe with me. No one will know that Wil Townsend owns more than a denim jacket and a cowboy hat." They both laughed. She loved his laugh. It was sincere and from the heart.

They had just finished their salad and soup when the main courses arrived. They tasted as good as they looked. The fish was fresh, and the sauce was a perfect complement. By the way Wil dug into the steak, it appeared that there was nothing wrong with that either.

They chatted merrily during the meal, laughing and smiling at each other. Marie hadn't felt this comfortable with a man in quite some time. She loved every moment of it. Wil, too, was actually enjoying himself. She was different than any woman he had been with before, including Maggie. Marie was sure and confident. She was mature and sincere. But he couldn't say she was shy. He knew that right from the get-go. That first night when she stood up to him, he knew this woman had guts.

They passed on dessert and settled instead on coffee. That is to say, he had coffee, and she had herbal tea. She was inwardly glad to see that he was responsible enough to forego the alcohol before their long ride home in the dark back to Grants Pass. It reconfirmed her trust in him.

"I thought you wanted to talk about your house?" he asked.

"I did," she replied, caught off guard. "I mean, I do. But we are having such a wonderful time; I don't want to bring work into it."

"Oh, I see," he said, half believing her.

"I'll be here a couple more days. Couldn't we meet again?" she asked, looking up at him with girlish charm.

"Sure," he said, grabbing the check that had been left on the table. "Only next time, you pay."

They left the restaurant and walked out to the parking lot. The moonless sky was full of stars. Before Wil opened the door to let her in, he pointed out Mars, Jupiter, and the constellations Orion, Andromeda, Pleiades, and Cassiopeia.

"You're a man of mystery, Wil," she said. "A man of hidden talents." He smiled back at her, and she melted inside.

He flipped on the radio. "What kind of music do you like?" he asked.

"Oh," she answered. "I've learned to like just about anything." Then she hastily added, "Anything except opera!"

"Well, little lady," he said. "You don't have to worry about that in this town. But I'll tell you one thing. You better like country, 'cause there ain't much more than that here.

She laughed. "I don't mind country as long as it's not too twangy."

"Let's see what we've got," he said. Fumbling with the buttons, he tuned into the local country station. LeAnn Rimes was singing "Looking Through Your Eyes."

"You like this?" he asked.

"It's perfect," she said as she scooted closer to him. He looked over at her and smiled as LeAnn sang her romantic love song. LeAnn was singing the feelings of Marie's heart. "Love just took me by surprise," LeAnn sang, but Marie was feeling it, living it. She had never heard the song before, but the words could not fit more perfectly. She knew then why being with Wil made her feel like a schoolgirl. Their chemistry matched. She was sexually attracted to him, but more than that, she loved him.

The ride back to Grants Pass seemed surreal after her self-revelation. Her mood was soaring. This was so different from her normal life. It was almost dreamlike. She hadn't been wined and dined in so long; she almost felt guilty for feeling pleasure. "I so missed this," she thought to herself as all her daily stress faded away. She looked over at Wil. He really was handsome. His profile was comforting. He was smiling. Was it because of her? She hoped so. Secretly, she hoped the evening would end with the two of them in bed. She wanted to have sex with Wil. He could bring about such a sensuous thirst in her. Would he make a move? "Please, please do," she chanted to herself, trying to send her message to him telepathically.

Wil pulled the pickup into a hotel parking space close to her room and turned the motor off. She scooted over to her door and waited for him to come around and open it for her. She thought about the night ending like this. Everything had gone well. He seemed interested in her, but she could not tell if he wanted to take the relationship to another level, specifically the sexual level.

It was difficult getting out with her tight skirt. She was grateful that chivalry was not dead and clung to Wil's extended hand. She was also glad that his truck had a running board. He walked her to her room. She invited him in, but he declined.

"Damn, he's going to be a gentleman," she thought. "Well, this is it. It's now or never."

"Wil," she said, looking straight into his deep brown eyes. He looked down at her, and her knees got weak. "We are both adults. We've both been hurt by love and don't want to get hurt again. We just had a lovely dinner. The whole evening has been wonderful. I really don't want it to end just yet. Come in for a bit. Maybe we will just talk awhile and say good night. But maybe it will be more. I have to be honest with you. You have awakened feelings in me that I had forgotten about. You can't tell me that you don't feel it, too."

There, she said it. She had opened the door to her heart and laid it all out on the table. She was praying that he would accept her invitation and that she hadn't made a fool of herself. She had never been so bold with a man.

He was finding it hard to believe that she was saying everything that he was feeling. "I feel it," he said and moved close to her. He put his arm around the small of her back and pulled her tight to him. He breathed in her fragrance. This time he didn't care if she felt the fast-growing hardness in his groin. He kissed her hard on the lips and tasted her sweetness. His tongue gently grazed her teeth and searched out her tongue. She kissed back with built-up passion and wanting.

When their lips finally parted, she was breathless. "Let's go in," she said as she put the key in the door. This time he put up no resistance.

Without breaking their embrace, they entered the tiny hotel room. Their mouths hungrily explored each other's as they kicked off their shoes and made their way to the bed. He pushed her down onto it, quickly took off his jacket and shirt, and lay next to her. He unbuttoned her blouse and pulled it off. Her breasts were ready to burst out of her bra with her every panting breath. He reached around her back and undid the hook, freeing her breasts. Marie let out a moan.

"My God," he said. "You've got beautiful titties."

She looked up at him with a seductive smile. Reaching down, she unsnapped his jeans and started to push them down. He took the hint and pulled them off, letting them fall to the floor. Then he reciprocated by unbuttoning her skirt and pulling the zipper down. Without breaking their embrace, he pulled it off and let it fall to the floor as well. She pulled off his boxers as he pulled off her panties.

It was happening. It was actually happening. She could feel her heart racing. She felt the primitive hunger in her belly and the wanting between her legs. For her, all the years of sexual abstinence and pent-up desire were released with uninhabited abandon.

Wil could not get enough of her fire. Her suppleness was like nothing he had felt before. Her breasts were as soft as satin. He cupped them in his hands and gently sucked her nipples, getting pleasure as they hardened at his touch. He kissed her breasts and laid down a trail of kisses on her smooth, fragrant skin as he worked his way up to her neck. He inhaled her sweet scent, and it drove him mad. He nuzzled his face into her hair and started to kiss her again.

Marie reached down and grabbed his rock-hard penis with her hands. Its firmness felt strange after all this time, but it felt good. She wanted him inside her. She pushed herself to him, and he responded by grinding against her. His hands eagerly explored her delightful body, moving from her neck to her backside and back again.

Somehow through her erotic fog of sexual desire, she had a sobering thought. Sex had not been part of her life for so long that she had no pregnancy protection, and she certainly didn't want to get pregnant now. How stupid of her not to think about that until now. "Wil," she whispered in his ear. "I'm not on any kind of birth control and—"

He interrupted her by placing his finger across her lips. He whispered back, "Don't worry; I had a vasectomy years ago." She relaxed, and with her hands, she guided his manhood into her already wet sex. The full feeling was elating. He drove himself into her again and again, firmly, slowly, passionately. Each thrust brought her higher and higher. She could feel her climax approaching as her pleasure reached new heights. The sleeping bear had awoken. Together, they erupted into spine-tingling orgasm.

They lay there physically spent. They were two people, a man and a woman, who desperately needed to be loved, right then, right there. Their lovemaking had been like a symphony, well played and in perfect sync. They gave each other what no one else had been able to give them for such a long time. They had fed on each other's bottled up emotional and sexual needs and had been satisfied.

Lying together for a while, side by side, motionless, without speaking, catching their breath, they slowly floated back to reality. Wil glanced over at the bedside clock. It was well past midnight. He got up and started to get dressed. She watched him silently and smiled a broad smile.

"You look like the Cheshire cat," he said.

"I just feel so good," she said, propping herself up on some pillows, allowing the sheets to fall and expose her breasts. A single strand of her long, dark hair fell gently on top of one, as if pointing to the ample bosom.

"I'll second that," he said, his attention drawn to her exquisite titties. They still glistened with sex dew from their intense, erotic romp. "And you look good, too," he chuckled back.

Suddenly she got serious and covered herself with the sheet. "Wil," she said, "I don't want you to feel obligated to me because of this."

"I know," he said. "You got your life. I got mine."

"But I want you to know how much it meant to me." She found it hard to express herself without coming right out and admitting that she loved him.

"You talk too much," he interrupted. "Now get some sleep, and call me later. We really do have to talk about your house before you go."

"OK," she said. "Good night, and thanks for a wonderful evening…all of it."

He combed his hair back with his hand, but those few stubborn strands fell forward and brushed against his forehead. He turned and walked toward the door. As he turned the latch and opened it, he looked back at her and gave her a tip of an imaginary hat. "You're welcome, ma'am, but the pleasure was all mine," he said and walked out.

She closed her eyes and relived the amazing sexual encounter of the last few hours. "I can't believe it," she thought, pleased with herself. "I just had sex with Wil." It was better than she could have ever imagined. It was so different than with Charles. Having sex with Wil opened up a part of her that was almost animalistic. She wanted him again. She wanted him bad, rough, and raunchy. She could tell he wanted it, too. She felt as if he'd been holding back and thought about what it would be like the next time. She was sure they had made a connection, satisfying some base need they both had. They had gotten along so well all night. Their lovemaking seemed like the natural thing to do. "Don't over think this," she thought to herself. Whatever it was, it felt good, really good. She quickly fell into a deep, restful sleep.

CHAPTER NINE

MARIE AWOKE REFRESHED THE NEXT MORNING, TENSION FREE and relaxed. It was nearly ten. She was usually up before dawn. She felt slightly guilty, not because of what she had done the night before but because she had missed the sunrise and slept away the morning. Her activities of the past evening were a source of great delight. Making love to Wil had been everything she had hoped for and more. His touch was strong and powerful, yet he was a gentle lover, ever conscious of her feelings and needs. No, she felt no guilt about that, only happiness.

She thought of calling him right away but decided she shouldn't. No commitments, no obligations. That was the way they left it. Take it nice and slow; there was time. A man like Wil wasn't inclined to commit to a lifetime after only one encounter. No, their relationship would have to mature like a fine wine. And it would; she was sure of it. She sensed something in his passion, a need that she fulfilled. Yet there was still caution around him. One day at a time, that was how she would win him over.

She decided to spend the rest of the day writing. After her libidinous session the previous night, her head was filled with a myriad of sexual thoughts and ideas that could be incorporated into a wonderfully erotic story.

She showered, dressed, and went to the restaurant for a late breakfast, giving the maid time to clean her room.

When she returned, she was surprised to see that a small bouquet of spring flowers had been delivered in her absence. The card had three words on it. It said, "Until next time." Her heart did a flip.

She called Wil's business number but only got an answering machine. "Poor guy," she thought. "He stayed up half the night and had to go to work in the morning." She left a message thanking him for the flowers and asking if he would meet her for lunch the next day, her treat. She gave him the name of the little sandwich shop on *G* Street and told him to meet her there at eleven thirty. She asked him to call if he couldn't make it; otherwise she would see him there.

That being done, she settled in for a day of writing. It was a beautiful day, and she had already wasted half of it. So she set up on the balcony, overlooking the Rogue River. Her fingers flew over the keys, creating page after page of erotic, *X*-rated tales. By nightfall she had four new stories. At this rate, she would have a book in no time. Room service delivered dinner. Tonight it was cheese pizza. It didn't matter. She was happy, happier than she had been in ten years. She felt as if she had been given a second chance at life, a new house, a new man, and possibly a new career.

Wil was feeling much the same. He also had missed the sunrise, waking at eight. He still said his little prayer of thanks for the beautiful day. Only this time he had something else to be thankful for, Marie—funny how things turn out. When he first saw her, he had no interest in her. Now, he wanted to be with her whenever he could. He wanted to take care of her and protect her. Their first sexual encounter had been great, exciting and passionate. She was so willing and so much in need. She pleasured him without guilt or commitment. Poor woman, had it really been ten years? "Well, it won't be another ten years," he pledged to himself.

He wanted her to know that she was special. The flowers had been ordered in hopes that she wouldn't feel awkward the next time they met. But he didn't want to appear to be a smitten puppy, thus the short but meaningful message.

He had a full day of work ahead and was trying to finish up loose ends so that he could devote all of his time to Marie's house. He vowed to build it as if he were building his own, with extra supports and strength. Her happiness and safety had become important to him.

When he returned home that evening, he heard her message inviting him to lunch the next day. Just the sound of her voice was enough to get him excited. He closed his eyes and imagined he was holding her close, smelling her female scent and imagining their naked bodies entwined in passionate lovemaking. Thoughts and images of the night before danced in his mind's eye.

"Lord, have mercy! It's got to be a woman." An intruding voice woke him from his fantasy.

Wil snapped back to reality and opened his eyes to find Duke staring at him with a perplexed look on his face.

"Who is she?" Duke asked, his voice tinged with excitement.

"None of your damn business," Wil responded gruffly.

"But it was a woman you were thinking about just now. Wasn't it, Dad?"

Wil could feel his face reddening at being caught in such a compromising situation by his son. "Ain't you got better things to do than butt into my personal life, Junior?"

"I haven't seen you look that pie-eyed since we bought that little colt in Denver," Duke chided. "It's got to be a woman or a horse. Now which is it? And what's her name?" He wasn't about to give up, knowing full well it was a woman.

Then, putting two and two together, he said, "You were out with her last night, weren't you?"

"So what if I was?" Wil said, giving in to his son.

"I knew it," Duke said. "I knew something was up when I saw that you washed the truck."

"What are you doing home anyway?" Wil asked. "I thought you were taking them folks out for a full week."

Duke shrugged his shoulders. "They had enough nature. Besides, it rained pretty hard on us the other day, and the lady was coming down with the sniffles. We decided to come back early." Seeing the concern on his father's face, he added, "Don't worry, Dad; they paid for a full week." Relentless, he asked again, "Now, who is she? Do I know her?"

Wil could see that his son was not going to give up. Stubborn he was, that boy. He must have gotten that from Maggie. "Well, not that it's any of your business—'cause it ain't—her name is Marie."

Duke's face could not conceal his surprise or his delight. "You mean Marie Trousdale? The fish-eating vegetarian?"

Wil nodded affirmatively.

"What happened? By the way you were acting on the trail, I would have never put the two of you together." The wheels in his head were spinning. "Hey, wait a minute," he said. "I know that look. You two didn't…I mean you, and her, you know. Did you?"

Wil's face got stern. "Now just get your mind out of the gutter. It wasn't like that. It was different."

Duke's face broke out into an ear-to-ear grin. "Dad, don't worry. I couldn't be happier. I like Marie. She's nice. She's a lot nicer than the women around here that I've seen you with."

"Hey, wait a minute," Wil interrupted. "Don't go readin' nothing into this. It was just one night. We ain't gettin' married or nothing like that."

"Yeah, right," Duke said sarcastically. "We'll see."

Wil was feeling uncomfortable at the thought of a lifetime relationship. Memories of the pain Maggie had caused came flooding back. He wanted to end this conversation.

"Enough prophesizing. Go upstairs, and wash off that trail dust," he said to his son. "You smell ripe."

Duke started to laugh, gave his under arms a smell, and obediently headed up the stairs.

Marie arrived at the restaurant at 11:20. She was seated at a table near the back. She saw Wil's truck pull into the parking lot at eleven thirty exactly. She liked a man that was punctual. He entered and nodded shyly as he sat down. She could tell by his demeanor that he was all business. He was carrying a set of blueprints under his arm. Wil looked at her and smiled. She smiled back. The unspoken and unseen connection was still there. She didn't imagine it.

A young, aproned waitress appeared from nowhere and asked if they were ready to order.

Marie ordered an avocado sandwich and a glass of juice. Wil ordered a turkey club and a Coke.

"I'm glad you could make it," she said after the waitress had left.

"Couldn't pass up a free lunch," he joked.

"The flowers are beautiful; thank you."

"Glad you liked them."

"I'm leaving in two days," she said.

"I know," he responded solemnly. An uncomfortable sadness covered them like a blanket.

"So, what do we need to talk about?" she asked, trying to conceal her sadness at the thought of going back to her other life.

He rolled out the set of blueprints and started to point out features of the house. It was the first time she saw the layout, and she was impressed. She liked it and told him so.

"I know you only got six months before they take your house. So, we'll get the basement dug then pour it at the same time the septic is being put in and the well is being dug. After we frame it up and get the roof and siding on, you'll have to come back to pick out the rest of the finishes, like flooring, cabinets, electrical and plumbing fixtures, and appliances. That will be in about three months. Can you swing a trip back here then?" he asked.

Her face broke into a smile at the thought of returning to paradise, to him. "You bet," she said, looking deep into his eyes. "I'll miss you," she said, taking a chance.

He looked at her and smiled. "I'll miss you, too," he said sincerely. "Heck, three months ain't nothing. You'll be back before you know it."

The waitress brought their food. While they ate, Wil talked about technical things, like plumbing and heating. Marie gave him the names of the alternate-power equipment companies she had found on the Internet. He was still reluctant, but she was persistent. He promised that he would follow her wishes and that the house would be "off the grid."

By the end of lunch, they were laughing and joking like old friends. Marie picked up the tab, as she promised. Wil walked her to her car.

"So, I guess this is good-bye for now?" he asked.

"I guess so," she said sadly. "I'm gonna call the airlines and see if I can catch a flight back tomorrow. I haven't been gone this long in quite some time. I'd like a day or two to get back into the swing of things before I go back to work."

"Well, have a safe trip," he said. "I'll call you a week or two before I need you back up here."

"Great," she said. Both of them just stood there like a couple of kids.

"Oh, what the hell," he said as he grabbed her and planted a long, sensuous kiss on her lips.

She put her arms around him and kissed him back. She wanted this moment to last forever. She felt so safe and secure when he held her in his arms.

"I'll miss you," she said after he broke their embrace. She turned quickly to conceal the tears that were forming in her eyes. She got in her car and drove away.

Once again, Wil found himself staring as she drove off.

Marie was able to get a seat on the morning flight. Tears were falling down her cheeks as she packed. She was unprepared for the deep emotions she was experiencing at the thought of being separated from Wil. Three months, a lot could happen in three months. She would handle it like she handled all the sadness in her life. She would immerse herself in her work. This time she had two jobs. She was a project manager, *and* she was an author.

She affirmed to finish the book before her return to Oregon. A friend in New York had introduced her to a publishing agent about a year ago. He had given her his card. Where did she put it? At the time, she never gave it a thought. Suddenly, she was anxious to get home. She wanted to finish the book and get it published. She didn't want to be a project manager anymore. The pressure and constant demands of the job were becoming unbearable. It had become a demanding world that she no longer wished to be a part of. She longed for her future life in her Oregon home. She longed to live close to Wil.

CHAPTER TEN

—∿—

CINDY WAS STANDING BY THE CURB AND GREETED Marie as she stepped out of the cab. "Welcome back. How did it go?" she asked.

"Hi, Cindy," Marie replied happily as the two women hugged. "It went great." If Cindy only knew… "I got a contractor all lined up. He promised to have the house completed before I have to get out of here." She thought it best not to mention her romantic involvement with Wil.

"That's good news. Hey, where did the flowers come from?" Cindy noticed the bouquet of flowers Marie was holding; they were the ones from Wil.

"Oh, just a courtesy from the hotel," Marie said, lying. "I couldn't bear to leave them behind." The last part was true.

If Cindy was suspicious, she didn't show it. She was a trusting girl and had no reason not to believe Marie. She picked up one of the bags as they walked to Marie's half of the duplex. "I was just picking up today's mail. The house is open. I just watered your plants. I wasn't expecting you until tomorrow."

"I know," Marie said. "I did what I needed to do, so I decided to come home early." She opened the door, and the women walked inside.

Cindy put the bag down. "Well, I'll let you get unpacked. Nothing new around here, same old stuff. I don't think it has sunk in to anyone yet that this whole block will be leveled in less than six months."

Marie shook her head. "I suppose most everyone will wait till the last minute, as usual." She walked Cindy to the door and gave her another hug. "Thanks for watching over things for me."

"No problem," Cindy said and walked out, closing the door behind her.

The first thing Marie did was find an appropriate vase for Wil's flowers. They would be a constant reminder of him and their passionate night together, at least until they wilted. She unpacked quickly and threw a load of clothes in the washer. She checked her answering machine. Most of her friends and family had known she was going to be gone, so she was not surprised when there was just a handful of messages. There was one from her insurance agent, another from her dentist's office confirming her appointment for next week, and one from her nephew Justin. He told her, in his sweet, little voice, that he missed her and loved her and he wished she could come to visit him soon. He ended with a little song he made up about his cat. How she loved that little boy. She would have to call Madelyn soon. But it was nothing that couldn't wait awhile.

That being done, she got busy looking for the old stories she had written in high school. The attic had a pull-down ladder for access. She grabbed a flashlight and headed up.

There was a pull-string light at the entrance. It was the only light and just gave off a dim glow. In the time that she had been living in the duplex, there had been little reason for her to go to the attic. Usually it was just to get or put back the boxes marked "Christmas Stuff." It was dusty and dirty up there. She would eventually have to go through all the boxes before she moved anyway. The attic contained only personal items. Everything else was in storage.

Moving the flashlight from box to box, she purposely avoided lingering on the box marked "Andy," knowing full well that it contained pictures and toys that used to belong to her precious, little son. She had long ago gotten rid of his clothes and most of his toys. But some things were just too meaningful. They were things like drawings that Andy had made for her and Charles—Mother's Day cards, his favorite stuffed animal, his baby book, things that would only mean something to her. There was a box marked "Charles" as well. This, too, was avoided.

Finding the box marked "High School Memories" was not a difficult task. She blew off the dust and opened it. Shining the flashlight inside, she smiled as she picked up a dried wrist corsage that, when fresh and fragrant, she had worn to her senior prom. Avoiding the temptation to leaf through her old scrapbook and yearbooks, she dug down to the bottom of the box. There, in a well-worn notebook, with hand-lettering that said *"Dirty Stories of a Rich Girl,"* were her stories. The pages were yellowed with age but were completely readable. She pulled the notebook out and put it under her arm as she closed the box and put it back on the stack.

Back downstairs, she began to read. There they were, in black and faded white, sixteen stories in all. They had been typed with a typewriter and would have to be entered on the laptop. This would give her an opportunity to freshen them up a bit. She had a slightly different view of life now than she had when she was in high school, a more mature view. She was not as naïve as she was back then either. Besides, they had been written as stand-alone short stories. The book needed some direction and flow, continuity. Now she was glad she had come back from Oregon early. It gave her a few days to work on her book before hitting the road and becoming a project manager again.

Wasting no time, she plugged in the laptop and got to work. She worked feverishly until the wee hours of the morning, breaking only to eat the Chinese takeout that she had delivered.

It was all coming together, and it looked good.

For the next two months, she worked. By day, she was Marie Trousdale, project manager, straightlaced in a business suit. By night, she was Sheila Exotica, porno author. That was the pen name she chose. She always liked the name Sheila. No way could she put her real name to the book. Being an *X*-rated author was not something she wanted to advertise, in spite of the fact that she hoped it would become her bread and butter. Even Ann Rice had used a pen name for her erotic Sleeping Beauty series.

The drudgeries of her day job became a heavy burden. This supplied the incentive to write faster and get the book done. She had called the publishing agent from New York and told him her idea. He was very interested and had her e-mail him a few chapters. Within hours of receiving the stories, he had called her back and told her he could guarantee her a book deal once the book was complete. They agreed on his fee and a signing bonus for Marie. He faxed a contract, which she signed and faxed back. He told her he would take care of the legal end. All she had to do was finish the book.

Marie managed to spend another weekend with her sister, Madelyn. As usual, it was after a brutal workweek. A week that involved lost luggage, which was found and delivered to her two hours before an important business meeting; a special vegetarian meal that never made it on board; two flights with screaming babies; and a three-hour flight sitting next to the world's most fidgety person, not to mention the normal work fires that needed to be put out. By the end of the week, she was frazzled. Lately, it seemed like this was becoming the normal travel week.

The plane was one hour late landing in Detroit. It took another forty-five minutes to get the luggage and the rental car, and it was a forty-minute drive to her sister's house. She was supposed to arrive at Madelyn's by five in the evening. It was nearly seven by the time she drove the rental car around a curve and Madelyn's house finally came into view. It looked like an oasis in the desert. Justin's welcoming kisses were sweet as sugar. Madelyn had prepared a special veggie meal and had the guest room made up. Marie felt comfortable there. It was almost like a second home.

The first night, after dinner, Marie, her sister, and her brother-in-law were sitting around the living room enjoying an after dinner aperitif. Marie was feeling very relaxed and decided to talk to her sister and brother-in-law about her plans to publish *Dirty Stories of a Rich Girl.* Madelyn was pleased that her big sister had taken her suggestion. "You know," she said, "If the book is a success, you will have to tell Mom and Dad. How do you think they'll take it?"

"Dad will love it. And Mom will never know until I am rich and famous," Marie answered. "Unless you tell her, after all, it was your idea" she quickly added.

"My lips are sealed," Madelyn replied. "I'm not the one who is going to drop this bomb."

"No," Marie said. "I'm sure we both know who will." She was thinking of one of their other sisters, who could not keep a secret if her life depended on it.

Madelyn looked at Marie, and as if in one voice, both said, "Annie!"

Annie was the baby of the family, and try as she might, she just couldn't keep her mouth shut.

Jake was excited and aroused just thinking about it. His first comment was, "You know, they say it's the quiet ones you have to watch out for." After a brief pause, he added, "You don't happen to have a few chapters I can read, do you?"

Madelyn had seen how burnt out Marie had become and could see that she was excited about the chance to get out of project management. Her sister's happiness was Madelyn's only concern.

Marie debated whether or not she should tell them about Wil. After another drink, she decided she would, thinking, "What the hell!"

"There's something else I think you should know," she said cautiously.

Madelyn and Jake looked at her with wide-eyed wonder.

"I met a man," she said offhandedly, waiting for a reaction. She didn't have to wait long.

Her sister and brother-in-law turned to stone for a moment as their jaws dropped. Then they both bubbled with excitement, asking a million questions at once. Madelyn wanted to know who he was, where she met him, what kind of job he had, and other personal things. Jake had one thing on his mind.

"No shit! Did you guys do the nasty?" he asked, percolating with excitement.

After Marie calmed them down, she told them the whole story. She started with her first meeting with Wil at the Wonder Bur and told them about the adventure trip in the mountains, the near encounter at the cabin, and the final enchanting evening at the hotel.

Madelyn could see love for this man in her sister's eyes. She couldn't have been happier. For so many years, she had watched Marie turn inward and away from male companionship after the death of Charles. She had prayed that the right man would come along and release Marie from her solitary shell. Madelyn wanted her sister to find a man that would make her as happy as she was with Jake. When Marie had finished her story, Madelyn gave her a big hug. Both women were on the verge of crying.

"Oh for crying out loud," Jake interjected. "You two are too much. She got laid and by a cowboy to boot. Ride 'em cowgirl! Yee-haa!" With that, he made a mock rocking motion, simulating riding a bucking bronco, flailing one arm up in the air and slapping his leg with the other.

Marie and Madelyn broke off their embrace and stared at Jake. They picked up the throw pillows from the couch and pelted him with them. Soon they were all laughing and toasting Marie's new romantic relationship.

It had been two and a half months when Marie got the call from Wil.

"Marie?"

She recognized his voice immediately, and it made her weak in the knees. "Wil," she said with surprised pleasure. "How are you?"

"I'm fine," he answered. "Are you ready to come back?"

"You're kidding?" she said with astonishment, her skin tingling. "You really mean it?"

"No, I'm not kidding, and, yes, ma'am, I mean it," he said proudly, wishing he could see her face. "I think you'll really be pleased."

"I have no doubt," she said, having every confidence in him. She quickly grabbed her Day-Timer and checked her schedule. "Today is Friday. I have to be at a client site next week until Wednesday. How about Thursday? That way I can stay until Sunday."

"That'll work," he said. "Oh, by the way, don't bother renting a car. I'll pick you up at the airport. Just let me know what airline and what time."

She knew what that meant. Wil planned on spending a lot of time with her. She couldn't be happier. She had missed him terribly. Obviously, he missed her, too.

"You got a deal," she told him. "I'll call my travel agent right away and call you back with the flight information. Will you be home for a while?"

"I'll be here all night. Duke and I just had dinner, and we're planning on watching a John Wayne movie, *Rio Bravo*."

"Great," she said. "Tell Duke I said hello. By the way, did you tell him about us, about that night?"

"Didn't have to," he said. "He guessed."

She smiled to herself. "He's a clever boy. I'll call you back as soon as I can."

"Later," he said as they hung up.

Marie was floating on a cloud. She could not believe her good fortune. Not only was she close to finishing her book and had a guaranteed book deal, but also her new home was becoming a reality. It was framed. That meant the walls were up. She could walk around in it. How exciting! The best part, of course, was that she would be with Wil again. Life had certainly made a change for the best.

She called her travel agent and made the flight and hotel reservations. After getting the information, she dialed Wil's number.

"Hello," she heard him say before the phone completed one full ring.

"Wil, it's me."

"So, when do you come in?"

"I get in at noon, United Airlines."

"I'll be there," he said. Then he added, "And bring something like that little outfit you wore that night. I thought we could go to that seafood restaurant again."

"Well, I'll see what I can do," she said smiling. "He is just a romantic at heart," she thought. Her breasts began to tingle with anticipation at the thought of another intimate encounter with her man of the West.

"See you then," he said. There was a slight hesitation. She could tell he wanted to say something more, so she waited. "And Marie?" he said finally.

"Yes, Wil," she answered softly.

"It'll be good to see you."

His words touched her heart. "It will be good to see you, too. I've missed you," she said, saying the words that he found too hard to say.

That weekend she put the finishing touches on her book. She had thirty-five steamy chapters of raw, sensuous, wantonly sexual, erotic stories. She had previously sent a couple chapters to Madelyn and Jake to get their opinions. Madelyn was amazed that those words could come from her sister, whom she had idolized in a pious sort of way. Subject matter aside, even she had to admit they were good. Jake read them hungrily and begged for more.

The workweek started on a sour note. There were flight delays and missed deadlines. The client was ready to cancel the contract with the company she worked for. And this was only Monday. Tuesday wasn't much better. By Wednesday, she had performed her magic, and the client was happy. A new timeline had been agreed to. Wednesday night, she could hardly sleep, knowing that in the morning she would be flying to Oregon and into Wil's waiting arms. She was glad that soon she would not have to pull any more rabbits out of the hat. Soon, she hoped, she could quit this job and make a living from her book earnings.

Thursday's flight went amazingly smooth. The plane was practically empty. She had all three seats in her row to herself. Breakfast wasn't too bad. Surprisingly, the airline had remembered her vegetarian meal. She always ordered a fruit plate on the morning flights.

The plane taxied to the gate, and the engine stopped. As she walked off, she saw Wil waiting, grinning cheerfully. He was wearing his jeans, Levi's jacket, and black cowboy boots. His thick, dark hair was sticking out in back from under his cowboy hat. He was just as she remembered him. When she was near enough, he swooped her into his arms and kissed her passionately.

"Wow," she said when he let go of her. "What did I do to deserve that?"

"Nothing," he said tenderly. "I'm just glad to see you."

"I'm glad to see you, too," she said with all sincerity. "More than you'll ever know. It's been a bitch of a week."

She told him about her workweek while they waited for her bag. Wil was sympathetic. He had no idea she had to put up with so much bullshit, and he told her as much.

As they walked out to the parking lot, Marie noticed that he had washed the truck again. "Did you wash it just for little ol' me?" she teased with an exaggerated southern accent.

"Nah, just got bored and needed something to do." He was not a very convincing fibber.

"Please," she said. "I've put up with bullshitting men all week."

Wil's eyes got wide, and they both started to laugh. They were both feeling the electricity of the unspoken affection and love they shared for each other. They felt complete for the first time in a long time.

It was a beautiful Oregon day. Summer was in full swing, and the leaves of the trees were shimmering with sunlight. The mountains were green with trees, ferns, and other undergrowth. Springtime growth was all around, and the buds on the Douglas firs were maturing into fine new branches.

They pulled off the freeway when they reached the Grant's Pass exit. They approached the hotel, but Wil didn't stop.

"Hey," she said with alarm. "You missed the hotel."

"You ain't staying there," he replied.

"Where are we going?" she asked.

"You're going to stay with me and Duke."

She looked at him suspiciously. He saw that she was getting uncomfortable.

"Don't worry," he assured her. "It's not what you think. We got a little guesthouse out back. You'll be staying there. No sense in you spending money at that rat hole. That's for tourists. You're not a tourist anymore. You live here."

"It's a nice hotel," she protested.

"It'll be OK," he said. "Trust me. You'll see."

And she did.

Wil was right, as usual. He set her bags down in the bedroom and showed her around. The guesthouse was lovely, all knotty pine inside. It had a cozy feel to it. There was a little kitchen area off of the living room, a good-sized bedroom, and a bathroom with a shower. The floors were all hardwood.

"Did you build this?" she asked.

"Yep," he replied. "Me and Duke built it for my mother. She lived here until she passed away."

"I'm sorry," she said with sincere sympathy.

"Don't be," he said. "She lived a good, full life. She died in her sleep one night a few years back. Never was sick or nothing, just passed on. Now we just use the place when we have company. Only got a two-bedroom house, and Duke is too big to share a bed with. Besides, he snores."

They both started to laugh.

Just then a black cat walked in through the open front door. He was immense. It was the biggest cat Marie had ever seen. "And who is this?" she asked.

"That's Spot," Wil announced. Turning his attention to the feline monster, he said, "Spot, no one invited you in. Where are your manners?"

The cat ignored the scolding and boldly walked up to Wil and began to rub up against his leg. Then he did the same to Marie.

"He likes you," Wil said.

Spot continued his rubbing ritual between them. "He has got to be the biggest cat I ever saw. He's beautiful," she said. Spot was purring so loudly that she could hear it. "What kind of a name is Spot for a cat?" she asked. "Besides, he's all black."

"Look at his chest," he said.

She bent down to pet the purring feline and noticed a half-dollar-sized white spot in the middle of his massive chest.

"Aren't you a handsome guy," she said as she scratched the cat's head.

"Now you've done it," he said. "Now he'll never leave you alone."

"That's OK," she said. "I love cats. Just figured it wouldn't be fair to have one with all the traveling I do."

He looked at his watch. "Why don't you change, and we'll head out to the house. It's not that far from here. That way we can head into town tomorrow morning, and you can pick out your fixtures and things."

Wil's house was about halfway between her property and Grant's Pass. She looked at her attire. She was dressed in business-casual clothes, almost like the first night she had met him.

"OK, I get the hint," she laughed. "I'll pull out the old flannel shirt and jeans. I'll blend."

"I just want you to be comfortable," he said. "We might decide to take a walk. You can't do much walking around there, dressed like that."

He was right, and she agreed.

"Just come on up to the house when you're ready. Duke made us a picnic lunch to take up with us."

"Oh, don't tell me," she said. "Tuna sandwich and a candy bar."

"No, Miss Smarty Pants," he teased. "Avocado sandwich and a candy bar, for you anyway."

He gave her a peck on the cheek and walked out the door.

CHAPTER ELEVEN

—⁂—

MARIE UNPACKED IN A HURRY AND CHANGED HER clothes. It felt good to be back in her flannel shirt, jeans, and boots. She was becoming comfortable in this attire and thought she could quickly grow accustomed to dressing like this all the time.

Grabbing her trusty ball cap (she would have to get a cowboy hat soon), she walked out the door and headed toward the big house. There was a large, treelined yard between the two homes. A concrete sidewalk edged with colorful flowers divided the yard in half. On one side there were dozens of trees and a picnic table. Nearby, a hammock hung between two large madrone trees. They afforded it ample shade from the hot afternoon sun, their red bark giving contrast to the dogwoods, oaks, and Douglas firs. The other side of the yard had a few trees and neatly cut grass, except for where two horseshoe stakes protruded out of bald, sandy areas. In her mind, she pictured Wil and Duke playing and smiled. She was sure Wil had many wonderful memories of watching Duke grow into a man. For a quick moment, she was both jealous and sad, feeling cheated out of that experience with Andy.

She refocused and gazed beyond the homesite and saw a barn. Two horses were standing under the shade of a large oak to the far end of the adjoining corral. She recognized them. They were the horses that Duke and Wil had ridden during the mountain adventure.

"What a cozy place," she thought as she sauntered down the walk. Secretly she wished that her new home would have the same safe, secure vibration she was feeling here.

As she approached the door, Spot, who immediately began begging for scratches by rubbing up against her leg, greeted her. "Hi, Spot," she said in greeting as she bent down to grant the feline's wish. Spot immediately began to purr. She looked up as she heard a screen door squeak open. Wil was standing there, holding a picnic basket.

"I must say, you're really starting to blend in. You almost look like an Oregonian," he teased with a twisted smile as he walked toward his truck. She followed close behind him. She loved looking at his sexy swagger. It made her melt inside.

"I think you're starting to approve of me," she said with trepidation, admiring the view.

"I guess I am," he confirmed solemnly, without turning around. Marie breathed a sigh of relief.

She told Wil about her visit with her sister and brother-in-law and their reaction to the news about the two of them. She carefully avoided any hint or suggestion about the book. She wasn't sure how he would react if he knew she moonlighted as an *X*-rated author. She didn't want to throw that possible stumbling block in the way of their blossoming relationship at this point. Besides, who knows, the book could be a flop, and no one would be the wiser.

But she tried not to think about the book in that context. This was to be her ticket out of her present job. If this didn't work, she didn't know what she would do. To be able to live here in heavenly Oregon, next to Wil, she would be willing to take a job at McDonald's. No, she wouldn't go that far. That would be something, wouldn't it? She tried to imagine a vegetarian at McDonald's. She would draw the line there. Even Paul McCartney had drawn the line at McDonald's when he was offered an advertising contract with the company.

The ride to the property didn't take long. Surprisingly, Wil's house was very close to hers. You could even say they were neighbors by Oregon standards. As they pulled into the property entrance, Marie could see that a great deal had been done since her departure. The trees along the driveway had been trimmed back, and all of the fallen branches had been removed. The road showed evidence of a new layer of gravel and looked welcoming. Of course, you couldn't see the house from the road, but the land no longer looked like a bereft piece of the planet, waiting for some charitable life-form to take pity and become its caretaker.

As they crossed the newly reinforced bridge, her home came into view. She was awestruck. Even in its unfinished state, the log siding made it look inviting. The house looked sturdy and solid. The windows were large. There would be a view from every room. As they pulled the truck around to the back, she could see that there was a large two-car garage attached to the house. Next to the garage was a modest-sized back porch, with sliding glass doors that opened into the dining area. Or so she assumed, trying to recall the blueprint layout that Wil had showed her months before.

She was speechless with excitement and happiness. Wil turned off the motor and got out of the truck. Marie bounded out of the truck and ran up to him, embracing him in a bear hug, thanking him excitedly as tears began to roll down her cheeks. She found it hard to find the words to express her gratitude for the obvious care and attention he had expended on the house.

"Heck," he said modestly. "It ain't nothing yet. You haven't even seen the whole thing. Besides that, it's not finished yet." He gently released himself from her grip and escorted her up to the porch by the arm.

To Marie, it was her palace, her Camelot, finished or not. This was her house. She could feel an emotional attachment already. It was special. It was, after all, a gift from Charles. At times like this, she felt like he was invisibly working to make her life easier, to give her some happiness and peace after all the years of pain and suffering.

As they walked toward the sliding glass door, she thought she could see the basement walk-out on the opposite side, beyond the porch railing. She was right. As they stepped through the slider, they entered into a spacious dining/living/kitchen area. The room had an open and airy feel. The house was brightly illuminated with natural sunlight, thanks to the large windows. Wil led her around to the kitchen part. A skylight let in even more light. Shadows from nearby tree branches swaying in the breeze outside were dancing on the plywood floor. She looked up to see the trees through the skylight and felt a positive rush of energy enter her body. It was exhilarating. She was meant to be here. Building this home *was* her destiny, to be sure.

As the tour continued, she was led to the east end of the house. She stepped into an oversized master bedroom. At one end of the room, the walk-in closet and bathroom were framed in.

"I put the bedroom facing east, so you could catch the sunrise from your bed. I figured you to be an early riser, since you were up early that morning at the cabin. So I thought you would appreciate it," he said.

"It's perfect, Wil," she voiced. She walked around the room, looking at the view from three windows that faced east, south, and north. The south window was actually another sliding glass door that opened out to a deck under construction. "Sunrise is my favorite time of the day. Everything is brand-new and fresh."

Wil agreed wholeheartedly. He walked up behind her and embraced her gently from behind, kissing her softly on her neck. She closed her eyes as she giggled and basked in a satisfying feeling that enveloped her whole being.

Even though it was only framed, she could picture the finished product. Seeing the floor plan on the blueprints looked OK. But seeing it three-dimensional was amazing.

They left the bedroom and walked through the expansive, high-ceilinged living area. At the opposite end of the master bedroom, in front of the garage, opening up to the west and south, was a second bedroom and a bathroom, smaller than the master bath but still a good size. It separated the bedroom from two more rooms on the north side of the house.

"What are these?" she asked. "I don't remember seeing these rooms on the blueprints."

"Well, I changed things around a bit. Figured you might want a laundry room and office upstairs. I added a few more feet on the house, so they wouldn't be cramped. I won't charge you for the extra square footage—my gift to you."

"Laundry! Of course," she exclaimed. "I never thought about doing housework up here." She chuckled. "Every time I have been here before, we were on vacation. I guess I have to start thinking about the real world. Thank you for thinking about it."

"You don't mind then?" he asked.

"Mind?" she responded. "I don't mind. I feel stupid for not thinking about it myself."

With that, he moved in closer to her and grabbed her around her waist, pressing her body against his. He could feel her breasts pressing into his chest. "Don't ever call yourself stupid," he admonished. "You're one of the smartest ladies I know." He lifted her chin so that they were face-to-face. She looked into his eyes. He bent his head and kissed her gently on the forehead and then the lips, lingering there for a while. She embraced him and kissed him back.

Feeling that if he didn't break away soon, he would have to do her right there on the plywood floor, he pushed himself away from her. In an attempt to get his mind off of that thought, pleasant as it was, he said, "Hey, let's eat. I'm starving."

Marie breathed in hard, as if being awakened from a trance. She straightened out her shirt and smoothed back her hair. She had been feeling the sexual heat as well. "Yeah," she agreed. "So am I. Where shall we set up?"

"I know a nice, little shady spot over by the creek," he said. "Come on."

On the way to the creek, he grabbed the picnic basket and proceeded down toward the creek. Marie was close behind. About forty feet up the creek was a flat, grassy area, about twenty feet in diameter, surrounded and shaded by trees and bushes, giving it privacy and coolness. "Here we are," he announced as he put the basket down.

"Let me help," she said and began to take things out of the basket. As on previous occasions, the two worked in perfect harmony. Within a few minutes, a blanket had been spread, over which a small, plastic tablecloth was laid. Duke had gone all out this time. Besides the sandwiches, he included fresh vegetable strips, fresh fruit salad, and, of course, the candy bars. The plates were paper, and the flatware was plastic, but to them, it looked better than fine china. Once the spread was laid out, Wil dug into the minicooler and produced a small bottle of Chardonnay, which he presented to Marie, and gabbed a beer for himself.

When all was in readiness, they sat down and prepared to eat. He opened her wine and poured it ceremoniously into a plastic cup. He popped open his can of beer and said, "Let's make a toast."

She grinned in agreement and held up her glass. He continued. "To your house. May you always be safe and happy within its walls."

"That was beautiful, Wil. I'll drink to that," she said as plastic hit aluminum. They both took a healthy swallow. Then she continued. "Now it's my turn."

He nodded with approval and listened.

"To you, Wil Townsend, for bringing me a peace and happiness I haven't known in a long, long time. I'm glad I met you, and I'm glad we are friends."

Looking slightly embarrassed by her praise, he clinked his can to her glass and took another swig of beer. She was hoping, in her mind, that they could become more than friends. Not that they weren't already. Even though it was still a one-way love, they did have carnal knowledge of each other. But their relationship was free and open. She was still hopeful that Wil would fall in love with her. But it was best to take it slow. She felt he was still reluctant to give himself completely. The hurt left by lost love is never forgotten. She could be patient. He was worth it.

Although she had never felt as if she was betraying Charles by having desire for Wil, or, for that matter, for making love to him, being with someone other than Charles still gave her a strange feeling. But making love to Wil was a different experience altogether. Besides, being physically different from Charles, he had his own sexual style. It was totally unlike Charles but just as satisfying to her, perhaps even more.

That was what was still nagging her in the back of her mind. Sex with Wil was better than with Charles. Or was it? Could it be that she had been without it for such a long time that anything would feel good at this point? She had never had complaints about Charles. But Wil, oh, Wil, he had a sort of animal magnetism. He was more self-confident. He seemed to anticipate her needs and give her new desires. Sex with him was uninhibited and satisfying for sure. She was waiting in excited anticipation for the next dinner out. She was hoping it would end the same way as the first.

Lunch was enjoyable. The sound of the babbling creek was harmonized by a plentiful assortment of songbirds. It was a beautiful day; the sun was out, and there was just a smattering of clouds dusted across the sky.

After they had eaten their fill, Marie started to clean up and put things away. Wil helped. She liked that, a man who wasn't afraid to help out with domestic chores. He was not a man who was used to a woman waiting on him hand and foot. There had been no wife, except for the brief time Maggie had been with him, but Marie was sure that he had always been there to help out his mother with kitchen duties, being as he was an only child.

They decided to have another drink before going back up to the house to gather the pertinent information they needed to decide on home furnishings tomorrow.

They sat side by side on the blanket, watching the creek as hundreds of gallons of clean, clear water rushed past them on its way to feed into some distant creek or river. Wil looked down at Marie. She looked so peaceful and serene, not to mention beautiful and desirous. A slight breeze blew past and bathed him with her subtle essence. There it was again, the perfume with the haunting aroma that gave him lustful desires for the woman sitting next to him. He turned to look at her as she turned to meet his glance. The unspoken desire was there, the electricity between them powerful.

He reached out and put his arm around her. She moved closer to him. She turned her body toward him and pressed herself against him. He did not resist. Reaching around her, he grabbed her bottom firmly and squeezed it hard. She could feel her pulse racing and her anticipation growing. She reached up and knocked off his cowboy hat. She ran her fingers through his thick hair and pulled his head down toward hers. She kissed him hard, with open mouth. He kissed her back, and it began.

Within minutes, they were naked and making love on the blanket. His mouth moved to her beautiful breasts, teasing her nipples with his tongue and making them hard. She was bathed in waves of heated passion that had been awoken from a ten-year slumber. She held his manhood and stroked him as it hardened and grew at her touch. He explored her smooth, soft body. His hand moved down her back and caressed her round ass. His fingers moved down to tease her between her legs. He could feel that she was wet and ready for him. Gently, he slipped a finger into her as she groaned with pleasure, his hunger and craving for her rising with every stroke of her hands on his hardness.

He rolled her over and spread her legs apart as he positioned himself between them. Tenderly, he guided his hard, throbbing member into her waiting sex. His thrusts were met with hungry fervor. She felt her pleasure rising from deep within her. Their sounds of passion added a new chorus to the song of the creek and the birds. She struggled to keep her climax from peaking. He could tell she was ready and whispered, "Come on, girl; let it go. Come for me." His low, sexy voice brought her over the edge, and she exploded with blissful abandon. Sensing her pleasure, he let his orgasm burst forth with a primal grunt. He came so hard he thought his head would explode. After the rush, they lay for a moment, staring up at the sky through the trees; neither one could move.

Turning to look at her, he said apologetically, "I don't know what it is; I just can't keep my hands off you."

"That's OK," she said. "You know, you don't have to apologize every time we make love or you have a sexual desire for me. I have sexual needs and desires, too. I'm not a prude who frowns on sex. Just because I haven't been with a man since my husband died doesn't mean I never think about it or want it or like it."

He grinned at her knowingly.

She thought of *Dirty Stories of a Rich Girl*. Anyone who read it might say she thought about it quite a bit. She continued. "What makes you think I haven't been thinking about sex with you more than once or twice? I admit, when we first met, I never thought it would ever come to this. But now that I know you, I like you. I could even say I love you." The words slipped out without her thinking. She quickly added, "But I like the way it is now. We are forming a good kinship here; I don't want to jeopardize it by attaching restrictions and commitments to it. We'll just let nature take its course and see how it turns out. Who knows what'll happen? But in the meantime, don't apologize or feel guilty for what we do. I want and need it as much as you."

Love, she said it. Could it be? He felt the same way but had always been a man of few words, depending more on actions. This was just one more example of how they complemented each other.

"Why is it you always find the right words to say?" he said tenderly, leaning over and kissing her gently on the forehead as he brushed her hair over her shoulder. He, too, felt that their relationship could grow into something more, and like Marie, he wanted it to. It was a daily struggle to keep his deep emotions for her at bay; he was fearful that either she would reject his advances or, worse, sever the ties of their relationship completely. Maybe now he could let loose a little. She was willing to give it a try, and so was he.

He pulled her naked body close to him. They lay there, entwined in each other, basking in the lovely afterglow of their lovemaking.

Slowly they got dressed and repacked the picnic basket. He wanted to continue showing off his work to her. They walked a few hundred feet farther up the creek.

"What's that?" she asked as a small house-shaped building came into view.

"What do you think it is?" he teased.

"I don't know. Looks like a child's playhouse or something."

"That, my dear lady, is your battery house. And those pipes coming out of the back are going to be the connection to the turbine, which, I might add, hasn't arrived yet."

"Oh really?" she asked, bursting with excitement. "What do I need a battery house for?"

"You city folk," he said offensively. "Did you even research how this thing works before you *demanded* that I install it? What do you think, you flick on the wall switch and the power just generates on the spot? You have to store the power. It gets stored in batteries."

"Well, I didn't even think—" she said sheepishly.

He cut her off. "I know you didn't. Probably saw it in some yuppie magazine or on some trendy TV home show."

"No need to get all bent out of shape," she said. "It *is* a good idea. I won't be dependent on anyone for anything out here. Where are the solar collectors?"

He shook his head. He had to agree with her on that one. He hated to be dependent on anybody for anything. "Those will be on the south side of the house. They will be used for hot water and some incidental electrical lights that will not be dependent on the turbine power."

"I love it," she said cheerfully. Her cheeriness was contagious. Soon his sour face had turned to a smile. He loved to see her happy.

Eventually they managed to make it back to the house and talk about all of the things she needed to make decisions on the following day. There were cabinets to pick out, colors to choose for paint, and fixtures, flooring, and appliances to select and buy. He took measurements as they spoke. It would be a full but exciting day.

By the time they returned to his house, the sun was beginning to set. Unknown to Marie, but previously arranged by Wil, Duke had brought home pizza, one with cheese and mushrooms, the other a meat eater's deluxe. All they had to do was heat them up. Since Wil lived halfway between her property and town, it would have been an extra twenty-minute drive to town for anything more substantial. She had been on an adrenaline high all afternoon. The excitement of seeing her new house and the unexpected but totally climactic sexual encounter earlier had left her mentally and physically exhausted. Pizza and a soft, comfortable bed—alone— sounded like a plan.

Duke came in just as Wil was taking the now-hot pizzas out of the oven. He had been out in the barn, feeding the horses. When he saw her at the table, his face broke out into a grin. Extending his hand to greet her, he said, "Marie, nice to see you again."

He had a handsome face. She could imagine that Wil was as handsome at that age. Both men appeared to be chiseled out of the same stone by a common artist.

"Hi, Duke," she replied, smiling back. "It's nice to see you again, too. And thank you for the wonderful lunch. It was perfect."

"Glad you enjoyed it," he said. "I hope Dad hasn't been working you too hard out there on the property. He can be a slave driver you know."

Wil interrupted. "Now that'll be just about enough out of you. Besides, I pay you for being my slave."

Marie looked at Wil then at Duke. "Have you been working on the house?" she asked.

"Yes, ma'am," he replied. "Every day. Heck, this is the first afternoon I've had off since you left."

She turned to Wil. "Wil," she said. "All work and no play are not good for a boy his age."

"All right," Wil conceded. "I don't see him complaining on payday. Besides, good, hard work never hurt nobody. It's good for him, builds character."

"His character is just fine," she defended.

"I don't mind, ma'am," Duke said. "I haven't seen Dad this excited about a job in a long time. If you don't mind me saying so, since I'm sure he hasn't told you so himself, I think he's sort of sweet on you."

"That's it. That's it," Wil broke in. "I can do my own talkin'; thank you."

She laughed as father and son verbally bantered. The battle ended when the two men agreed that it was time for a beer.

After helping with the clean up, Marie excused herself. She really was beat. It had been a full day. Wil said he wanted to head into town early the next morning. He invited her to join him and

Duke for breakfast at six. He said the guesthouse had its own phone line and asked if she wanted him to give her a wake-up call.

She laughed and teased him, reminding him that she, too, was an early riser. She asked if he wanted her to call him in the morning. She said her good nights. Wil walked her to the guesthouse and left her with a passionate good-night kiss at the door.

She changed into her nightie, brushed her teeth, and snuggled into bed. She thought about her life and how it had changed though the years. She again felt the gratefulness of having been given a second chance at happiness. Pleasant thoughts filled her head as she floated off into a peaceful slumber.

Lying in his bed, Wil thought of the day's events and of his relationship with Marie. All totaled, they had only spent a handful of days together, yet he felt as if he had known her all his life, as if they had always been together. When they made love, it was as if there was an unspoken communication that transmitted secret thoughts to each other to fulfill their desires. Sex with her was natural and passionate. She had a fire burning deep inside her that had not been fanned in a long time. He had sparked the flame with the heat of his own passion. They had made love twice now, this last time better than the first. They gave all they had to each other sexually, but there was no pressure for emotional commitment.

It wasn't that their relationship wasn't full of as much emotion as passion; she hinted about love but didn't really say she loved him. The thought of lifelong love scared him. He was comfortable with their relationship the way it was right now. He always felt that if it was working, you best just leave it be. But he found himself becoming increasingly obsessed with her. To his dismay, he felt that he needed to protect her. And worse yet, he felt he needed her in his life. This feeling grew stronger every time he saw her. It was an unfamiliar feeling, and it was driving him crazy. Was he falling in love despite his best efforts not to?

On the other hand, he was sure that she liked the house. All the days of hard labor and painful attention to detail had paid off. He was feeling good about that. Lying there in bed, he realized that the bitterness that he had been carrying with him since the day Maggie left was finally losing its grip. Being with Marie did that to him. He closed his eyes and imagined the soft touch of her body and the fragrant smell of her skin as he drifted off to sleep.

CHAPTER TWELVE

CREAMY ORANGE HUES, BOLD PINKS, AND SILKY LAVENDER tones blended in the eastern sky when Marie awoke to the sound of a rooster crowing. A red, digital "5:01" glared back at her from the bedside clock. She dragged herself out of bed and headed toward the bathroom. As she walked past the window, she could see several lights on at Wil's house. "Surely, they can't be up and around already," she thought. Looking closer, she saw movement in the kitchen. What time did Wil say to be there for breakfast? Oh yeah, six. One hour, plenty of time.

At 5:55 a.m., she knocked at Wil's kitchen door. A smiling Duke greeted her. Wil was over at the stove, flipping pancakes.

"Good morning," she called out cheerfully.

"Morning," Wil replied. "Sleep OK?"

"Slept like a baby," she said. "Can I help with anything?" She noticed the table had already been thoughtfully set; she saw butter and real maple syrup, and there was a glass of orange juice at every place setting.

"You can just sit your pretty, little self down," Wil said, half-commanding.

She glanced at Duke for confirmation. He nodded and held a chair out for her.

"You know," Wil said. "We usually do bacon and eggs. The pancakes are in your honor, Ms. Vegetarian."

"Well, you certainly won't die of weakness without your morning fix of animal flesh," Marie said as she sat down.

Duke's face went sour. "You certainly make it sound gruesome."

"To a vegetarian, it is," she said without hesitation.

"All right, all right," Wil interrupted. "Enough of that philosophical talk. The day is just starting. Let's eat." He put a huge, steaming plate of griddle cakes on the center of the table. "Dig in!"

Duke poured heaping mugs of hot black coffee for himself and his father. To Marie's surprise, she was served a cup of chamomile tea. It was a cheery and lovely breakfast. She felt right at home.

"That was just perfect," she said as she helped Duke clear the table. "Thank you."

Wil looked at his watch. It was six thirty. "You ready to go?" he asked Marie.

"I was going to help Duke clean up."

"Ah, he's a big boy. He knows how to clean the kitchen by himself. Don't ya, Son?" He glanced in Duke's direction but didn't give him a chance to respond. "We got a full day ahead. The trip to Medford will take an hour in itself."

"OK, I guess I'm ready then," she replied.

A full day was an understatement for the bustle of activities they went through that perfect Oregon day. By the time they were done, Marie's head was spinning with paint and stain colors, appliance sizes and functions, floor coverings, and tile designs. They had been to numerous stores in both Medford and Grants Pass. Besides appliances, paint colors, and floor coverings, she had selected windows, doors, cabinets, and lighting and plumbing fixtures. And although Wil did not approve of everything she had chosen, she did listen and take his advice on a few important items, like window types and doors. These were inconsequential to her, and she relied on his construction experience in these matters.

As they pulled into the long, winding driveway at Wil's house, the sun was low in the western sky, giving everything a warm, welcoming golden hue. They had picked up Chinese takeout in Grants Pass. He dropped her off at the guesthouse, so she could freshen up while he went home to heat up the food. He said he was good at that. Dinner was quiet, tasty, and almost romantic. Duke had gone out for the evening. They were alone.

After dinner, the two settled on the couch to watch a little TV. Marie made herself a cup of herbal tea. Wil had a beer. Sitting next to each other, they could feel the sensuous heat between them building. Wil reached up and put his arm around her shoulder, pulling her in close to him. She didn't resist and put her head on his chest. She could feel his heart beating strong and fast in his chest. She looked up into his stoic face. He looked down at her and kissed her gently on the lips, his hair falling in front of his face. She reached up and combed it back as her lips met his hard with passion, tasting him with her tongue. She couldn't help herself, and he didn't want her to. She reached down. Her hand pushed on hard-stretched denim and felt his throbbing manhood underneath. His fumbling fingers unbuttoned her blouse and released her bra hooks, throwing both aside aimlessly as he succeeded. Gently he cupped her ample breasts, tenderly rolling a nipple between his fingers, feeling it grow firm at his touch. They were necking and petting on the couch like a couple of school kids.

Suddenly he sat up, looking disheveled. "Hold on. I'm way too old and way too big to do this on the couch. This is my house; let's go upstairs and do this right."

She caught her breath, smiled, and agreed. "I'll race ya," she called out playfully. She leaped up and started running bare breasted up the stairs.

She could hear him growling and running close behind. At the top of the stairs, he caught her and swooped her into his arms as she squealed in delight. He carried her to his room, nuzzling his face into her hair, breathing in her scent. He set her down on his bed and stripped off his clothes. Unsnapping her jeans, he pulled them off in one quick tug. He stepped back and admired the view.

There she lay, wearing only her panties. His desire grew, as did his manhood. She reached out for it, and he moved toward her. Sitting up, she grabbed it with both hands. She stroked it as she kissed the tip. Then she slowly put her mouth around it and sucked in its entire length. He moaned and grabbed the back of her head with his hands, pulling her closer. She gently twirled her tongue around the tip before going down on it again. He tasted delicious, and she could tell he was really enjoying it. His pleasure was turning her on.

Suddenly, he pulled back and said, "Hold on. I want you to enjoy this, too. Turn around and bend over the bed." He grabbed her by the hips and lifted up her ass toward him and positioned himself between her legs. He reached down with his fingers and felt that she was wet and ready. He thrust his hardness into her from behind, and she moaned with euphoric delight. They made passionate love that crested and climaxed over and over again. After they had their fill of lovemaking, they drifted off to sleep in each other's arms.

Marie woke to the sound of a car door closing. She looked at the clock. It was two in the morning. "That must be Duke coming home," she thought. Suddenly, she remembered her blouse and bra that had been carelessly thrown on the back of the couch in the heat of passion.

"Wil, Wil," she said as she tried to wake the sleeping giant in bed next to her.

He woke with a start. "What!" he called out in surprise.

"Duke is home, and my blouse and bra are downstairs," she said with concern.

"So?" he said groggily. "Your point is?"

"I don't want him to see them. You need to go down there and get them."

"Don't you think he's ever seen a lady's bra before?" he said, scratching his head and slightly irritated at being woken up for such a trivial matter.

"I don't want him to think..."

"To think we had sex." He finished the sentence for her.

"Well, yes," she said sheepishly as she jumped out of the bed and began pacing the floor nervously.

"My Lord, girl," he said. "What do you think he thinks? I told you he already knew about us. In fact, he planned to be away so we could be alone tonight. Don't you see? He already knows, and he doesn't care."

"But I don't want him to think I'm some kind of sex fiend."

"But you are," he said as he reached down and grabbed himself under the covers.

She picked up the pillow and threw it at him.

"All right," he said. "If it will make you feel better, I'll go get it."

"Thanks," she said, putting on a sweet face. They could hear Duke in the kitchen fixing a snack. "Hurry up," she added.

He threw on a pair of pants and went downstairs. She could hear him talking to Duke but couldn't hear what they were saying. About five minutes later, he came back upstairs with her blouse and bra in his hands.

"Thanks. I better get back to the guesthouse." She hugged him and started to get dressed.

"You can spend the night if you want," he said.

"Thanks, but I think it's best if I go back." She had finished dressing and was headed down the stairs.

"I'll walk you over," he said.

She agreed, feeling good that he was so thoughtful.

As they passed through the kitchen, Marie said, "Hey," to Duke, who was busy downing a sandwich and a bottle of beer.

Wil walked her across the yard to the front door of the guest-house. "So, what do we do tomorrow?" she asked.

"You can sleep in for one, at least until seven." He laughed. "I thought we could do a little horseback riding after breakfast. There are some nice trails off the property that go off into the foothills out back. Then we're going to dinner at that little seafood place in Medford."

"Sounds nice," she said as she yawned.

"Go to bed." He kissed her forehead and pushed her through the door.

He walked back to the house, grabbed a beer, and sat at the table with his son.

Duke looked at him with a smirk.

"What are you looking at?" Wil asked.

"I saw her bra on the couch," Duke said smiling.

"Big fucking deal," Wil said. "So we had sex. What did you think we would do?"

"I'm not saying nothin'," Duke said, grinning from ear to ear. "I think it's cool."

"You're damn right it's cool," Wil said as he leaned back in his chair, took a deep swig of his beer, and thought about Marie.

Saturday started out bright and sunny. Marie tried to sleep in, but being the early riser that she was, she tossed and turned for a half an hour and could only manage to stay in bed until six. Between being with Wil and being in such a beautiful setting, she found sleep impossible once the dawn broke. She showered, dressed, and decided to visit the horses in the barn.

"Morning," she heard as she opened the barn door. Duke had just finished feeding the horses.

"Good morning," she replied. "Do you guys always get up this early?"

"Not my choice, but Dad wouldn't have it any other way. Says you should greet the sun every day, or else the day is wasted." He leaned against the barn wall. "What are you doing up so early?"

"Oh, I don't know," she said. "I usually get up early anyway. And it's just so beautiful here; I couldn't stay in bed. Is Wil up and around?"

Duke started to chuckle. "Are you kidding? He's been up for hours."

She joined in his laughter.

He turned to her, suddenly serious. "Marie?"

"Yes?" she said, not knowing what to expect.

The younger version of Wil hesitated for a moment then continued. "I hope I'm not getting personal, but I just wanted to tell you what a difference you have made in my dad's life."

She looked surprised. "Well, thank you, Duke. That is a very nice thing to say. But I really haven't done much."

"You don't understand," he said. "Dad hasn't had an easy life, what with his own dad dying when he was young. He took care of Grandma all those years, and then, well, I guess you know the story about me and my mother."

"Yes, he told me," she said compassionately.

"Well, there hasn't been much joy in Dad's life. He's a hard worker and has had to work hard for everything he has."

"Your father is a wonderful man, Duke. And he has gotten a lot of joy from you. He's very proud of the man you have become."

"You see, that's what I mean," he said, his eyes twinkling like stars in the clear Oregon sky. "You see that in him. Not many people do."

"Wil puts on a rough exterior. He doesn't let people see the other side of him."

"But you did; you do!"

"I guess I do."

"Well, I just wanted to say thanks for bringing happiness into Dad's life. No matter what happens in the future, you made him happy, even if it's just for a short time."

"Thank you, Duke," she said sincerely. "About the future, I don't know. We are just kind of playing it by ear. We live so far apart. We have different lives. It seems to be working just the way it is, no commitments."

"Maybe things will change once you move out here," he said hopefully.

"We'll see," she said, hoping in her heart that he was right. She decided to change the tone of the conversation. "So what about you? A handsome, young man like you has got to have lots of girlfriends."

"Aw, heck," he said, blushing. "I played the field for a while. Not much to choose from around here. But I got me a special girl now. She lives just on the other side of Selma. We've been going out for about a year."

"Are you serious with her?" she asked.

"Kind of," he said. "'Bout like you and Dad. We just let it happen. No commitments."

"You got a good head on your shoulders, Duke. You are your father's son."

"Thanks, ma'am. That's quite a compliment." He looked out toward the house and saw Wil standing on the back porch. "Looks like Dad has breakfast ready."

"Good," she said. "I'm starving."

Wil had prepared another excellent breakfast, French toast with fresh strawberries, juice, and coffee or herbal tea, depending on preference. Marie was impressed and told him so.

After breakfast, Wil and Marie headed to the barn to saddle the horses. Wil's horse was a proud buckskin gelding. His name was Pal. It was the same horse he had ridden on the adventure trip. Marie was going to ride Rex, who was also the same horse she had ridden before, those many months ago.

The ride was leisurely and enjoyable. Wil was more of a tour guide this time, pointing out plants and trees and telling her interesting facts about the history of the land and the animals that roamed it. She was amazed that he was so knowledgeable. Then she remembered Duke had said how at home he was in the mountains.

They returned from their ride at about two in the afternoon. After putting up the horses, she helped him prepare some sandwiches, and they spent the rest of the afternoon relaxing in the yard.

Dinner at the Medford restaurant was once again delicious and delightful. Wil looked exceptionally handsome and was much more relaxed than the first time they went out together. Marie took extra care in preparing for her date, and her efforts did not go unnoticed by Wil.

On the way back, the two conversed about her house and its estimated completion date. She would not be returning until it was done. The city planned to take her present home in about three months. Wil was confident that he could get the new house ready by then but offered the guesthouse as an interim solution should he fall behind schedule. She agreed. They set a date for Duke and a friend to move her belongings. Wil said that her things could be stored in his barn if her house wasn't done.

The two were still talking when he pulled the truck up in front of the garage. She was feeling melancholy and didn't want the evening to end. She invited him in for a drink. He accepted.

They sat together on the couch, him with a beer, her with a glass of juice. He noticed that she was unusually quiet. "What's the matter?" he asked with concern. "Didn't you like your dinner?"

"Of course I did, silly," she said, fighting to hold back the tears.

"I was just thinking about going home tomorrow and leaving this…and you, all behind."

"Hey, don't get all mushy on me now. We both got a lot of work to do in the next three months. I got a house to finish, and you got a lot of packing to do. Time will go by quickly; you'll see. Before you know it, you'll be back. And then you won't have to leave. You'll be one of us, an official Oregonian."

She managed a smile but could not stop the single tear from running down her cheek. He held her face gently in his hands. She looked so fragile and so beautiful. He kissed her cheek where the tear had left its trail. That solitary, tenderhearted gesture was all she needed to let the floodgates open. She sobbed openly as he held her in his arms.

"I haven't felt like this in so many years," she said. "I had forgotten how wonderful it was to be held like this. I feel so safe and protected when I'm with you."

"I haven't felt like this ever," he confessed. "And don't worry; I'll never let anything bad happen to you. Not if I can help it. That's a promise."

She knew he was not the kind of man to give vacant promises. She was starting to feel better. He turned her face to his and wiped away the tears with the back of his hand. "Now let's not end our evening like this. Did I tell you how pretty you look in that dress?"

She was smiling now. "Yes, I think you did, once or twice."

"Good," he said. "Then let's go in the bedroom and take it off. I like what's underneath much better." He reached under the dress and cupped one of her breasts in his hand.

"Oh, Wil, you are hopelessly incorrigible," she said with a smirk, "but loveable."

Moving his hand from her breast to her hand, he led her into the bedroom. There they undressed each other and made amorous, ardent love, as if it were their last day on earth.

He slipped out in the middle of the night without disturbing his sleeping angel. She *was* an angel to him. She was a gift from God to repay him for all the years of painful loneliness, all the years of thinking he was destined to be solitary and hopelessly loveless for the rest of his life. He wanted to tell her he had fallen in love with her. But he was afraid. What they shared was special. It was wonderful. It felt too good to be true. He felt if he confessed his love, it might break the spell.

The next day the sun shined brightly in an azure blue sky, but it was a sad day for two people so in love and yet so afraid of the feeling. They hardly spoke on the way to the airport. She insisted that he just drop her off at the curb of the airport and not come in and wait with her. It would be easier that way, she told him. Tears were filling her eyes as she kissed him good-bye. They poured down her face in a stream as she waved and watched him drive off.

CHAPTER THIRTEEN

—◆◆◆—

MARIE ARRIVED HOME IN THE AFTERNOON. SHE WAS still feeling
sad and missed Wil terribly. As usual, Cindy had piled up her mail
on the kitchen counter. She sorted through it as she listened to the
messages on her answering machine. There were only two. The first
was from Justin, Madelyn actually, but Justin spoke first. He sang
another new song for her, told her he loved her, and said he had
a surprise for her when she came to his house again. Madelyn got
on then and said that she figured Marie would need some cheer-
ing up when she returned home. Her sister could read her like a
book. Madelyn ended with a hint of some exciting information
about their brother-in-law Tom's new baby-to-be. Marie had a
trip planned to an East Coast client the following week and had
planned to spend the weekend with her sister's family. Madelyn
said she was saving the news for the visit. It had to be good. Marie
was curious as a cat but resisted calling Madelyn and prying it out
of her.

The second message was from her book publisher. The book had gone through editing with very little changes. They were overnighting the edited version to her for her approval. They left a number for her and her agent to call to discuss the publishing date. She couldn't believe it. It was really happening. About the same time she was listening to the message, she noticed a large box that was sitting on the kitchen table. "It must be the book," she thought. She opened the box and looked inside. Not only was the edited version of her book in there, but there were sketches of possible cover designs for her to choose from. It was so exciting. It was actually becoming a reality.

She unpacked her clothes and began to read the edited version of *Dirty Stories of a Rich Girl* by Sheila Exotica. She was pleasantly surprised to see that none of the substance or explicit descriptions had been edited out. Most of the changes were punctuation and grammar corrections.

Her travel didn't begin until Tuesday. This gave her Monday to call her agent. Together, they called the publisher and made all the final arrangements for the book. She was astonished to learn that they had planned a book-signing tour and a couple of television appearances for her; one of them was a local morning show in Detroit. The publisher loved the book.

Although this definitely brightened her mood, it added an extra burden to her already jam-packed schedule. At least the tour wouldn't start until she had completed her move to Oregon. She was moving. She had forgotten. There was so much packing to do. Should she have a garage sale? Most of what she had would not look right up there. She decided to sell the furniture and move only personal items and what she still had in storage. That was solved; now to get ready for the busy week ahead.

It was a normal, hectic workweek. The only thing that kept her going was the knowledge that she would be seeing her sister and her family over the weekend.

She was able to wrap things up early with her last client of the week and caught an earlier flight to Detroit on Friday. It was about four in the afternoon when she pulled into her sister's driveway. Little Justin came running out to greet her. She scooped him up in her arms and gave him a big kiss.

"Auntie Ree!" the little boy said excitedly. "I have a surprise for you. I drawed you a picture." He was so full of energy and love; it was contagious.

"Did you really?" she answered back. "Let's go inside, and you can show it to me."

His little feet hit the ground running, and he was off in a shot.

Jake came out to get her bags. They greeted each other with a hug and a kiss. She could see Madelyn waiting at the door.

The sisters hugged, and Madelyn made a comment about how much more relaxed Marie looked. Jake said it was because she was getting some. The sisters shot him a dirty look. But Marie had to agree that he was probably right.

She was grateful for the distracting sounds of Justin calling her from his bedroom. She still felt uneasy about discussing her relationship with Wil. After such a long period of abstinence, she felt almost sinful enjoying sex.

That evening over dinner, Marie brought up the subject of Tommy and Naomi. "OK," she said to her sister, "what's the news you have to tell me about our dear brother-in-law?"

Her sister's face broke into a sinister smile. "Well, you know we had the girls over for the weekend last week."

"Oh, I didn't know. How are they?" Marie asked.

Her sister continued. "Katie is almost as tall as I am and as pretty as ever. Tommie is a real handful and looks more like Shelly every day. But that's not what I wanted to tell you."

"Please," Marie said emphatically, "the suspense is killing me."

"OK. We were talking about Naomi's baby, and Tommie blurted out that they know the baby is a girl."

"A girl!!" She was overjoyed. "Shelly had to have something to do with that. Don't you think?"

"She had to," Madelyn said, turning her eyes heavenward. "Way to go, Shelly."

"I guess the old guy just doesn't have it in him to make boys, eh?" Marie said. "Do you think they will have another, just to try and give Tommy his son?"

"No way," Madelyn said. "I talked to Naomi when she came to pick up the girls, and she said that this was it."

"Well, there is some justice in the universe," Marie voiced.

"Amen to that," Jake said, getting his two cents in.

"I haven't told you the best part," Madelyn said, sparking her sister's interest. "I made arrangements for the girls to spend the night the next time you come."

"Did you really?" Marie shouted. "Do Tommy and Naomi know I'll be here?"

"Of course they do," her sister responded. "You know, Naomi is not really a bad person. She's good to the girls."

"Yeah," Marie admitted. "It's just unfortunate that she fucked our sister over."

"Really." Madelyn went on. "If Tommy had met her after Shelly died, I'm sure we would all love her. She's really sweet."

"You are too forgiving," Marie said, thinking about the times Shelly had called, crying about the affair her husband was having.

"Marie, Shelly isn't coming back. Naomi is the mother figure in the girls' lives now. We have to get used to that and make the best of it."

"I know you're right. It's just so hard." Marie was fighting back the tears.

Madelyn could see that her sister was close to crying, and she felt helpless to stop her. "I know what you're going through. It took me a long time to be able to forgive her for what she did to our family. But I had to for the girls' sake."

"Believe me," Jake interjected. "She's right. I was there."

Madelyn had walked over to her sister and hugged her. Both sisters were crying now.

"Oh, no," Jake said sarcastically, waving his hands and shaking his head like an old woman. "Now I've got two crying women. Lord, help me."

His animated motions caught the women by surprise, and tears and sobs turned to bursts of laughter.

"So," Jake said, now that he had lightened the mood. "What's up with your book? Did you bring any more chapters for us to read?"

"No, I'm sorry," she said. "But soon you will be able to pick up a copy at the store."

"Are you kidding?" Her sister was bubbling with excitement.

"No, I'm not kidding," Marie assured her. "The book went through editing and should be released in about three months. They even have a book-signing tour and TV appearances for me."

"That's wonderful," her sister said, adding, "I think."

"What do you mean?" Marie asked.

"Are you going to appear like that?"

Marie looked at her attire. She was in her normal business dress. No one seemed to share her fashion sense, first Wil, now her own sister. "What's wrong with what I'm wearing?"

"Nothing, if you were publishing a business manual. You're putting out an *X*-rated book. Do you want all the perverts in the world to know your true identity?"

"You're right, Maddy," she said with realization. "I hadn't thought about that. What am I going to do?"

"Lucky for you, you have a sister who used to be in the salon business. I still have some wigs, and we can work on some makeup. And, by all means, we need to get you some different clothes."

Marie turned to Jake. "Isn't she wonderful?"

"In every way," he said with a suggestive wink.

"Well, there's one pervert who knows who I am," Marie retorted.

She seldom wore makeup, and it took a little practice for her to get the sultry, sexy look down. But after much effort, and with Madelyn's expert assistance, she learned how to make herself up.

"This takes forever," she complained. "How can women do this day after day?"

"Not all women are blessed with good looks like you and I," her sister replied sardonically. "They need to give Mother Nature a helping hand."

"I guess we can thank Mom and Dad for that," Marie added. The sisters laughed.

By the end of the weekend, Marie had a totally new identity for Sheila Exotica. Business Marie was hidden behind a short red-haired wig, plenty of heavy eye makeup, and ruby-red lips. The sisters had gone shopping and chose some suggestive-looking black blouses to wear with Marie's newly purchased black leather pants. Madelyn had wanted her to wear fishnet hose and spiked black heels, but she refused. Marie said she had a hard enough time walking like a lady without adding to the degree of difficulty and had given up wearing heels long ago. They settled for black-tinted hose and flats. She thought of her comfortable ropers, flannel shirts, and jeans, which made her think of Wil.

Jake was impressed with the completed alter ego. "Wow," he said when Marie walked out of the bedroom in her Sheila persona. "I can't believe it's really you, Marie. Even your parents won't recognize you."

"Good," she said, pleased with the transformation. "Just the effect I was hoping for."

Sunday evening as Marie was packing to go home, Madelyn came into the guest room with an inquisitive look on her face.

"So?" Marie asked.

"So what?" Madelyn replied.

"You look like you want to ask me a question."

"Am I really that transparent?"

"Like glass."

"Well, inquisitive minds want to know about you and this Wil character."

Marie burst out laughing. "He's a character all right."

There was a long pause. "Come on, spill," her sister demanded.

"What? There's nothing to tell. We aren't serious or anything like that."

"There's obviously something going on between you two. I haven't seen that gleam in your eyes since…" Her sister hesitated.

"Since I met Charles." Marie finished the sentence for her. "It's OK. You can say it. Lately, thinking about Charles doesn't make me sad anymore."

"Because of Wil?" Madelyn asked.

Marie thought for a moment. "Mostly because of Wil. The time I had with Charles will always be special and precious to me. But now I have this new kind of life with Wil. He is so different from Charles. He looks different. He talks different. He dresses *way* different. We do different things. It's a whole different lifestyle up there. When you first meet him, he seems cold and aloof. But that's just a cover. He's been hurt by love, too. When he was a teenager, he got a girl pregnant and married her."

Madelyn looked shocked. "Is he still married?"

"Heavens, no," Marie said. "I'm no home wrecker. She left him and her infant son to make it big in Hollywood."

"Oh, the poor guy," her sister said sympathetically. "How could a mother leave her baby?"

"My thoughts exactly." Marie continued. "Anyway, to make a long story short, she got mixed up with the wrong crowd and OD'd. Wil raised his boy himself. He's had a hard life. Nothing has been easy for him."

"So, he has a boy. How old?"

"Duke is hardly a boy anymore. He's in his twenties. He works with his dad. You should see the two of them together. They have a great relationship."

"The son likes you?"

"He's a great kid. Yeah, he likes me. Last time I saw him, he thanked me for bringing joy to his dad's life."

"He sounds like a good son. And what about you and Wil, is the sex is good?"

"You are like a bulldog with a bone." Marie smiled, thinking of their last encounter. "The sex is fantastic!"

"So, are you going to get serious with this guy?"

"Maddy, I wish I could answer you. Sometimes I feel like if I can't be with him, I'll die. When I have to say good-bye to him, it hurts inside. I feel alive when I'm with him. But I'm not sure how he feels about me. We both have been alone for such a long time. We have different lives. He's not a very vocal person. We like it the way it is now, no commitments."

"Marie, who are you trying to convince? Me or you? I can tell. You want it to be more. Why don't you just tell him how you feel?"

"I can't do that."

"Why not?"

"It's just not the right time."

"What does he think about your book?"

"He doesn't know about it," she confided.

"So, that's it. You better tell him before he finds out from someone else," her sister warned.

"Who would tell?" she said. "Besides, the book could be a flop."

"Don't underestimate yourself, my dear," Madelyn said as she put her hands on her sister's shoulders. "That book is hot stuff. I think you're going to surprise yourself."

"I hope so. But I'm not going to say anything to Wil just yet. I'll give it some time and see what happens," she said as she zipped up the suitcase. "Done. Let's go watch some TV."

CHAPTER FOURTEEN

—〰—

WIL WAS RIGHT. AUGUST AND SEPTEMBER WENT BY very fast. Marie immersed herself in her work, and the time passed like a swift-running stream. On the weekends, she and Cindy would search for heavy-duty boxes and had begun the arduous, laborious task of packing. She had decided that a great deal of what she had could be sold at a garage sale. Starting a new life meant new things. Cindy, too, had some salable merchandise. Some of it was her boyfriend's. Since she was moving in with him, she had decided that his bachelor-type furnishings and mismatched dinnerware would have to go. Knowing how precious Marie's time was, she had graciously volunteered to conduct the sale on a weekend that Marie was in Detroit.

It was almost the beginning of October. Marie had to be out of the house by October fifteenth. Duke would be down in a week to move her. She looked forward to seeing him again. His facial features and body-build were so similar to Wil's. Looking at him always made her feel as if she was looking at a young Wil. Her thoughts drifted to her hunky mountain man. They had been speaking on the phone every week, so he could keep her abreast of the progress on the house.

The boiler and turbine had been delivered and installed the week after she left, and even Wil was impressed with them. The solar panels had been put in place. The well and septic tank were hooked up to the house. By the middle of September, the house was nearly done. All that was left was interior painting and floor coverings. Wil figured it would work out just about right. Everything would be complete by the time Duke arrived back in Oregon with her things. Her excitement was growing now, not only because of the move, but to be with him again. The feeling was mutual, and he had said as much the last time they spoke.

Her book was in printing and would be released to the public about one month after she moved to Oregon. It would hit stores just in time for Christmas shoppers. She still hadn't told Wil about the book. She didn't want to tell him unless she had to. And that would only be if the book was a hit. Early reviews had been good. She had gotten a couple of advance copies of the book and was thrilled beyond belief to see it bound and printed. She hurriedly sent one off to Madelyn and Jake. Madelyn said the book was good, but it was not her "cup of tea." Jake thought it was hot, the best thing since sliced bread, and guaranteed her it would be a best seller.

Everything was falling into place. Sometimes she was afraid to breathe for fear that it would all disappear. She feared it was all some kind of dream and waited for the pinch to awaken her. She tried not to think about it but to just accept that her life was now different, different even than it had been just a mere six months ago, before she made the decision to move to Oregon, before she decided to write her book, and before she met Wil. Funny, now she could not imagine her life without him in it.

Compared to how quickly the last two months had gone by, the week before Duke arrived seemed to be endless. There were multiple problems at work that needed her constant attention. She visited three different clients in three different parts of the country. She would no sooner close a meeting with one client before she was off to the airport and another client. She arrived late at the hotels and was at the next site early for all-day meetings. By the end of the week, she was stressed out and burned out. She got home late on Thursday evening. A message from Wil on her answering machine said that Duke's flight would arrive at nine in the morning. He gave her the airline and flight information.

She had taken Friday off to supervise the move. It was midnight before she was able to get to bed. She fell into a deep sleep as soon as her head hit the pillow. She awoke at seven and couldn't believe she had slept so late. She walked through the airport door barely five minutes before Duke's plane landed.

Duke hugged and kissed her as she greeted him. It was the first time he had been so affectionate. She was beginning to feel a maternal attachment to the boy, a boy who had grown up without a mother. She had not, of course, met Wil's mother, but she instinctively knew the type of woman she was, caring, loving, and nurturing. This was evidenced by the virtues and morals of both Wil and Duke.

Duke introduced his friend John, a pleasant-looking young man about his age. On the way home, they stopped at *U*-Haul to pick up the truck that the boys would drive back to Oregon. It not only had to move her belongings but tow her car.

The weekend was a flurry of activity and hard work. By Sunday evening, her house was empty and her life in California was over. She had a suitcase full of clothes, her laptop, and a few files. She would be traveling all week, spend the weekend with her sister and her two nieces, and then fly home to Oregon. "Home to Oregon," the words seemed unrealistic. The actuality of living in Oregon still seemed unnatural. She was anxious to leave California and all of its memories but apprehensive about the move. What if she didn't like it? What if it didn't work out with Wil? What if? What if? She decided to forget the "what-ifs" and accept it. She was moving to Oregon, and no matter how long it took, her relationship with Wil would only get stronger, end of story.

For a change, the workweek went exceptionally well, which was good, since she was taking the next two weeks off to get settled into the new house and didn't want to leave her backup with a handful of problems while she was gone.

The welcome at her sister's house was doubly good as she was greeted by not only her sister and her family but also her two nieces, Katie and Tommie. It had been almost a year since she had seen them, and the change in them was remarkable. Madelyn had been right. Katie seemed to grow more beautiful as she got older, and Tommie looked more and more like her mother. She wondered if Tommy saw the resemblance and if looking at Tommie made him feel guilty about what he had done to Shelly.

The weekend was perfect—good weather, lots of giggles and laughs—until Sunday afternoon, when Tommy came to pick up the girls. It was the first time he had come face-to-face with Marie since she had sent the now-famous (or infamous) letter.

The girls greeted their father at the door and let him in. Marie was sitting on the living-room floor, playing with Justin. Madelyn and Jake were in the basement.

"Hi, Tommy," she said, trying to be cordial.

"Hey," he said dryly.

"How's it going?" she said pleasantly, trying to make small talk. The tension was so thick you could cut it with a knife.

"OK," he painfully replied. "Come on, girls. Get your stuff. Let's go."

The girls obeyed, running downstairs to give Madelyn and Jake a kiss good-bye. Tommy stood there like a stone while the girls gathered their bags and gave Marie a final loving hug and kiss before walking out. Tommy left without saying good-bye. Luckily the girls were too young to notice what an ass their father had been to their aunt.

Marie, on the other hand, felt hurt by his coldness. "Why should I be the bad guy in this," she thought. She wasn't the one who had the affair. She wasn't the one who was flaunting a mistress in front of his dead wife's family. The nerve of him! The more she thought about it, the more angry and hurt she became. Finally, it became too much for her. She ran to the guest room and burst into tears. She wasn't sure what made her cry, his actions or the thought of Shelly's last days with that ass. How dare he treat her that way?

She took consolation in the belief that someday he would get his. She just wanted to be around to see it.

When she ran to her room, Justin had something was wrong and ran downstairs to tell his mother. Madelyn quickly came upstairs and went into her sister's room. Marie explained what had just happened. Try as she might, she couldn't stop crying. By now Jake was in the room, too. The three of them talked it out. Madelyn said she knew exactly what Marie was feeling. It had taken her a long time to be able to talk to Tommy or be around him and Naomi and not come home and have a good cry. Jake corroborated her story and said they used to buy tissues by the case. Then he tried to cheer her up with a few jokes. Finally, she calmed down, and the three of them hugged. Marie told them how much she loved them and thanked them for being there for her and understanding. Once again, her younger sister had been more like a mother than a sister.

The weekend over, she lay in bed, thinking about her trip the next day. Tomorrow evening, she would be in Oregon. She was taking Wil up on his offer to stay at his guesthouse while she organized her new home. The thought of once again being in Wil's company comforted her. Her attachment to him was growing stronger by the day.

The flight to Oregon was long and required three plane changes. She breathed a sigh of relief as the plane taxied to the gate at the Medford airport. A smiling Wil greeted her with open arms as she entered through the gate. She felt the familiar, reassuring safety of his powerful embrace. She breathed in his smell. He always smelled like the forest. His scent was rugged and untamed. It was truly Wil.

The rest of the world, with all of its pain and misery, disappeared when he held her. She forgot her sorrows and her job, her very being encircled by his strong arms. The incident with Tommy had made her despondent, and she needed Wil more now than ever.

He could tell something was not right. "You're trembling," he said with concern. "Is everything OK?"

She wanted to tell him about Tommy but not here in the airport. "I'll tell you when we get in the truck," she responded.

"Did I do something to get you upset?" he said almost apologetically. There was a worried look in his eyes.

She looked at him lovingly. "Oh, no, Wil. It's not you at all." She clung to him even tighter.

He grabbed her bags and put them in the back of the truck. Neither one spoke until they were on the freeway and well on their way toward Grants Pass.

"Now," he said firmly. "What's got you so uneasy?"

She felt as if a pressure valve had been released and began to tell Wil about her sister Shelly and her valiant but fatal struggle with breast cancer. She told him about Shelly's beautiful daughters. Then she told him about the affair Tommy had with Naomi and how they were now married and expecting their own daughter. She finished with what had transpired over the weekend.

Wil was appalled that a man could do that, not only to his wife but to her family and, most of all, to Marie. He had known men like that. It made him sick. He hated to see Marie in such an emotional state. It disturbed him in a protective sort of way.

Just telling him about it made her feel better. But she could see he was disturbed by her story. She assured him that she was feeling better now and that just being with him made it better. He saw that she was still visibly shaken. They were just getting off the freeway at the Grants Pass exit. He pulled the truck off to the side of the road.

"What are you doing?" she asked with surprise.

"Come here, you poor thing," he said tenderly, motioning for her to slide over close to him. As she did, he enfolded her with both arms. She melted in his grasp and broke into sobs. He looked down at her. She reminded him of a wounded fawn he had once found in the forest when he was twelve. He had brought it home and nursed it back to health. Could he do the same for her? He would try.

Being held like this was healing to her. Indeed, just being in his presence was washing away the sadness she had felt from the day before. Now everything was OK. She was with him. She was in Oregon. She was safe at home.

"Oh, Wil," she said once she had composed herself. "I really needed that."

"I know," he said with his crooked smile. He was pleased that he could help in some small way. She smiled back. He pulled the truck back on the road and drove off.

Being at Wil's was a comfort, and she did not feel out of place at all. He took her bags to the guesthouse and told her he thought it best if she spent a quiet, restful evening at home. But she insisted on going out to see her house.

Nothing could have prepared her for the surprise she received when she saw the completed project. Wil had obviously put in extra time and personal attention to detail. It was perfect, better than she could have ever imagined. It was ready for her to move into it. She would, of course, have to buy curtains and landscape around the house. But, other than that, everything was in, from the kitchen appliances to the washer and dryer. Duke had even parked her car in the garage. She was even more surprised to see that all of her belongings were neatly stacked on the other side of the garage.

"I can't believe my things are here. I thought you were going to store them in your barn," she said in wonder.

"Well, we figured we had the stuff in the truck; no sense unpacking it and packing it back up when you got here. Saved us a step."

"Oh, Wil," she said in amazement. "This is wonderful. You did a fantastic job. Everything is perfect. I feel like I live here already."

"You do, darlin'," he said as he handed her the keys. She took the keys from him and gave him a hug.

"Thank you," she said wholeheartedly.

"My pleasure," he responded, kissing her passionately on the lips. "Feel like breaking in the bedroom?"

She smiled coyly. "That would be *my* pleasure," she said as she took him by the hand and headed toward the bedroom.

Her bed was set up, and there was a pile of blankets stacked next to it. Wil grabbed the top blanket and spread it over the mattress. He stretched out his arms, and she ran into them. They fell onto the bed together, and within a minute, they were naked.

"I missed you so much," she confessed as he kissed her neck and slowly moved down to her heaving breasts. She ran her fingers through his long sideburns and up into his hair as he licked her belly and headed toward her dark triangle forest. He lapped up the sweetness of her love juice. She had forgotten how heavenly the feeling could be. She bent her head back, arched her spine, and opened her legs wider to give him free access to her most private parts. His tongue circled her clitoris and sent shivers up her spine. She moaned with delight and pulled his head in closer. She felt his whole mouth engulf her as he sucked her honeypot. She felt his fingers slide into her, and she pushed up against them. Pleasure penetrated her being as she wrapped her legs around him. Feeling that she would come right then and there, she grabbed his head and said, "I need you in me right now."

He looked up and smiled. He slid up on the bed and situated himself on top of her, his hard penis rubbing against her thigh. She was so wet that his cock slid in her easily. He thrust it in deep as she writhed and moaned with delight, meeting his every drive with force. Within moments, their sexual momentum crested in explosive orgasms.

"Wow," was all Marie could say as Wil gently rolled off of her and lay next to her on the bed.

"Welcome home, darlin'," he said.

She turned to face him and smiled. She covered herself with the blanket and snuggled under his arm.

By the time they returned to Wil's house, Duke was already busy in the kitchen making dinner. "Hey, Marie," he said as he stopped what he was doing and came over to greet her.

"Hi, Duke," she said as they hugged. "Smells good. What's cooking?"

"Thought we could have some salmon tonight. I know you eat fish. I also have baked potatoes, salad, and corn on the cob."

"Sounds yummy. I'm starving. What time do we eat?"

"It'll be ready in about half an hour."

"Good. That will give me time to change into some Oregon clothes. I want to make sure I *blend*," she said, exaggerating the word "blend" as she shot a look and a smile at Wil.

He returned the smile. "Need any help?" he asked her. Duke could not help but snicker.

"I don't think so," she replied, shaking her head, embarrassed. "But thanks for asking."

After dinner, the three of them spent some time out in the yard. The trees had started to turn their autumn colors, and although the air was crisp, it was not uncomfortable to be out in a light jacket. The sunset was incredibly beautiful. Puffy pink and lavender clouds floated across a red-and-orange sky.

"I love it here," she said.

"I'm glad," Wil said, and he meant it. "We got a full day tomorrow. I think we should all hit the hay early."

She looked sad. "I'll miss being here with you two," she said remorsefully.

"Heck, you don't live that far. We'll be out to see ya anytime you want to make us dinner," Wil said. Then he added, "Just none of that tofu stuff."

"Don't worry; even if it is tofu, you'll never know," she said.

They talked out the agenda and task assignments for the next day and said their good nights. Wil walked her over to the guesthouse to make sure she had everything she needed.

She wanted to tell him what she needed was to be sure he would be in her life from now on, but she held back. Instead, she thanked him again for building her such a beautiful home. They kissed and said good night.

Inside the guesthouse, she suddenly felt very tired. Between travel and the excitement of the new house, she was exhausted. She quickly changed into her nightie, brushed her teeth, and fell onto the bed. As soon as her head hit the pillow, she fell into a deep, peaceful sleep.

CHAPTER FIFTEEN

—ᴡ—

"HEY, UP AND AT 'EM! WE'RE BURNING DAYLIGHT!" Marie's restful slumber was disrupted by the military-like sound of these words coming out of the living room. She woke up, disorientated for a second before she remembered where she was. She looked at the clock by the bed. It was six in the morning.

"OK," she called out to the living room. "I'm up."

She heard the sound of clunking cowboy boots on the hardwood floor. Wil stuck his cowboy-hatted head through the door of the bedroom. "I can't believe you are still in bed," he said incredulously.

"I can't believe it either," she said. "I guess I was more tired than I thought."

Remembering the emotional state she was in when he picked her up at the airport, he felt a touch guilty and said, "I guess you needed it."

She got out of bed, rubbing the sleep from her eyes. "I'm up now. Just give me about half an hour to wash up and get dressed."

"Half hour!" he exclaimed. "We could be at your house and have half the stuff inside by then."

"Well, that's just too bad. Go play with your horses for a while," she said teasingly. "I need half an hour." She let out a big yawn and motioned him out with a shooing hand.

"Women," he said, shaking his head and walking out the door.

Once they got to her house, the heavy work began. She began directing the men and telling them which room to set the boxes in. Thank goodness she had labeled them well, which helped to defuse the chaos. Wil did a lot of complaining about his poor, aching back and made comments about women and the useless stuff they saved. Duke was having fun teasing his old man.

It was about three in the afternoon before everything was out of the garage. What little furniture she'd brought from California was put in place. Wil hung pictures when and where directed. Clothes were hung in the closet. Marie's home office, including her laptop, was set up and ready for work. Most of the boxes were unpacked. Others would have to wait for the new furniture to arrive. And some, she had decided, would just have to wait until later.

Duke, always the thoughtful son, had brought sandwiches, fruit, and the ever-present candy bars for lunch. But after a full day of hard work, they were all famished. Marie suggested that they all go into town for a pizza, on her. Wil wouldn't agree unless she bought the beer as well. She consented.

She planned to go to town to buy the new furniture she needed the following day and decided to stay at Wil's until it arrived, so she grabbed some fresh changes of clothes before leaving.

She took a quick, final tour of her new house, which now contained all her worldly possessions. It was already getting a cozy feeling of home. She would take joy in living here. It felt good. She felt that Charles and Andy were there but not just in their pictures, which hung on the wall. The feeling was not a restricting or threatening aura. It was peaceful and free. It was almost as if Charles had planned for all of this to happen, the move from California to the beautiful house on the property that he provided. He may have even had a hand in finding Wil to take care of her. She liked to think so. In any event, she was grateful and said a silent prayer of thanks to the "Great Spirit" as Wil liked to say. She was picking up a lot of his ways lately.

She needed a man like him now. She had developed into a different kind of woman than she was when she and Charles were married. She was more intense and dimensional, wiser and more mature, less naïve about life, and hardened by her experiences, yet she still maintained a certain innocence and vulnerability. It was because of that innocence and vulnerability that she needed Wil. He was many things, but no one could ever say he was innocent and vulnerable, except in matters of the heart pertaining to her.

"Good-bye for now, my beautiful house," she whispered as she blew it a kiss. "Thank you, Charles," she added as she closed the door behind her.

Within one week, Marie was settled into her new house. She had selected rustic-looking furniture and carried the theme throughout the house. It was a style both attractive and functional, and what was most surprising was that Wil approved.

Wil and Duke had already begun building the barn and living quarters. They were on site every day. This gave Marie and Wil the opportunity to see each other frequently and maintain their personal relationship and their frequent sexual trysts. When she was not traveling, she made lunch for the boys and sometimes dinner. Wil had brought a little barbecue over, and on some occasions, he and Duke grilled chicken or steak while she supplied the rest of the meal. The guys had to have their meat in some way, shape, or form for it to be a real meal. Once in a while, she would fool them with a totally vegetarian meal, like stuffed manicotti. She got no complaints.

Marie was able to work from home almost every other week. Life in Oregon agreed with her. She didn't mind the remoteness or the long trek to town for staples. On the days that Wil was not there, she would walk the creeks and property by herself. The mountains and the streams bestowed tranquility. She had found numerous resting stops that afforded a beautiful view and a peaceful setting. One afternoon she had found a wild blackberry patch that had sweet blackberries the size of her thumb. On Wil's insistence, she always took the handgun that he had bought her and some pepper spray for the bears. She was learning to be cautious in the wilderness. He was teaching her well.

Her relationship with him was steady and intense. Most days, he would spend the night with her, and the sex got better each time.

Her book was ready to hit the streets. The book-signing tour would begin December first. She planned to end her career as a project manager on Thanksgiving. This would give her a week or two before the tour. Marie had insisted that she be home at least two weeks every month. They had agreed. Wil would never notice the difference, since he was accustomed to her taking off for weeks at a time with her current job. Besides, he had completed the barn and living quarters and no longer spent his days at her house. They went out for dinner every Friday night and would alternate houses but always spent the night together. On occasion, they would see each other during the workweek. Their relationship was becoming very comfortable. There were still no verbal commitments or admissions of love, but neither one dated anyone else.

If the book was a flop, she had already gotten enough up-front money that between what she was already given, what was left of her savings, and what she had gotten for her California home, she would only need to get a part-time job to live comfortably. Her cost of living was much lower in Oregon. It was doable. She thought maybe she could do bookkeeping on the Internet. So regardless of what happened with the book, she didn't have to go back to being a project manager. She didn't have to work for anybody anymore. She was self-employed. It was a feeling of being reborn.

Marie was having a hard time finding the right person to be her hired hand and live in the living quarters, or, rather, Wil was having a hard time finding the right person. An ad in the local paper had gotten good results. But Wil had insisted on doing the interviews, since he knew more of what the job would entail. She wanted to get horses, but Wil stood firm on getting the hired hand first. So far, no one had passed his tough specifications.

"Wil," she said, after yet another hopeful was rejected. "I think you're being too hard on these guys."

"Hard, hell," he answered back in an aggressive tone. "These yahoos don't know the difference between horseshit and horse food."

"Can't they learn what they don't know?"

"And who's gonna teach them? You?" he retorted. "I don't have time to baby-sit these assholes."

He was getting upset, and she could see the veins in his forehead beginning to pulsate and his brow narrowing. She didn't like this side of him, but she couldn't get angry. She knew he was just being protective, and it felt good to be cared for like that.

"Well, we've got to find someone and soon," she said. "I'm going to be traveling quite a bit the next couple of months, and I don't want to leave the house alone. Not with all of my things in it."

Wil agreed and thought about it in silence for several minutes. Marie knew better than to say any more. It would be like stirring up a hornet's nest. Finally, he spoke. "Tell you what," he said, as if the light bulb just went on. "Duke can move out here till we find someone."

She was surprised. "Not that I wouldn't want him here, but what about you? Don't you need him to do things around your house?"

"I can do 'em. I'll just get up earlier or start work later. Besides, he'll be closer to that little gal he's been seeing."

"Someday, I'd like to meet her," she said. "What did you say her name was?"

"Amber, like the stone," he answered.

"That's right. Amber." She let the name float off her lips. "That's a pretty name."

"Yeah, and she's a pretty, little thing, too," he added.

"Anyway," she said, getting back to the business at hand. "If you really don't mind Duke moving out for a while, you better see how he feels about it first. Don't you think?"

"He'll do it," he said with fatherly confidence and authority.

She liked the idea of Duke being out there. It would mean an even closer connection to Wil. To be honest, she really wasn't looking forward to having a stranger living on the property with her. No matter how much checking she did on someone, that person could still turn out to be a weirdo. Sooner or later, she or Wil would find the right person.

She would feel safe with Duke there, almost as safe as if Wil was there. She was happy with the decision and just hoped that Duke would go for it.

Thanksgiving was a happy occasion. Marie made a turkey and all the fixings. Although she didn't eat the bird, it was tradition, and she was never one to force her beliefs on anyone. She had invited Wil, Duke, and Amber.

She found Amber to be a sweet, young woman, who seemed to have genuine affection for Duke. She was appropriately named. Her amber-colored hair was shiny and hung past her shoulders. She was taller than Marie imagined, about five six, taller than Marie by two inches. She was slight but looked athletic. Amber was very friendly and down-to-earth. She shared a love of nature with Duke. They made a cute couple. And she helped out in the kitchen without being asked. Marie liked that.

Marie had more than a beautiful, new house to be thankful for this year. She was embarking on a new career, a new life, and a new love. It was hard to keep the revelry of leaving her old job to herself. Although she was still apprehensive of making it as an X-rated author, she was greatly relieved to have the stress of project management removed from her life.

Duke had agreed to move into the living quarters and had most of his things in there already. He would move in the day before she hit the road for the book-signing tour. Neither Duke nor Wil knew the real purpose of her travel.

The book had been released on November first and had made a remarkable impression on the critics. Although it was described as raunchy, rough, salacious, sexy, and steamy, never once was it referred to as pornographic. The critics loved it. It had been touted as the most erogenous book ever written by a woman and described as deliciously erotic from a feminine point of view. Everyone was curious to know who Sheila Exotica was. There were no pictures or biographical information about the author in the book. The only personal note was the dedication. It read simply, "To Maddy." The book was already selling well. The timing of the tour was perfect.

December first arrived, and she started the two-week book-signing trek. It was understood by all involved that her true identity and personal facts were to remain anonymous. The travel and hotel arrangements were much the same as the travel she had done as a project manager. Only this time, there were no whining clients or fires to put out.

She had hooked up with a representative of the publishing company, who would be her personal agent and accompany her on all tours. Grace Santos was a pleasant gal, midforties, recently divorced, and at her sexual peak and proud of it. Santos was her maiden name, which she took back as part of the divorce. She was a hot-blooded Latina, by her own admission, and spoke with a slight Hispanic accent. She and Marie got along great.

She loved Marie's book but was surprised to see that Marie was nothing like what she had imagined. She nodded in approval when she saw Marie transform into the full regalia of her alter ego.

"Now that's what I call one hot tamale," Grace said when Marie walked out of the bathroom as Sheila.

"Do you really think it will be OK?" Marie asked, still a little self-conscious of her appearance.

"Honey, the men will want to sleep with you, and the women will want to be just like you," she said honestly.

The tour was a series of one-day trips up and down the northeastern part of the country. It was sponsored by a major bookstore chain and widely advertised. There were long lines of eager readers, men and women, who had many thanks for Marie. Some thanked her for putting a spark back into their marriage. Some were grateful for the ideas it had given them and their mates. Women were grateful for a sexual book that didn't depict women as bimbos. Most times the men were just eager to meet the woman who could write such stories. And in every store on the tour, the book sold out.

The two women traveled in the evening and slept in late in the mornings, mostly because of exhaustion. Marie signed books from one to six most nights. The second week started in Boston, and they had Sunday off. They traveled around the city like a couple of tourists and enjoyed the break. That night at dinner, Grace gave Marie good news.

"Did you hear, darling?" Grace said over a glass of wine as they perused the menu.

"Hear what?" Marie was curious.

"Your book hit the *New York Times* best-seller list this week. You premiered at number seven."

"Are you serious?" Marie was overwhelmed. "I can't believe it."

"Believe it, sister," Grace said. "You are a hit. Or I should say Sheila is a hit." Grace raised her wineglass in a toast. "To Sheila, may she live long and prosper, anonymously, of course."

"Of course," Marie confirmed as she lifted her glass of ginger ale. "Waiter, I'll have the lobster," she added.

Her happiness was dampened slightly by the inevitable thought of having to tell Wil about the book. How would he react? As raucous and adventurous as he was in the bedroom, he had never shown an interest in pornographic literature. Well, he would have to accept it, if he wanted to keep seeing her. If not…well, that was a flip side she didn't want to contemplate.

She loved him; that was certain. The possibility of losing him was not a pleasant thought. But she had to do what she had to do to make a living. Surely he would understand that she couldn't go on as a project manager. Since her move to Oregon, he had seen her return from trips burnt out and weary. He had seen her put in long hours at her home office, taking care of project details. He'd taken pity on her more than once and taken her out to help her unwind after a long, laborious week.

Marie thought about those times. They were becoming a regular item at the Wonder Bur these days. They sat at Wil's regular table, and the women no longer gave her dirty looks as they passed by. They knew that he was smitten with her and they didn't stand a chance. They had accepted it and her.

She would deal with him when she returned. For now, she refused to let it spoil the enthusiasm and joy of her success. Tonight she was a *New York Times* best-selling author, and nothing could spoil that.

The rest of the tour went exceptionally well. News of the book making the best-sellers list ignited more sales. The book climbed up the charts to number two. The mystery that surrounded the life of Sheila Exotica was fuel to the fire. Stores could not keep the book on the shelf. Magazines such as *Playboy* and *Penthouse* called, requesting interviews. Even *Cosmopolitan* and *Vanity Fair* called. After discussing the offers with Grace, she agreed to be interviewed by both of the latter. She felt that they would keep the interviews tasteful and would appeal to women. After all, women were bigger readers than men. The interviews would be held during one of her touring weeks so as to keep her home a secret. She was scheduled to do the Detroit morning talk show in January. While there, she could be interviewed at an undisclosed, neutral location.

By the end of the two weeks, Grace and Marie had become amicable friends. She liked Grace. Grace didn't get personal and ask questions that she didn't want to answer. Grace knew where she lived, but that was about it. Everything was kept on a business level. They would meet up again in Detroit, after the holidays. Marie would do the talk show, and they would fly south for the start of her next minitrip. This time it would cover the southern half of the East.

They said their good-byes and parted at the airport. Marie boarded the plane and began contemplating how she was going to break the news to Wil that she was the mysterious, sensual, best-selling author Sheila Exotica.

CHAPTER SIXTEEN

—ₘ—

MARIE HAD LEFT HER CAR IN THE AIRPORT parking lot, and she was glad of that little fact. It would postpone the confrontation with Wil. She decided to do some Christmas shopping in Medford before returning home. Christmas was only two weeks away, and she had not even started her shopping. Most of the gifts for her family would consist of gift certificates. But she wanted to pick out something nice for Wil and Duke.

Wil was busy building another house, which would keep him occupied every day. The two had no plans to see each other before the weekend. On the way home, she made the decision to delay telling him about the book until after the holidays. This was the first time in a long time that she had felt the Christmas spirit, and she didn't want to chance ruining it with his reaction to her dirty, little secret.

It was all she could do to keep it a secret. Grace called from time to time to tell her how well book sales were going. *Dirty Stories of a Rich Girl* had climbed the best-seller list to number one. Marie was beside herself with joy and pride. But she could not share her happiness. She told Wil and Duke that she had taken vacation time to explain why she did not travel or work during the holiday weeks.

Christmas was a happy and special time. A huge Christmas tree that Wil and Duke had cut and brought down from the forest dominated the living room. It glistened with lights and tinsel. Wil had spent Christmas Eve at her house, so he could be with her and Duke on Christmas morning. She gave Wil some new power tools that Duke said he needed. He was surprised and overjoyed. She gave Duke some horse equipment she saw him eyeing in town and some gift certificates to restaurants, so he could take Amber out.

Duke gave Marie some new flannel shirts from the western clothing store he had heard her say she liked. The best presents of all came from Wil. One gift was a picture of the two of them that he enlarged and put in a beautiful, wooden, western-style frame. It was a picture that Duke had taken when the three of them were horseback riding that past fall. The mountains and trees in the background were in full fall colors. Marie and Wil were side by side on their horses. They were both laughing and obviously enjoying themselves. There was an unmistakable look of love in their eyes.

She remembered when the picture was taken. It was one of those days when everything had gone right. The weather had been perfect. Wil had just given her Rex to keep as her own horse. She had gotten fond of him and he of her. He always seemed to perk up when she was riding him. Wil noticed this, too, and figured they were meant for each other.

The other gift was wrapped in a tiny box. Inside was a pair of antique ruby earrings that were set in delicate gold filigree.

"They're beautiful!" she exclaimed as she took them out of the box to look at them more closely.

"I'm glad you like them," Wil said shyly. "They were my mother's."

"Oh, Wil," she replied. "I can't possibly accept these. Are you sure you want to give these to me?" She could feel the tears welling up in her eyes.

"Oh, for crying out loud," he said as he put his arm around her and pulled her close. "I can't think of anyone else that they would look prettier on."

"Thank you," she said sincerely and kissed him on the lips.

He embraced her and returned her kiss passionately.

"Excuse me," Duke interrupted, clearing his throat. "Would you two like to be alone? Should I go to my room?"

Wil broke away from her. "Just sit there, and keep your mouth shut," he said as he pulled her even closer. "You can watch if you like. You might learn something."

"Oh, please," Duke exclaimed. He got up and went to the kitchen to get something to drink.

Marie had to suppress the guilty feelings she felt inside when accepting the earrings. She wanted to come clean with Wil. She didn't like keeping things from him. But her inner self kept her from divulging the secret. The gift of the earrings meant that he was committing himself to her. His love for her was growing day by day. She could feel it. Her love for him was all consuming.

The week between Christmas and New Year's, they traveled to Brookings, a small, coastal city on the Pacific Coast. To get there, they traveled through the redwood forest. It was her first time. She was in awe of the magnificence and beauty of the mighty redwood trees.

They spent three glorious days walking the beach, watching the sun set on the Pacific Ocean, and making love.

Up until now, the weather had been exceptionally warm for winter. But that was the way Oregon was. On the way back from the coast, the wind began to blow, signaling a change in the weather. Within a day, a fresh blanket of snow covered the ground and gave the Douglas firs a postcard appearance. It was beautiful. Because of the snow, the two decided to spend a quiet New Year's Eve together in front of a roaring fire at Wil's house. Marie made dinner, and the two settled in for the night with a bottle of wine for her and a bottle of scotch for him.

At the stroke of midnight, the sound of distant firecrackers and car horns could be heard. Wil embraced her tightly and looked into her eyes. "Happy New Year, darlin'," he said before he kissed her tenderly.

His act of affection touched deep in her heart. She kissed him back and wished him the same. The sense of happiness, joy, and sincerity she felt at that instant was overpowering. She felt like putty in his strong, masculine arms. She fought to keep back the tears of joy. But the guilty feelings began to hedge around the corners of her mind. "This just isn't the right time to tell him," she thought. Keeping the secret was the hardest thing she ever had to do in her life.

Two days into the new year, Marie hit the road again. The book held its position at number one and was still selling like wildfire. Grace was as energetic as ever and anxious to tour. The two met up in Detroit. Marie planned to stay at Madelyn's house as she had always done before. Grace had declined an invitation to stay at Madelyn's, stating that it would cramp her style. She had some male acquaintances in Detroit that she planned to look up.

The television appearance went extremely well. Marie was nervous as a cat, but it didn't show. The hosts stuck to the predefined questions, and no hint of Sheila's true identity was leaked. Marie was amazed and impressed at all the preparation and manpower it took to put on the show. The show aired later that day. Afterward they found out that it received notably high ratings.

The following night, Saturday, she agreed to go to a local club where another of her sisters, Diana, was a singer in a band. Marie did not like bars or clubs as a rule. She didn't really count the Wonder Bur. She didn't like the smoke-filled atmosphere or the loud, rowdy people who frequented these places. She could never understand why Diana had chosen this for her career. Both Diana and her husband, Paul, were in the band and had spent almost every night of their five-year marriage in the club.

But, being the good sister that she was, she had agreed to make an appearance. By now the whole family knew about the book. As predicted, Annie had been the one who spilled the beans to Marie's parents. And just as they thought, her father was proud; her mother was embarrassed. The family had been told not to let out the fact that she was really Sheila. Marie was worried about Annie, but she knew that since Annie lived in a remote area of northern

Michigan, she wouldn't have many opportunities to discuss it in public. So far, Annie had been true to her word.

During a break between sets, Diana came down to sit with Marie. A friend joined them, and that's when Marie found out.

"Marie," Diana said in her raspy stage voice, "I want you to meet a good friend of ours. This is Mortimer Jablonski, Morty for short. Morty, this is Marie."

"Oh, you don't know what a pleasure it is to met you," Morty said as he held out a sweaty palm.

Morty was a somewhat pudgy, bizarre-looking guy in his late twenties, with greased-back black hair; a face full of pock-marks; thick, black-framed glasses; multiple piercings in his ears, from which hung an assortment of mismatched earrings; and outrageously trendy clothes. He looked uncomfortable in his skin, and there was something about his smile that made her feel uneasy. He chain-smoked designer cigarettes, light-ing a fresh one before butting out the old. Marie didn't know or care what kind they were, but they were wrapped in dark brown paper, not white like domestic ones. His aftershave was overpowering, and combined with the cigarette smoke, she had trouble breathing.

"Nice to meet you," she said politely and extended her hand. Morty's hand was sweaty, and his shake was weak and limp. She made a mental note to wash her hands as soon as possible and threw Diana a puzzled look.

Diana got the message and started to explain. "I know you told us not to tell anyone. But when Morty told me he had read your book and raved about how great it was…Well, he said it was the best book he had ever read. I just couldn't help but tell him that Sheila Exotica was my sister."

"That's right," Morty said. "It's my fault, not hers. I dragged it out of her. And when she told me you would be here tonight…well, I just *had* to meet you. Will you sign my book?" Morty reached into his jacket pocket and pulled out a well-worn copy of *Dirty Stories of a Rich Girl*. "I've read it a hundred times."

"I'm flattered," was all she could think to say. "Diana, you and I will have to talk later." She smiled a fake smile that told her sister she was in trouble. Taking the book, she signed it with a pen that Morty also provided. She wondered if Morty used the book for sexual recreation and if any of the pages were stuck together. By the looks of it and Morty, she could only guess that he had. She wished she had a pair of rubber gloves.

"Oh, don't worry," Diana said lightheartedly. "Morty is cool. He won't tell anyone else. I've known him for years. He's cool, really."

Somehow that didn't make Marie feel any better. But what was done was done. She just hoped that Morty was really "cool" and kept his big, fat mouth shut. She couldn't shake the creepy feeling she got from this guy.

She handed the book back to Morty, who was grinning from ear to ear. "Are you writing another book? You know, I am your most totally devoted fan. Please tell me you're writing another book."

"Well, Morty," she spoke articulately, "I hate to disappoint my biggest fan, but I don't know at this point."

"Oh, please, please, please say that you will. I'm just so totally devoted and in love with that girl in the book, Jana. She could do me any day. Nasty girl."

"Fat chance of that happening," Marie thought to herself, thinking that this guy was just a little too weird. Poor Morty looked like he would have trouble getting any girl to sleep with him.

"Well," Diana said. "Break time is over. Paul is giving me the eye." She looked at her sister. "You gonna stick around? It's my last set. A bunch of us are going to Morty's afterward. He has the coolest house on a lake."

"Oh, please come," Morty begged.

Marie saw this as a cue to leave. "No, I'm sorry. I gotta go," she said, faking sincerity. "I got a lot to do tomorrow. I'm flying out tomorrow night. But it was nice meeting you, Morty." She leaned over and gave her sister a kiss on the cheek. "See ya, Diana. Say good-bye to Paul for me."

They all stood up at once. Diana reached over to give her sister a hug. As the two embraced, Marie whispered in Diana's ear, "Please, don't tell anyone else."

"Sorry," Diana said apologetically. "It won't happen again."

Marie walked out without looking back.

Diana turned and began to walk toward the stage but Morty pulled her back. "Your sister is amazing. Where did you say she lived?"

"Oregon," she answered. "Remember? I told you she just moved there from California. She's out in the middle of nowhere. I don't know why she wants to live there all alone like that. But, she seems to like it."

Marie walked out to the parking lot and got into her rental car. Her head was pounding, either from the smoke, the music, or the

meeting with Morty. Maybe it was all three. Her clothes reeked of cigarettes, and so did her hair. She would have to shower before going to
bed. Her stomach felt queasy, too. No wonder she hated these places.

The next morning, Jake prepared one of his famous breakfasts
for her. He had been a short-order cook right after high school. It
was a talent he had never forgotten. His specialty was breakfast.

"Jake!" Marie exclaimed as she took a bite. "These have got to
be the best hashbrowns you've ever made."

"Thanks. How's the omelet?" he asked.

"Perfect, as usual," she replied.

"So, how was it last night?" Madelyn asked as she put a cup of
herbal tea in front of Marie and joined her at the table.

"You won't believe this," Marie said as she put her fork down.
"Diana told some creepy guy that I was Sheila Exotica."

"Are you kidding?" Madelyn couldn't believe her ears.

"No, I wish I was," Marie continued. "His name is Morty."

"Oh my God," Madelyn said, eyes wide. "You mean Mortimer
Jablonski?"

"Yeah, I think that was his name. You know him?"

"Not really, but we met him once at Diana's. She said that his
dad is some big exec for an oil company in Texas. Morty is a trust-
fund-baby; filthy rich. He's also a religious fanatic slash weirdo that
likes to drink. He read your book?"

"Yeah, not only that, he said it was the best book he had ever
read. He carried it with him. I had to sign it. You should have seen
it. It was all dog-eared."

"Probably jerked off to it," Jake shouted from the stove.

"Jake," Madelyn scolded.

"No, Maddy, that's what I thought," Marie said.

"Ew, I can't believe it," Madelyn continued. "That guy gives me the creeps."

"Yeah, he gave me the creeps, too. He said he loved my book. Called himself a 'totally devoted' fan."

"Well," Jake said as he walked toward the table carrying two plates of food. "Let's just hope that's all she told him." He set one plate in front of Madelyn and began to eat from the other.

"I think she would have told me if she told him more," Marie said, only half-convinced.

"I think she would have," Madelyn agreed.

Marie thought for a moment. "You know, he didn't look like a religious freak to me."

Madelyn looked at Jake, "Didn't Diana say he got in some trouble as a kid and went to an all boys Catholic boarding school during high school?"

"Yeah," Jake replied. "She said those nuns really did a number on him. Still can't shake the Catholic out. He goes to church on Sunday and stuff, I guess."

"Not only that," Madelyn added, "He is a sex freak and has a big penis."

Marie looked at Madelyn with stunned surprise. "How do you know that?"

"Diana told me, of course," she answered.

Marie let out a loud, "Ew-w! How does she know?"

Before Madelyn could speak, Marie had changed her mind. "Never mind, I don't want to know."

"Hey, let's change the subject," Madelyn broke in. "Did I tell you the latest goings-on with Tommy and Naomi?"

"No," Marie said, feeling a little better. "Do tell."

"Naomi had the baby two weeks ago, cutest little baby girl. Anyway, I found out that Tommy has been taking a lot of out-of-town trips. You know what that means?"

"You don't think he is up to his old tricks again, do you?" Marie asked.

"I don't know for sure, but Naomi sure seems worried about it."

"I guess a leopard can't change his spots," Marie said. "What a total asshole."

"Naomi went into this relationship with her eyes wide open," Jake said. "She should have known."

"Can't say that I feel sorry for her," Marie added.

"I do," Madelyn said. "I told you. I've gotten to know her, and she really is a nice person. And the baby is so cute."

"Well, I agree with Jake," Marie said. "She knew that Tommy was the cheating kind when she married him."

"For the girls' sake, I hope he isn't cheating on her," Madelyn said.

"I do, too," Marie agreed.

"So, when will we see you again?" Madelyn asked with a sad look.

"Next month the tour goes from Michigan down to Kentucky and swings around up to Minnesota. Then it works its way back to Michigan."

"Good," Madelyn said. "Then I don't have to cry when we say good-bye."

CHAPTER SEVENTEEN

—◊◊◊—

THE REST OF THE SECOND TOUR WENT BETTER than the first. Calls for talk shows were coming in daily. Some of the tour dates had to be rescheduled to accommodate the television appearances. The mystique surrounding Sheila Exotica was a definite plus. Marie was beginning to enjoy her fame and popularity, even if it was in the persona of Sheila. In fact, that made it better. Sheila had become quite the celebrity. She was even getting fan mail. The book signings never failed to draw a crowd. A couple of the mall signings had been very close to mob scenes, and security had to be called in.

Professionally, she was doing well. Her emotional life was a different story. She was in constant turmoil thinking about Wil. She realized that she could no longer postpone her talk with him. Each time she called him and had to lie about what she was doing ripped at her heart.

Finally, the tour was over, and she was exhausted. She and Grace said their good-byes at the airport and went their separate ways. Wil was picking her up at the airport. She knew this was the time to reveal her new vocation. Perspiration beaded on her forehead as the plane taxied to the Medford airport gate.

To make matters worse, Wil was waiting with a bouquet of flowers. The two greeted each other and kissed. On the way to the baggage claim, he could see that something was bothering her.

"What's wrong?" he asked as they waited for her luggage to come around.

Upset that he could pick up on her distress, she said, "Nothing."

"Bullshit. Don't give me that," he demanded. He knew her all too well. "Did that asshole brother-in-law do something to you again?"

"No," she said nervously. "I didn't even see him."

"Then what is it? Did I do something?" he asked.

She could tell he would not let this go. "Oh, no, Wil," she said, feeling guiltier by the minute. This was going to be harder than she thought. "Believe me. It's not you. I don't want to talk about it now. I'll tell you on the way home," she replied.

As she spoke, her bags came around on the conveyer belt. Wil grabbed them, and they walked to the truck without saying a word.

Once they were on the freeway, he looked at her and said, "OK. We're on the way home. What's the problem?"

The moment of truth had come. Her mouth was dry as a desert. She didn't know where to start. She closed her eyes, took a deep breath, and spoke.

"I don't quite know how to tell you this, except to just say it," she began.

He looked baffled. "Should I pull the truck over?" he asked.

"No," she replied. "I'd rather you didn't." She hesitated.

"Well?"

"I've been keeping a secret from you," she confessed. God, she hated this.

"I think I better pull over," he interrupted.

"No, no, please don't," she insisted. "This isn't easy for me. I'm just going to say it." She took another deep breath. "I quit my job."

The tension washed away from Wil's face, and he began to smile. "Is that all? That's great news. What's the problem?"

"Wait, Wil. Let me finish. I quit last November."

The puzzlement returned to his face. "Then what have you been doing? Where have you been going?"

"I wrote a book, and I've been on book-signing tours."

"You have? Nothing wrong with that. Why are you so upset?" he asked with confusion etched in his face.

"It's the kind of book that it is, Wil." She chose her words very carefully. "Have you ever heard of *Dirty Stories of a Rich Girl*? The author is Sheila Exotica."

He looked even more befuddled. "I heard of it. Smut book. One of the guys had a copy of it at the Blur the other night. It was disgusting. I saw the slut that wrote it on TV the other day. What's that got to do with you?"

"I'm Sheila Exotica," she said.

The color drained from his face. "Can't be you. She didn't look anything like you."

"It's me, Wil," she confessed. "I have a wig and wear a lot of makeup."

His face went blank as he stared at the road. This wasn't going well. She could see that he was trying to grasp the reality of it all. His silence was killing her inside.

"Wil, please, say something."

He looked at her, his gaze hard and cold. "Why would you go and do something like that?" Before she could answer, he added, "So, you've been lying to me these past couple of months."

His words cut to the heart. "Yes, I've been lying. But I didn't want to. Let me explain."

He cut her off. "Nothing to explain; you're a liar and a slut."

"No, Wil," she tried to expound. "I'm nothing like the girl in the book. It's all fantasy, honest."

"How do I know you're not lying now? I thought I knew you. I thought you were decent. How could you write such filth? To think I gave you my mother's favorite earrings."

A stream of tears began to tumble down her cheeks. She felt as if her heart had been ripped out of her chest. "I'm sorry," she said, sobbing. "I just couldn't be a project manager any longer."

"So you turned to sleaze? What got into you? Why didn't you tell me you hated your job that much? My God, a porno writer! Did you ever think of me and my feelings? You played me for a fool, Marie. Did you ever think about what people in this town would think of you when they found out?"

"But, Wil, that's why I invented Sheila."

"Don't say another fucking word," he said.

She knew that nothing she could say would change his mind. She just sat there and silently cried in the icy coldness of his emotions.

Not a word was spoken between the two of them until they reached Marie's house. Wil got out of the truck and grabbed her bags. He threw them on the front porch without speaking.

"Will I see you tomorrow night?" she asked, hoping against hope that the long ride to her house had calmed him down.

"I'll call you," was all he said. He got in his truck and drove off, leaving her standing on the porch in a cloud of dust.

But he didn't call. He didn't call the following week either. Marie was beside herself with regret. She questioned Duke, but all he knew was that she had made his dad mad, and Wil wouldn't talk to him about it either. She wondered if she should tell Duke the whole story but decided against it. Wil would only accuse her of trying to get Duke to take sides.

She was miserable. Her world had crumbled around her. She had been given a second chance at love and blown it. She couldn't blame Wil. He was a man of virtues. His wife had proven to be a slut. Both of the women he had cared about had betrayed him. She wasn't sure if it was the book or the lying that made him so angry. Maybe it was both. Since he wouldn't talk to her, she could only guess.

The next leg of the tour was scheduled to start in a few days, and still no word had come from Wil. She decided to leave for Detroit a day early, so she could spend it with her sister. She needed to be with family now more than ever. She felt alone and forsaken.

Madelyn could tell immediately that something was distressing her sister. "You look like someone died," she said when Marie arrived.

"Oh, Maddy," she said. "I really blew it this time." She burst into tears.

"Marie, Marie," Madelyn said, trying to console her sister. "Come on inside. It can't be that bad. What happened?"

"I told Wil about the book. Now he hates me."

"Oh, I don't think he hates you," Madelyn said, trying to make her sister feel better.

"Yes, he does. He was mad. I've never seen him so angry. He thinks I'm a terrible person. He called me a slut. He didn't call the whole time I was home." She was sobbing loudly now. "Maddy, it's over."

"Oh, hon. Come on now. It can't be that bad. It's not over. You know men. He just needs some time to let off steam. And you are not a bad person."

"You didn't see him…his face…the way he looked at me. It's over. I know it."

"You hurt his pride, Marie. He found out that you were not the person he thought you were. It must have been quite a shock. Give him time. He'll come around."

"I don't know." Marie sobbed. "I don't know what I'll do if I can't have him in my life. I love him, Maddy. I really do." It was the first time she had admitted this to anyone, the first time she said it out loud.

"I know you do," Madelyn said. "I could tell the first time you told me about him."

"You could?" This surprised her. She hadn't really fully acknowledged it to herself until now.

"I could see it in your eyes. When you talk about him, I see the same look that you used to have when you talked about Charles."

"Oh, Maddy," she cried. "That makes it worse. What am I going to do?"

Madelyn took her sister by the hands and looked her straight in the eyes. "A man's pride is strong, but it is easily bruised. You need to give him time to think about it. He needs time to realize how much more you mean to him than the book you wrote. Trust me. From what you've told me about Wil, I think he is as much in love with you as you are with him. He's a hardheaded, independent man, like most men. He'll come around. You need to call him when you get home."

"What if he won't talk to me?"

"Then you go over to his house, and you make him talk it out. If you love him, and he loves you, you'll make it work."

"He's never really come out and said that he loves me."

"Actions speak louder than words, my dear. His actions prove that he does. Did he read the book?"

"Not all of it." Marie was regaining her composure now. "He said someone had it at the Blur and he read part of it."

"Well, there you go. He probably read one of the more sexy parts. I'm not a fan of explicit sex, but when you read your book in its entirety, it all fits in. It's a very well-written story of an extremely sexually active young woman. It's not like you're promoting prostitution or anything."

"Maddy, you read my book?" Marie was in awe.

"Of course I did. You think I want Jake having all the fun?"

This brought a smile to Marie's face. "You're right. I'll talk to him when I get home. I'll make him talk to me. I'll make him understand," she said, trying to convince herself that she could but not really succeeding.

"That's it. Now go wash those tears off your face. Justin will be up from his nap soon, and he has a joke he wants to tell you."

"Thanks, Maddy. I love you."

"I love you, too, Marie." The sisters embraced.

Her book held steady at number one. Bookstores were selling out. She was becoming more comfortable in front of the TV camera. Everywhere she went, people wanted to see Sheila Exotica. Because the real Marie was nothing like Sheila, she could walk among the people as Marie and observe their reactions when they saw her on TV or in the bookstores after the signings.

There were the religious zealots who condemned her for the book, proclaiming it was the work of the devil and accusing her of being a perverted soul bent on corrupting America's youth. But so far, there had been no demonstrations against her. The cities for the next leg had to be carefully chosen. It would swing through the Bible Belt and into Florida. They didn't expect any trouble, but the book company was going to hire security guards, just in case.

The two-week tour was over, and she was headed back home. She was able to spend the night at Madelyn's. Her sister pumped up her confidence before sending her off. She also filled Marie in on the latest goings-on with their brother-in-law.

"I talked to Naomi the other day," Madelyn said casually after dinner.

"My, you two are getting pretty chummy these days, aren't you?" Marie asked.

"I guess so," Madelyn answered. "I like her. You know, I've had a chance to talk to her about what she did to Shelly and the family by having the relationship with Tommy. I explained to her why you wrote the letter. She understood and said that you are welcome in her house anytime. She even apologized for having the affair."

"Really? Why? Is the shoe on the other foot now?" Marie joked.

"Yes, yes, it is," Madelyn quipped.

"You're shittin' me?" Marie was dumbfounded but not totally surprised. "How does she know?"

"She hired a private detective, I think. She was very elusive about it. But I know it wasn't her that saw them."

"Tommy, the Shit," Marie declared. "So, now Naomi knows what it feels like."

"Yes, she does. And she has apologized over and over. She says she confronted him and he admitted it. She had proof beforehand, of course. She just wanted to see if he would deny it. He promised her he would break it off."

"Yeah, like he promised Shelly?"

"I didn't want to tell Naomi about that. Maybe this time he will."

"I wouldn't bet on it," Marie said.

The plane ride back home to Oregon was long and arduous. The drive from Medford to her home was even worse. Duke was home, chopping wood, when she arrived and approached her as she pulled the car into the garage.

"Hi, Duke," she said as he helped her out with her baggage. "How's your dad?"

"Miserable but he won't admit it," he replied. "He finally told me what was bugging him."

"He did?" she said. "How do you feel about it?"

"I think he's being a jackass about the whole thing, and I told him so. I understand why you did it, and I can see why you didn't want to tell him."

"You do?" She was delightfully surprised to hear this. For the first time, she felt that there was hope of reconciliation.

"Sure," he said. "I read the book. I got to admit, it's hard to picture you writing it. But I liked it. So did Amber."

"Oh, my. Does Amber know I wrote it?"

"She didn't at first. Neither did I when I read it. Dad just told me a few days ago."

"Duke, you haven't told anyone else, have you?" she asked.

"No," he answered.

"What about Amber?" She was getting a little worried now.

"No, don't worry," he assured her. "We figured if you went so far as to make up another name and wear that crazy getup on TV, you didn't want anyone to know who you really were."

She breathed a sigh of relief. "Oh, Duke. I love you. How did you ever get to be so smart?"

"Just lucky, I guess," he quipped shyly.

"Do you think your dad would talk to me if I called him?" she asked.

"Not right now," Duke said.

"Oh," she said, becoming disheartened again.

Duke quickly added, "Because he's not home. He's on an adventure trip. He won't be back for a week. Just left today."

"This time of year?" She was puzzled.

"Yeah, I thought it was kind of weird, too. It's just one guy by himself. The guy didn't even balk at the extra five hundred bucks for the off-season trip. Hey, money is money. I think Dad needed the time in the mountains anyway. He really does miss you, you know."

"I'm not so sure about that," Marie replied.

"Don't underestimate yourself," Duke said. "He's been like a bear since all of this happened. He's miserable without you in his life. Call him when he comes back."

"Thanks, Duke. I will."

Her spirits were lifted by this news. It gave her hope. She resolved to call Wil when he returned from the trip.

The week passed slowly. Finally, she noticed Duke was putting Wil's horse, Pal, back in the barn with Rex. Wil was back. Her fingers trembled as she dialed the number.

"Hello." The voice on the other end was emotionless and flat, but it was Wil.

"Wil, this is Marie."

"I know who it is."

"I just called to say…" She really didn't know what she called to say. "I called to say I'm sorry if I hurt or disappointed you."

Silence.

"Are you still there?" she asked.

"I'm still here." Good. He didn't hang up.

"Is it too late to start over? To be friends again, I mean," she asked.

"I still can't figure out why you had to write that kind of book," he said.

"Because I saw it as my way out. That's all."

"Hell of a way out."

"It's doing well."

"Good for you."

More silence.

"Wil, I want you back in my life. I miss you."

"I need more time, Marie."

"How much more time?"

"I don't know."

"Oh," she said, disappointed.

"We're still friends," she heard him say.

"Thanks," she replied. Her heart lifted with optimism.

"I gotta go," he said and hung up.

Well, not quite the ending she had hoped for. But at least it wasn't over. There was a chance.

He stared at the phone sitting on the desk and shook his head. It had been weeks since he found out about Marie's ugly, little secret, and it still upset him. He really didn't know why. He had been fuming mad when she told him that day in the truck. He couldn't believe she had lied to him all those months. She had to have been writing the book all along. How could she keep a thing like this from him? How could he be so stupid? How could he still be in love with her?

That's the part that made him the maddest of all. He still loved her. Life had just started to take on meaning again. He had even thought about asking her to marry him. Thank God, he didn't. At least now there were no real commitments between the two of them.

He was surprised when Duke told him he was being an idiot about the whole thing. He thought his own son would understand. It was Duke that got him to read the book. He read the book while she was gone. It was dirty, but it really was a good book. It had all the things that made it technically correct. But the sexual descriptions were almost too graphic. It embarrassed him to think that Marie had written it.

Now that he had read the book and had time to think about it, it wasn't as bad as it had seemed at first. He even felt a bit of pride that the book had become such a success. He wanted to forgive her. He really did. But he couldn't just yet. The wound was still too fresh. His pride had not yet healed. It still hurt too badly.

But thoughts of her floated in his mind every day. They had been together long enough to create treasured memories that he could not erase. Everywhere he went, he was reminded of her. He could not stop thinking about her, worrying if she was all right, wanting to protect her from everything evil and base in the world. Why hadn't she told him how much she wanted to quit her job? He would have supported her until she got something else going. Hell, he would have supported her forever, just to have her close to him and just to know that she would be there every night when he came home from work. He closed his eyes, and the image of her appeared before him in his mind's eye. He could smell her perfume. He remembered the softness of her skin, the feel of her lips, her breasts. Damn, he was beginning to feel like a character in that stupid book.

He decided to call her and talk about it some more. Maybe if he gave her a chance to explain, he could see it from her point of view. He let a few days pass before he called.

Marie answered the phone. "Hello."

"Marie, it's Wil."

"Wil, I'm glad you called." Her heart was in her throat.

"I wanted to give you a chance to explain yourself. Why did you feel the need to lie to me?"

"I lied because I didn't think you would understand, and I didn't want to lose you. I wasn't sure the book would be a success. If it failed, I wouldn't have had to tell you at all."

"Logical," he thought to himself. Then he spoke. "Well, you guessed right on that one. But I still don't understand."

"What don't you understand?" she asked.

"I don't understand why you had to write a pornographic book."

"It's not porn. The girl in the book is not a porn star or a hooker, just a real American girl, with a healthy sexual appetite. She promotes safe sex. We've done a lot of what she does in the book."

"Oh, come on. We never did it in a dressing room for heaven's sake."

"The acts, not the situations," she replied.

"How can you compare the two of us to her?"

He was getting mad again. Marie could picture the veins in his forehead pulsating.

"She's a damn sex fiend. She fucks men and women, and she uses sex toys. We make love."

His description of their intimacy made her smile inside. Then she began to wonder. "How do you know so much about the book?" she asked.

She had caught him. He had to admit it. "I read it."

"The whole thing?"

"Yeah, the whole damn thing."

She was too afraid to ask him how he liked it, but luckily, she didn't have to.

"It wasn't that bad."

She was smiling openly now. She could tell he was beginning to soften. "Does this mean you forgive me?"

"I wouldn't go that far. You still lied to me. I just wanted to hear why."

"Oh," she said, feeling depressed again. "I'm leaving the day after tomorrow. Can you come over before I leave?"

"I don't think so. I got a new job starting, and I gotta meet with the property owners for the next couple of days," he said.

"Will I see you when I get back?" She was getting desperate.

"Probably," he said. "Well, I gotta go. My dinner is ready."

She could hear the microwave chiming in the background. She wanted to tell him that she loved him and that her life was miserable without him. But she didn't. "OK. Well, then I guess I'll see you when I get back."

"Tell you what," he said. "What day do you get back?"

"Late on March fifteenth," she replied.

"I'll pick up some Chinese takeout and bring it to your house on the sixteenth, at six o'clock. OK?"

"Six o'clock is perfect," she said, feeling uplifted and redeemed. "Thanks." She paused for a moment and added, "Do you forgive me yet?"

"Almost," he said and hung up.

Marie breathed a sigh of relief. He was willing to give it another chance. She felt better and decided to go through some fan mail. Grace told her it was important to answer them personally.

The first two she opened were from fans who just wanted to tell her how much they loved the book, regular stuff. She quickly wrote out two short notes of thanks. The third was a little unsettling. The person who wrote it didn't sign their name. The letter was a graphic, sexual, description of what the fan wanted to do to Sheila. From the way the person described his own sexual attributes she could tell it was a man. He said that he loved her. Reading the letter made Marie feel ill at ease, but the ending made her skin crawl. It read, "See you soon."

She debated whether or not to let Grace know about it but decided against it. Besides, although it was postmarked Detroit, there was no return address. It would be impossible to track down the fan. She *was* popular in Detroit, but she had no new book-signings scheduled in Detroit for the next six months. Maybe it had been lost in the mail for a while. It was probably nothing and just part of being famous.

She wished she and Wil had already made-up. She wanted to tell him about the letter and see how he felt about it. She decided that she would tell him about it the night he brought the Chinese food on the sixteenth.

CHAPTER EIGHTEEN

—ɯ—

GRACE WAS WAITING FOR MARIE WHEN SHE STEPPED off the plane in Columbus, Ohio. Although the two women rarely spoke of their personal lives, Marie felt the need to tell Grace about Wil and his reaction to the book.

Grace was aghast that Wil could have such a provincial attitude in this modern age. "What is he, a caveman?" she said after Marie finished her tale.

"No, he's not that bad," Marie defended, feeling slightly hurt that Grace should be so judgmental of the man she loved. "Wil is kind of old-fashioned. He's just a sensitive man who has been hurt by love before."

"He needs to get with the times, baby," Grace said with a shimmy. "These are the nineties. Women can do whatever they want today. He should be proud that you are not a dependent, little waif that can't take care of herself."

"I know. But I don't think the nineties have hit Oregon yet. That's one of the reasons I love it there so much. Besides, I think he's over it now," Marie said. "He's bringing dinner out to my house the day after I get back."

"Yeah, the guy probably needs to get laid," Grace retorted.

"Really, Grace. He's not like that. Besides, he's an attractive man. There are plenty of women in Grants Pass or Medford he could have sex with if he wanted to."

"All men are the same, honey. They only got one thing on their mind, sex with a capital *S*. And thank goodness for that. You know what I mean? I always say a good man should keep his mouth shut and his dick hard."

"Too crude," Marie said, laughing.

The third leg of the tour started as successfully as the first two. Things went well in Ohio and West Virginia. The next stop was Louisville, Kentucky. There was a hint of a religious demonstration outside the bookstore in downtown Louisville. Just about half a dozen people were carrying signs that accused Marie of being evil and the devil's handmaiden. Security was called, and after a couple of hours, the demonstrators went home. Local media caught it, but it only warranted a one-minute spot on the local news.

Tennessee's and the Virginia's signings went without incident. But Alabama and Georgia were different stories. Everywhere they went in those two states, there were demonstrations. At first there were only small crowds or protesters; then, as the media picked up on it, the size of the demonstrations grew. In Macon, Georgia, extra security had to be called in, and Marie had to be ushered away with an escort before it got violent. It scared her, but Grace was undaunted.

"Don't worry, honey," she said. "This is great publicity. We could never afford to give you this kind of airtime."

She was right. News of the demonstrations made it into *USA Today* newspaper and onto CNN. Grace had been careful to shield Marie from giving interviews on the fly. Each interview granted had been timed and the questions reviewed and approved beforehand. The book was still at number one on the *New York Times* best-seller list. The number of people wanting their book signed still outweighed the demonstrators twenty to one. Letterman and Leno wanted her bad. Her agent was negotiating terms for the talk-show appearances.

Marie wondered if Wil was watching all of this and if it had fueled his fire against her or made him feel sorry for her. She missed him profoundly. She couldn't wait for the tour to be over and to have a nice, quiet evening with him at home. She missed their Friday night outings. She even missed the Wonder Bur, with all of its redneck men, big-haired women, stiff drinks, and twangy county music blasting out of the jukebox.

Why couldn't her life just be simple, quiet, and uncomplicated? Didn't she deserve it? Hadn't she paid enough dues?

The demonstrations ended when she was in Florida, and she was grateful for that. It was a peaceful ending to a tumultuous two weeks. Grace assured her that this would be the only troublesome tour. But she later admitted that the book company had hoped for this type of reaction, just to get some press.

Marie felt used and told Grace she didn't appreciate being made a public target. Grace justified the actions by restating that the book was still number one. She assured Marie that her safety was always primary and that she was never really in any physical danger. She told Marie that the book company had hired undercover security that was always lurking about. Grace said she didn't want to tell Marie before, because she didn't want her to be frightened. This comforted Marie to a degree but still made her feel uneasy.

The tour was over, and she just wanted to go home. She checked out of the hotel and met Grace in the restaurant.

"I have great news," Grace said as she sat down.

"What? I don't have to tour anymore?" she asked wearily.

"Are you kidding?" Grace said. "The fun is just beginning."

"OK," she said, preparing herself.

"I was up half the night getting this together."

She could see that Grace was excited.

"You're going to be on the *Late Show with David Letterman* tomorrow. The next day we fly to LA, and the day after that, you do the *Tonight Show with Jay Leno*."

"Grace, I can't," Marie insisted. "I'm tired. I want to go home. Why now?"

"We gotta strike while the iron is hot, sister," Grace said forcefully. "You're number one now. You're in demand. This is your fifteen minutes of fame."

"Can't it wait a week or two?" Marie asked.

"If we wait a week or two, you'll be old news. The demonstrations made national TV. You are *it*. Besides, you'll sell more books as a result of these two TV shows than you have so far on the whole tour. So, you go home a couple of days later. It will make what's his name hornier."

Grace's attitude toward Wil aggravated Marie. She rationalized that Grace had just gone through a divorce and was still bitter toward men. But still, Grace didn't know him and had no right to speak of him like that. "His name is Wil, and I miss him. I hurt him, and he is just about to forgive me. I can't do this to him."

"He'll get over it; believe me," Grace assured her. "This is your time now. You need to do this. Besides, it's all been arranged."

They arrived at the airport in plenty of time for Marie to call Wil and explain the change of plans. She hadn't spoken to him the whole two weeks she had been gone. She was so looking forward to seeing him and getting their relationship back on track. She had decided to tell him that she loved him. She didn't care if he reciprocated or not. She wasn't going to keep anything from him from now on.

She dialed the number and waited in anticipation of hearing his voice. The phone rang four times before the answering machine picked up. Damn. Now she would have to leave a message. She couldn't possibly explain it in a message. It would sound like she was trying to avoid coming home. She gave it her best shot.

"Wil, it's Marie. Something came up, and I'm not going to be coming home for another five days. I'm going to be on the *Late Show* tomorrow night and the *Tonight Show* two days later. I'll call you later and let you know when I'll be home. Please let Duke know, so he doesn't come out to the airport."

She hesitated for a moment, then added, "I miss you," before hanging up. "I love you," she whispered sadly after putting the phone on the hook.

Feeling melancholy and disappointed that she couldn't talk to Wil, she decided to call her sister.

"Maddy?"

"Hi, Marie, where are you?"

"I'm at an airport in Florida."

"Are you on your way home?"

"No," Marie said, disappointed. "We are extending the tour by five days."

She explained about the last-minute decision to do Letterman and Leno. Madelyn was ecstatic. Then she asked about Wil.

"Did you and Wil kiss and make up yet?" she asked.

"Kinda sorta," Marie replied. "We talked it out. I think he is beginning to understand why I did what I did. Duke has been a big help. He agrees with me, and I think he is trying to get his dad to see my side of it."

"Bless his heart," said Madelyn. "So? Does this mean you guys are getting back together?"

"Not yet really, Wil was on an adventure trip when I got back, and he was tied up with a new job the last couple of days I was home. But he's agreed to come over for dinner the day after I get home. He's bringing Chinese takeout."

"Sounds like you two are going to be OK. Do you feel better about it?"

"I did until this trip got extended. I hope he'll understand."

"I think he will. After all, it wasn't your doing."

"I hope so. I miss him so much."

"Young love," Madelyn teased.

"Ain't it grand?" Marie added sarcastically. "So, how are things out there in Motown?"

"Oh, we're just fine. I have to tell you, I spoke with Naomi again about Tommy."

"Oh really?" Marie said, uninterested.

"Tommy is being Tommy again."

"What do you mean?"

"Well, he broke his promise to Naomi, just like he broke his promise to Shelly."

This sparked her interest. "You mean he didn't break it off with his little tart?"

"No, this time Naomi caught him with his pants down, literally."

"No kidding?"

"She admitted that she had a PI on the case. She found out what hotel he was having his little rendezvous at and got a key from the desk clerk. She walked in on him in the middle of doing the nasty."

"Oh." Marie was enjoying this. "To have been a fly on the wall. What did she do?"

"She kicked his ass out."

"For good?"

"It's been a couple of days now, and she won't let him back in yet. She won't even let him see the girls."

"Wow, I'm starting to like her."

"She is fuming. I wouldn't doubt that she'll file for divorce."

This made Marie's day. Grace appeared and pointed to her watch. "Maddy, I gotta go. It's time to board. I'll call you in a few days."

The plane ride to New York was a three-hour flight. Marie slept through two hours. After checking into the hotel, she made arrangements to have her clothes laundered. Then she and Grace went shopping in downtown Manhattan. Sheila needed new clothes, and New York was just the place to buy them. In spite of herself, she had fun shopping with Grace.

Grace was in her element in New York. She still had friends and family in the city. She knew her way around and could speak the native language. She knew the subway system like the back of her hand.

The next day they taped the *Late Show*. David Letterman came backstage before the taping to talk to Marie, who was already dressed as Sheila. She was very nervous. Who would have ever thought she would be sitting there, talking to David Letterman like they were old friends? Dave was cordial and made her feel relaxed. They went over the allowed topics and questions to be used on the show. Dave was curious about the real person behind the wig and makeup. But under the watchful eye of Grace Santos, no secrets were revealed. The show was a success.

The flight to LA wasn't until the following morning, so Marie allowed herself to be talked into a night on the town with Grace and her friends. They had dinner at a gourmet restaurant that specialized in vegetarian cuisine. The food was delicious, and all the waiters were in drag. She was amazed that a man could have such a svelte body and look so good in women's clothes. Some of the men wore dresses that were so tight she couldn't imagine where they were hiding their packages. She couldn't help thinking about what Wil would say if he was there. He probably would have taken one look at the "ladies" and walked right out.

Marie did find it weird to walk into the ladies' restroom only to see one of the waiters walking out of the stall. She couldn't hide her surprised look. When the waiter passed her, he said, "Don't worry, honey; I squat."

Luckily the LA flight was early, and this gave her a winning argument for making it an early evening. If not, she would have been dragged to one of those nightclubs where you had to wait outside for an hour and only the privileged gained entrance. Although, with Grace's connections, they would have been let right in. To Marie, it would have been just like any other smoke-filled, loud bar, which she detested. Only this one would have been filled with trendy New Yorkers. Morty would probably fit right in. A room full of Mortys. She shuddered at the thought.

The flight to LA was long and boring. Marie had bought a couple of books at the airport bookstore but was finding it hard to concentrate. She missed her house. She missed Wil. She wanted to be with him and feel sheltered in his arms again. She missed having sex with him. It had been way too long, and her heart ached. She wondered if Wil felt the same way.

Wil returned home to find his answering machine blinking for attention. He listened to Marie's message with disappointment. He wondered how her plans could change so suddenly. He had missed her these past two weeks and was really looking forward to their date the following night. Her trip had given him time to put things in perspective, and he was more sympathetic to her feelings and reasons for doing what she did. He still didn't like it, but he understood now that she felt it was her only way out. Besides, he had no right to tell her what she could and could not do.

He knew now that she meant a lot more to him than he cared to admit. He knew that he loved her. He felt protective of her and worried about her safety, especially after seeing scenes of the demonstrations on CNN. He didn't want to live without her. He had built up enough courage to be able to tell her how he felt. Now he would have to wait five more days. It would be torture.

The next day he watched her on Letterman. Now that he knew Sheila Exotica was really Marie, he could see the resemblance. Marie was there, ever so slightly hidden behind all the gaudy makeup and that God-awful red wig. And those clothes, her boobs were practically popping out of her blouse. Only the body language and the sound of her voice gave him confirmation that it was really Marie. In a way, he was proud of her. He knew the book had made it to number one. She did it all herself. She sure was an independent gal. He kind of liked that, too. She was tough. She had proven that she could take care of herself if she needed to. Heck, she had been taking care of herself most of her life.

He ached for her. Watching her on TV just made it worse. She was there; he was a half a world away. He wanted to reach out and touch those protruding titties and bury his head in them as he had done so many times before. Four more days, could he wait that long? He would have to.

In LA, Marie and Grace were treated like royalty. They were put up at the Beverly Hilton and had a limo at their disposal. With the time change, they still had a good portion of the day to play after they checked in. Marie chose to just lounge at the pool and sip cool drinks. Grace had no choice but to join her. While the two were eating dinner, Grace got a phone call from the main office. The book company had decided that Sheila Exotica should do some book signing while she was in LA, which delayed Marie's flight home by one more day.

Pleasant as it was to be the center of attention, Marie still yearned to be back in Oregon and to get her relationship with Wil back on track. That evening, she called him to let him know she was delayed again and would be home the following evening. Melancholy filled her as she again got his answering machine. She left a short message telling him of the delay and how disappointed she was. She was beginning to wonder whether or not Wil was going to be excited to see her. It had been more than a month since they had been together. Did he find someone else? Or maybe he just didn't care anymore. Not knowing was killing her.

She decided to call Duke and let him know what day and time her plane came in. Again, she reached an answering machine. She left the information and hung up.

Doing the *Tonight Show* was almost like doing the *Late Show*. Jay was just as amiable and curious as Dave was. Only the audience was different. New Yorkers had a tendency to be high energy and dressed more fashionably, whereas Los Angelenos were more laid back and casual. It could have been because it was freezing in New York and sweltering in LA. Marie didn't care. She just wanted the show to be over, so she could get back to Wil.

The taping went well, and so did the book signings. Los Angeles welcomed Sheila with open arms and open wallets. *Dirty Stories of a Rich Girl* was a hot commodity, and the book company had to overnight a shipment to the bookstores Sheila was appearing at in order for there to be enough on hand when she got there.

Finally, the day arrived. She was going home. Grace and Marie embraced as they bid each other farewell. Grace told her how proud she was of her and that she really pulled this one off. Grace also thanked Marie for putting up with her and going along with all of the last-minute changes. She wished her luck with Wil and ran off to catch her plane.

Marie had to change planes in San Francisco and decided to call Duke.

"Hello," she heard. Finally, a real voice.

"Duke, it's Marie."

"Hi. I was just on my way to the airport. You haven't been delayed again, have you?" he asked.

"No, thank God," Marie said with relief. "This time I'm coming home. I'm in San Francisco and just wanted to make sure you got my message."

"Yeah, no problem."

"Duke, has your dad been around? I tried calling him, and all I got was his answering machine."

"He's been working long hours on that new house. I think he works late to keep his mind off of missing you."

"That's a sweet thing to say, Duke. I hope you're not just saying that."

"Trust me, I'm not," he said. "Listen, I gotta go if I want to get to the airport before you."

"Sorry," she apologized. "I'll see you in a while."

She wanted to ask him more about Wil but figured she could quiz the boy on the ride home.

Duke was there right on time when she arrived in Medford. On the way home from the airport, she got her chance. After asking the obligatory questions about how he, the horses, and Amber had been, she asked the question she was anxiously waiting to ask.

"So, how's your dad?"

"He's been pretty good actually," he said sincerely. "I think the talk you two had did some good. Although he was really disappointed when you called to say you wouldn't be home for a while."

"Really?"

"Really. He was upset at first. But I think he has really come around. We talk about you a lot."

"Yeah, like what?" She was curious.

"He really wants to understand what you are all about. Not that I know any more than him, probably less. But I think it makes him feel better to just talk. I told you, Marie. You mean a lot to him."

"I wondered about that for a while. I'm really excited to see him. Do you know if he is still planning on coming over tomorrow night?"

"Are you kidding? That's all he's been talking about for the last three days."

She couldn't help but smile and feel relieved.

The sight of her driveway looked like the road to paradise. "Home sweet home," she said as Duke made the turn. He just looked at her and smiled.

He helped her get her bags in the house and made sure she had everything she needed.

"I bought some juice and fruit in town yesterday. I didn't know what else to get. I'm still not sure of what a vegetarian eats," he said.

"Thanks, Duke. That was very sweet of you," she said.

"If you don't need anything else, I'm going to feed the horses and head on over to Amber's. There's a John Wayne movie on tonight that she promised she would watch with me."

"You are your father's son, Duke." She laughed. "Go ahead. I'm OK. I'll probably take a walk on the creek, relax for a while, and go to bed early. I'm bushed. And it feels so good to be home. I can't wait to sleep in my own bed."

"I guess that would be a bummer, all those strange beds," he thought out loud. "Well, call me at Amber's if you need anything."

"Have fun," she said. "And thanks for picking me up." She gave him a hug, and he walked out the door.

She unpacked and threw a load of clothes in the washer. She changed into her jeans and flannel shirt, threw on a jacket, grabbed her handgun and bear spray, and walked to the creek.

It was early spring, and the earth was awakening from a long winter's nap. Wildflowers were popping up all over. Leaf buds were making an appearance on the trees. The Douglas firs were bursting with growth, and their piney smell filled the air. Birds were returning from their winter homes and singing their praises of the season. The creek was flowing high with snow runoff from the mountains. Mother Nature's beauty was awesome. It made Marie feel as though she was the only human on Earth and nature's showy beauty was meant for her alone. She closed her eyes and breathed in the fresh Oregon air. It was crisp and cool. "How lovely," she thought. She felt so complete here. The only thing missing was Wil, and he would be there the next day.

It was nearly four in the afternoon when she returned. She noticed that Duke's car was gone. When she walked inside her house, she saw that her answering machine was blinking. She listened to the message. It was from Wil.

"Hi, Marie? Hell, I hate talking to a stupid machine. Well… ah…I just wanted to say welcome back. Ah…I wanted to let you know I'll be there at six tomorrow night with the Chinese, if you still want me." There was a long pause. "I missed you."

That was it. Damn, she had missed his call. She dialed his number but got the machine again. "He must have called from the jobsite," she thought. She'd try to call later.

There was a message on the refrigerator to call her sister Madelyn that she hadn't seen before; it was important. She dialed the number.

"Hi, Maddy, it's me. What's up?"

"Marie, I thought you'd be home by now. I've been trying to get a hold of you."

"Yeah, another last-minute change," Marie explained. "Spent an extra day in LA. What's so important?"

"Tommy's missing?"

"What do you mean 'missing'?" she asked.

"As in he went fishing with a couple of buddies, got drunk, and walked off into the woods. That's the last anyone has seen of him." Madelyn sounded concerned.

"How long has he been gone?"

"For three days now. Naomi is really worried."

"Are you sure? Are you sure she didn't have her family do their thing on him?"

Madelyn thought for a moment. "She wouldn't do that. At least I don't think she would."

"Never underestimate a woman scorned," Marie said. "If she didn't do it, I bet her old man had something to do with it."

"Now that's a possibility," Madelyn admitted.

"Well, let me know if he shows up."

"By the way," Madelyn said, changing the subject. "I saw you on Letterman and Leno. You were fabulous!"

"You really think so?" Marie said, feeling self-conscious.

"Absolutely. Jake thought so, too. I only wish I could tell my friends that Sheila is my sister."

"Don't you dare," Marie broke in. "One blabbermouth in the family is enough."

"Yeah. Well, listen, hon, I'll let you go. You must be exhausted."

"I am," Marie admitted. "I'm gonna take a shower and take a nap."

"I'll call you in a few days. I gotta know what happens with Wil," Madelyn said and hung up.

The shower felt utterly wonderful. She let the hot water wash away the tension that had been building up for weeks. After the shower, she dressed and laid down for a short nap.

Her own bed…was she dreaming? It was heaven. She felt as if she were floating on a cloud. She could feel her body melting into its cushiony softness. A few deep breaths and she gently drifted off into a lethargic slumber.

CHAPTER NINETEEN

—⁓—

MARIE ONLY INTENDED TO SNOOZE FOR AN HOUR or two. She was fully dressed and hadn't gotten under the covers. Perhaps it was the timbre of the rain gently hitting the window that soothed her into such a deep slumber. But the sound of an aluminum can hitting the deck brought her to startling awareness. She sat up instinctively, not quite sure if it was a sound from her dreams or from the real world. It was pitch black. She glanced over at her digital alarm. It was ten o'clock. She had been sleeping for six hours. She had only half heard the sound in that hazy state of consciousness between the two realities of sleeping and waking.

"Duke?" she called out. "Is that you?" She thought perhaps he had forgotten some important item to complete this evening's pleasures with Amber. His living quarters were not that close to her house, but she was a very light sleeper, and it was possible that a can dropped on Duke's porch could wake her.

There was no answer. She reached over and flicked on the lamp next to the bed. Its dim glow illuminated the room only slightly. She clicked it up one notch. She saw no movement and heard no other noise. It could have been a raccoon, a squirrel, or just a little mouse. Slipping her moccasins on, she climbed off the bed and headed toward the deck door. She flicked on the outside lights, hoping that whatever it was would be frightened away by the brightness.

Nothing stirred. Wil had taught her to be cautious of wild creatures. She grabbed the can of pepper spray that she always kept by the door, just in case this critter was bigger than a raccoon or squirrel and more deadly than a deer. Walking out onto the deck, she looked in all directions but saw nothing, not even the can. There was still a light drizzle of rain falling. She walked over to the barn and looked in the garage. Duke's car was gone. There were no lights on inside Duke's living quarters. She must have been hearing things.

Thinking nothing of it, she walked back to her house and locked the sliding glass door behind her, just in case. She set the pepper spray on the table. She was awake now and wanted to call Wil, but it was much too late for that. She knew him. He was up before the sun, but he also turned in early. He would be deep into sack time by now. Tomorrow would be here soon enough. She could call him first thing in the morning.

Hunger pangs began gnawing at her stomach. She realized that she hadn't eaten before she fell asleep. Duke had said that he bought some fruit. To her delight, there was a rather impressive assortment of fruit in the fridge. She grabbed an orange and a peach and walked over to the sink to rinse them off. While washing the fruit, she thought she caught a whiff of cigarette smoke. How could that be? Neither Duke nor Wil smoked.

"Must be more tired than I thought," she said to herself. First she thought she heard something; now she thought she smelled something. "I need rest," she said, trying to convince herself that it was just fatigue playing tricks on her. To play it safe, she turned on all of the lights around the outside of the house. She looked through every window for signs of movement. She saw nothing.

She sat at the kitchen table and ate the fruit. From the table, she had a clear view of the deck outside through the sliding door, and she kept scanning for movement. In the time it took her to eat the fruit, she saw no movement except leaves on the trees swaying in the breeze. She was beginning to feel more relaxed, so she shut all the outside lights off and closed all the curtains. She turned on a few more lights than normal on the inside. She decided to do a little reading and finish one of the books she had bought during her last trip. She only had a few chapters to go, and she didn't feel tired anymore.

She powered up the stereo and switched it to CD mode. Her CD player held six CDs at a time, and she usually kept it loaded. She pressed random play. Finding the book she was looking for, she settled into her recliner and started to read. She had read only a few pages when she heard the floor behind her creak. As she turned around, she felt a strong, gloved hand cover her mouth and nose. The hand was holding a handkerchief that had been saturated with some kind of chemical-smelling liquid. She struggled to get free, or at least turn to face her assailant, but she could quickly feel herself growing light-headed and faint. She blacked out in a matter of seconds. The trench-coated intruder swooped her up and carried her out to a waiting Jeep.

A light rain continued through the night and became steady by morning. Mortimer Jablonski was feeling pretty smug. He had clandestinely obtained the woman of his dreams. He had fallen in love with her the first time he read her book. Finally, here was someone who had the same sexual appetite that he did. Here was someone who loved sex and didn't think it was evil or sinful. Then, when he saw her on TV, he knew he had to have her. What a stroke of luck to find out that Diana was actually Sheila Exotica's sister. Once he knew that, it was nothing to find out everything about her. Diana trusted him—her mistake.

Sure, to everyone else she was Marie Trousdale. But Morty had met her. He knew her type. Inside, she really was Sheila Exotica. To Morty, she would always be Sheila. The name fit her. Not Marie. Marie sounded like a nun. Morty had endured enough of nuns. He shuddered when he thought of his Catholic school experiences and the nuns who seemed to always be named Sister Marie or Sister Mary something or another. His knuckles still hurt, thinking about the hundreds of times they had been whacked for some stupid, little thing he did that the nuns disapproved of.

He remembered the time Sister Marie Joseph caught him and Linda Grimmes with their hands in each other's pants behind the alter in fifth grade. He had been lifted by the hair and dragged to the mother superior's office. As punishment for being "dirty," he had to scrub the urinals in the boys' bathroom with a toothbrush every day for a month after school. The other boys never liked him and used to pee all over the urinals, knowing Morty would have to clean them. They were always jealous of him, because he had a man-sized cock by the time he was ten. The girls were always curious and wanted to see it and touch it. Morty liked that. He liked the way their eyes got wide when he persuaded them to stroke it and it grew even larger.

He still had a big cock. His was superior to most of the men he had seen. This made him attractive to both men and women. Gay men would pay him to let them suck it. He also got paid for anal sex. He wasn't gay. But if he closed his eyes while he was getting head, he couldn't tell if it was a man or woman sucking him off. A blow job was a blow job. And anal sex always felt good, as long as he was the top, and he always was. He had to draw the line somewhere, and getting a dick up his ass was where he drew his line. So fucking those gay assholes still felt like he was with a woman. Morty chuckled to himself; what a play on words. Besides, he usually got paid for it.

He liked sex. He liked sex a lot. He liked watching it, reading it, doing it. He could tell Sheila liked it, too. How else could she write that deliciously explicit book? All his life, he was told that sex was bad. His religious upbringing still had its grips on him. His parents practically had him committed when he was twelve. They caught him masturbating with a copy of *Playboy* magazine, a year after the Linda Grimmes incident. He used to pray that Jesus would take his sexual desires away, but in high school, he figured it was a gift from Jesus, not a curse. He still said his prayers; only now his prayers were in thanks for his gift and about his hope to always find sexual partners.

After accepting that his huge cock was a gift, sex had become a delicious, forbidden fruit. He couldn't get enough of it. He liked reading about it, watching porno movies, and, of course, actually fucking. Most of the time it was anonymous, one-night stand sex. He liked it that way, no commitments. Wham, bam, thank you, ma'am, or sir, whatever the case may be.

He knew now that his parents and the nuns were wrong. Sex was not evil. Screw them and their primeval attitudes. From now on, he called the shots when it came to sex. He felt in his heart that he and Sheila were sexual soul mates. Her book spoke to him. He would be her muse.

He threw out the cigarette he was smoking and lit another.

He laughed when he thought of that sleepy, little town of Grants Pass. Why, never in a million years would anyone in that town be able to outsmart him—bunch of hicks. Especially not that so-called mountain man that he had hired for the adventure trip. Morty didn't like him. He had an attitude. He thought he was better than Morty, him and his cowboy boots and hat. He reminded Morty of an overgrown kid, who'd never quit playing cowboys and Indians. Why, he'd be laughed silly in the circles Morty hung with back in Detroit. Who did he think he was anyway, telling Morty where he could throw his cigarette butts? He could throw them anywhere he damn well pleased. The cowboy had served his purpose though. If it weren't for "Grizzly Adams," he wouldn't have known about the cabin, stupid guy. The whole purpose of taking the adventure trip was to find some out of the way spot in the mountains to set up a campground but when Morty saw the cabin, he was ecstatic.

The fact that she lived alone, so far away from town played into his plan perfectly. She had that young stud living on the property. Morty had planned on taking care of him, too. Good thing the kid left for the night. He imagined Sheila and that kid acting out chapters of *Dirty Stories of a Rich Girl* after the day's work was done. Morty figured he had more sexual experience than that kid before he was twelve. He could teach Sheila a few things about sex, too. And he intended to. He had big plans for Sheila.

"I'll bet she never had a dick as big as mine," he thought to himself with pride. He reached down and stroked the bulge in his pants. It felt good. "It will be love at first sight."

He heard a moan from the backseat. He looked back and saw her stirring. She was coming to. That was OK. They'd be at the cabin in no time. Besides, he had her tied up pretty good with duct tape, and she was blindfolded. She wasn't going anywhere.

A month's worth of hard work was finally going to pay off. Secretly, Morty had been making trips to the cabin, stocking it with supplies that he figured he would need. Two weeks up there with Sheila ought to be about enough time. He had even brought up an old, manual typewriter, so Sheila could start writing her new book, the book he would costar in. He'd thought about a laptop, but there was no electricity at the cabin, and a battery wouldn't last long enough.

Sure, she'd be mad at first. But he'd be nice to her. He didn't want to hurt her. He would just help her write a couple of chapters in her new book. Besides, once she got a look at his massive manhood, she would be putty in his hands. He knew her kind. She craved cock. To be able to write the kinds of things she wrote, she had to. Besides, he loved her. She was his soul mate. He hadn't felt this strongly for a woman since Linda Grimmes.

Suddenly, he got a terrible taste in his mouth and a sharp pain in his head. He didn't want to think about Linda anymore.

He had been surveilling Marie's house since he got back from the adventure trip. She had been gone for a couple of weeks on a book-signing tour. He even saw the spot on CNN where the demonstrators nearly caused a mob scene. He had watched her on Leno and Letterman. When she was home, she never had any visitors, not even a boyfriend.

He had been careful not to show up in town. He was staying at a various hotels in Medford, where he made all of his purchases. He was just another face in the crowd there. He even took precautions with the rental car. Every week he would switch rental companies, so as not to draw attention to himself. This time he had the car for two weeks. No big deal.

It was raining harder at the top of the mountain, and he nearly ran the Jeep off the road a couple of times. Calling it a road was stretching it. It was an old logging road that hadn't been maintained in several years. There were deep ruts that filled with rainwater and mud.

"Perfect," he thought. "If this rain keeps up, they'll never be able to drive up here. Heck, it'll probably be days before anyone even knows she's gone." By that time the initial shock of the abduction would have worn off, and Sheila would be madly in love with him. She would enjoy the couple of weeks with him. He would see to that. Then they could spend the rest of their lives together, whereever they wanted.

CHAPTER TWENTY

—ɯɯ—

THE HEADLIGHTS OF THE JEEP REVEALED A BUILDING up ahead, the cabin. "Finally," he thought. Slowly he pulled the car through the opening in the log fencing, which allowed him to get as close as he could to the front door, and parked.

He ran out and opened the cabin door. He lit the two camp lights he had stashed just inside. He left one in the cabin and set the other one outside. A soft glow bathed the inside with an eerie golden hue. He propped open the front door. The rain was not blowing hard enough to blow in, but it was making the temperature pretty cold. He would have to work fast to get Sheila inside and get a fire going.

By now, Marie was fully conscious and squirming around. The blindfold around her eyes had loosened somewhat but still blocked any view. She gave a muffled scream when Morty put his arm around her and pulled her out of the car.

"Don't worry," Morty said gently. "You're safe. I'm not going to hurt you."

She eased up slightly and whimpered. She had heard that voice before. Where was it? Was it someone from the tour or someone from town? Where, where?

She felt the rain hit her head as she was being directed to walk. Her ankles were bound with tape. She could feel it pulling as she stretched it, taking tiny steps as directed.

"Easy now," he said as she reached the threshold. "Watch your step; you're going inside." He grabbed her by both shoulders to steady her.

As she walked, she caught the aroma of his aftershave. "Morty," she thought. "It's got to be him. The smell of the cigarettes, the horrid odor of that aftershave…What's going on?"

She was thinking fast, processing her options. "Stay calm. Don't struggle. Find out what he wants. Make him think you won't bolt."

She felt herself directed forward. Her foot hit a chair. Heavy hands turned her around and forced her down into it. "Sheila, do you know who I am?"

She nodded her head affirmatively. "Sheila," she thought. "He's calling me Sheila."

"OK," he said. "So I can take off your blindfold, and you won't be surprised?"

She shook her head obediently to indicate that she wouldn't be. The thickly folded bandanna was lifted from her eyes. The light was not blinding, but it took a moment or two for her to focus. She still felt a little light-headed.

It was Morty all right, smiling from ear to ear. She looked around. She knew this place. It was the cabin Wil had brought her to on the adventure trip, where she first realized that she loved him. Wil, where was he? He wouldn't even know she was gone until tomorrow. Or was it today? It was still dark outside. She figured it had taken less time to get up here by car than by horse. It must be the middle of the night. Would Wil realize what had happened to her? She prayed to God that he did.

Scanning the room, she could see supplies everywhere in the little cabin. She looked back at Morty. There was still a piece of duct tape across her mouth, and her hands and feet were bound together with the sticky stuff.

She looked at Morty, who was in front of the fireplace. He was still smiling. "Hi," he said as if greeting an old friend. "Isn't this place cool? Some old mountain man brought me up here. No one usually uses this place this time of year, so I thought it would be perfect. You just sit tight, and I'm going to make us a nice fire." There was already a bunch of kindling wood and paper in there. He had thought of everything. He took his lighter from his pocket and lit the bundle. There was a stack of wood piled up on the side of the hearth.

"Old mountain man," Marie thought. "He must mean Wil."

Then it clicked. Morty was the guy Wil brought up here a month or so ago, the guy who paid extra for the off-season trip. Good. That meant that Wil had met him. She couldn't imagine that this guy wouldn't stick out in Wil's memory. She hoped that he would be able to put two and two together and figure out this guy didn't fit in. So when the cops asked the routine question of, "Did you see anybody strange around here lately?" Wil should get a clear picture of Mortimer Jablonski.

Obviously Morty didn't know that Marie and Wil knew each other. Of course, why would he? They hadn't seen each other since then. Just as she was starting to feel a little more at ease, she realized that Wil would not even begin to look for her until nighttime, when he showed up for dinner. And even after that, he had to get to the cabin. She could hear the rain coming down harder now. Even blindfolded and bound, she had felt the car slip under Morty's control on the way up. If it kept raining, the road was sure to be washed out by nighttime. Wil would not be able to make it up until the road was passable. She began to worry again. A lot could happen between now and then.

What did he want? And why did he call her Sheila?

The fire had started to burn brightly now under Morty's tending. She could feel the heat against her face. She hadn't realized how chilly and damp it was until now, and she started to shiver.

Morty noticed and grabbed a blanket off one of the cots. "Here, Sheila," he said as he wrapped it around her shoulders, the smell of his sickening cologne wafting across. "This will keep you warm."

She looked at him, wide-eyed, thinking, "I wish he would stop calling me Sheila."

He sat back and looked at her. "I'm not going to take the tape off of your mouth until I explain."

Marie looked at him blankly.

"I love you, Sheila," he confessed. "I know you don't love me like I love you now. But you will after we get to know each other a little more. I want to help you write a couple of chapters for your new book. I'm going to costar in it with you. We're going to write a few chapters about making love together."

She looked at him incredulously.

He was offended by the look, and his face straightened slightly. "I've got something that you love, my darling. Look at this." With that, he unzipped his pants and pulled out his penis, letting it lay flaccid in his hand.

She did a double take. Madelyn had said it was big, but that word seemed inadequate now. It was huge, not only in length but in girth.

"Bet you've never seen one this big before, have you?" he said proudly.

She shook her head. The only place she'd ever seen a penis of that caliber was in *X*-rated movies, never one in the flesh, so to speak.

"We'll have fun with this later," he said as he put his member back in his pants and zipped up his fly.

"I bought you something," Morty was saying. She was still trying to get over the sight of his huge penis. The sound of his voice brought her focus back. She looked at his face like a frightened fawn. He got up and walked over to a duffel bag by the fireplace. He unzipped it, fumbled around in it for a while, and pulled out a jumble of black leather straps and buckles. She could not make out what it was.

He walked over to her and sat down in a chair next to her. Getting serious, he said, "Now, I know it's going to take some time for you to get to know me, and I don't want you to run away, so I got this harness for you. Let me help you put it on."

"Here's my chance," she thought. "He'll have to take this tape off to put that on me. I'll be able to make a break for it." She figured she could make it down the mountain before daylight.

"Oh," he said. "I almost forgot." He set the harness down on the table next to her and walked back over to the bag. He pulled out a chain. Not a heavy one, but one like you might find in a grocery store in the pet aisle, one that people bought to tie their dogs out in the yard. He ripped opened the plastic bag and removed the chain. He wrapped it around the center log beam that supported the building.

"There," he said proudly. "This way you can move around in every direction. Now, let me help you."

He pulled a sizeable hunting knife from its case, which hung from his belt, and walked toward her. "Hold still, and let me cut the tape." He looked at her sternly and added, "Now, be good. You promise?"

She nodded emphatically.

He started to cut away at the tape around her wrists but changed his mind. "Oh, I think we'll put it on this way," he said. He sat down and moved his attention to her ankles.

"You know," he said as he was cutting. "I thought maybe you might need some persuading that we should be together. Trust me, my love. You and I were meant to be together. You'll see."

He continued to concentrate on cutting the tape. "It's a good thing I got these at the porn store in Detroit. I'd never be able to find them out here. Good God, how can you stand it out here? There's absolutely nothing to do. I was…"

She felt the tape being pulled away from her ankles. The tape around her wrists had been cut enough so that she could free her hands. In a swift motion, she bolted up straight. Morty, surprised by her action, also stood up. Marie raised one knee and caught him square in the crotch. He doubled over in pain. Marie jumped for the door, but in the dimness of the camp light, she stumbled and tripped over a duffel bag. Searing pain gripped her as Morty grabbed a handful of hair and pulled her head back. Hot, smarting pain spread across her face as he slapped it with his free hand.

"That was a stupid thing to do, Sheila," he said sternly.

She could feel the blood dripping from her nose and began to whimper and cry under the duct tape.

"It wasn't supposed to be like this. Why are you making me hurt you?" Morty was confused. He was losing control of the situation. "Well, I'll have to be more firm," he said. Memories of how the nuns at the boarding school were "firm" with him came rushing back. The beatings and other physical abuses surfaced and soured his stomach. "I learned from masters," he thought. "I know exactly how to break her." Taking no pity, he pulled the tape on Marie's mouth off in a single, cruel, painful motion. He'd show her more pain before showing her kindness again.

She was crying loudly. He was feeling empowered by her pain and suffering. It felt good. He looked down at her and laughed. "I'm sorry, dear, but no one can hear you here."

He was bending her head back so far she thought her neck would snap. She tried to scream, but at that angle all she could manage was an open-mouthed moan.

"Now hold still," he commanded.

Marie was so frightened; she obeyed without hesitation. Who knew what else he had in that bag, maybe a gun.

He worked the buckles on the harness until it was secure around her torso and hooked it to the chain with a small padlock. All of the buckles were in the back. There was a strip of leather that wove them all together, which he tied into a knot. "There," he said, stepping back admiring his handiwork. "That 'ill hold ya."

She lay crying in a lump on the floor. She looked up at him and wiped her face. It was smeared with tears and blood. By the look on his face, she was convinced that he was insane and she feared for her life. "What do you want?" she begged meekly.

He looked surprised that she had asked this. "I already told you. I love you, and I know that I can make you love me, if you give me a chance. We can start by writing some new chapters for your book." Looking at her bedraggled appearance was disturbing him. This wasn't the way he intended it to be, but he could work with it. She was supposed to be sultry and sexy. He thought for sure she would surrender herself to him after seeing his huge cock. She didn't. This puzzled him. His cock had always been his golden key to anything he wanted.

He looked at her, crying on the floor, bloody. He took some paper towels off of the roll in the kitchen and moistened them with water from his canteen. He walked up to her to wipe off her face.

"Look at you," he said tenderly. "You're a mess. Let me clean you up."

She was furious. Her hands were still free. She closed her eyes and allowed him to come close. He started to wipe the tears and blood from her face. He had put the hunting knife back in its case, and it was hanging from his belt. If she could catch him off guard, she could grab it and…and what? Kill him? She couldn't even allow the killing of animals so that she could consume them for nourishment; how was she going to kill another human being? Even if she decided to, was she strong enough to do it? What other choice did she have? She thought for sure Wil would come to rescue her. But how long would that take? What could Morty do to her before then? It was her only chance.

He finished wiping her face with the paper towels. "There," he said, throwing them into the fireplace. "That looks better." He began to stroke her face and hair. He was still furious, but seeing her so vulnerable softened him, and he remembered that he finally had the woman of his dreams here with him. It was time to be nice. "You are so beautiful, Sheila. I love you." He tenderly brushed her hair away from her face and pulled her head close to his chest.

She allowed herself to move at his will. The smell of his after-shave mixed with the smell of cigarettes gave her a wave of nausea. She opened her eyes slightly. The knife was still there. Gently, she moved her arms up, hoping he would think she was going to embrace him. When her hand was close enough, she suddenly grabbed for the knife. She got it. Like a shot, she raised her arm to gain force for the blow, swinging the other arm between her and Morty to help gain momentum. She thrust the knife down, aiming for his heart.

He saw the flash of steel streak before his eyes. He put his arm up to defend himself. The knife missed its mark and was buried deep in his forearm.

"You fucking bitch," he cried out in pain.

She pulled it out and tried to slash his face. This time his hand clenched her wrist before she could complete her swing.

She knew she had blown it. She was defenseless now. The force of his backhand snapped her head back. Her nose started to bleed again. Her mouth filled with blood, and her lips began to swell. She was sent sprawling to the floor.

Morty got up and grabbed the bandanna that he had used to blindfold her. He quickly made a tourniquet around his arm. Then he searched for the duct tape, swearing and talking to himself the whole time.

Marie was hurting all over. She wiped her nose and her mouth with her sleeve. Her lips were stinging with pain.

"Stand up, bitch," he commanded, standing over her. She struggled to get to her feet. "I said stand up!" he shouted and grabbed a handful of her hair, lifting her up just like Sister Marie Joseph had done to him so many years ago. She was standing with her back to him. "Put your hands behind your back."

She did as she was told. She heard the sound of duct tape being pulled off the roll. In the next moment, her wrists were being bound with it. Once her hands were secured, he pushed her down into a chair.

Now that she was incapacitated, his mood became more relaxed. But he began to pace the cabin floor. "I don't understand you, Sheila. I don't want to hurt you. Why are you doing this?"

She looked up at him. Her swollen lip made it hard to talk. "I'm not Sheila," she said with deadpan seriousness. "My name is Marie."

He seemed not to hear her. He kept on rambling, trying to make sense of her actions and gain control again. "I know what it is. You're tired. Of course, that's it. You've had a long night, and you need some rest. This has just been too overwhelming for you. God knows I could use some sleep. Let's get you in bed. Everything will be different in the morning."

"I'm not Sheila," she said even louder.

This time he acknowledged her declaration. His face twisted into a distorted, gargoyle-like image. He walked up to her and leaned over, so his face was inches from hers. "You're whoever the hell I say you are, bitch. Now shut up, and get on that cot." She reluctantly obeyed.

Feeling more confident at the sight of her compliance, he grabbed the roll of tape off of the table and taped her ankles together. Then he tied them to the end of the cot with a piece of rope. He cut loose her hands, only to rebind them in front with rope. He then attached the other end of the rope to the head of the cot.

He threw a blanket on top of her and leaned over close to her face. The smell of his putrid odor was overwhelming. "Good night, my darling." With that, he kissed her on the forehead. "I had so hoped it wouldn't be like this. You sleep on it. You'll see. We'll have a good time. I really *am* a good fuck, you know."

Marie felt like throwing up. She remained silent rather than stirring his wrath again.

Morty began talking to himself again as he secured the cabin for the night. He was speaking in a very low tone. It sounded like passages from the Bible. Marie could just barely pick up a few phrases, but every once in a while, she heard a "thee" or "thou." He was reciting his nightly prayers.

He stoked up the fireplace before turning in. Once he got in his cot, he called out to her once again. "Sheila, tomorrow will be better. I asked God to make it better. I asked him to forgive you for your sins and make you see that you and I belong together. Now sleep, my darling."

Marie could only whimper. The bleeding had stopped, but she was in pain. Her face was swollen and throbbing. More importantly, she was frightened, more frightened than she had ever been in her whole life; never had she been the recipient of such violence. She truly feared for her life. Morty's moods could change in an instant. There was nothing left to do now but resign herself to the fact that she was at his mercy, at least for now. "Please God," she silently prayed, "please help Wil find me tomorrow." Within a few minutes, she could hear snores coming from across the room. She relaxed slightly and soon was overwhelmed with exhaustion and shock. She closed her eyes and, mercifully, fell asleep as well.

Although the clouds were heavy, Wil woke with a light heart the next morning. Tonight he would see Marie. He would tell her he understood why she felt she couldn't tell him about her book and apologize for being so chauvinistic and prudish. It's not like he didn't enjoy a good porn movie now and then. And the way she wrote the stories…well, he had to admit they were very well written. She had a way of making them erotic and graphic without being too crude or vulgar. He wondered if she got the message he left on her machine yesterday afternoon. She hadn't called back. Well, no news was good news. If she didn't call to tell him not to come, that was a green light. He would see Duke on the jobsite and ask him about her.

Duke stopped in at home to shower and change before going to work. He noticed that there was no movement in Marie's house and all the curtains were still drawn. It was early, but she was usually an early riser. His dad was the only one he knew who got up before her. He looked in the garage and saw her car. He figured she was just catching up on some much-needed sleep. She had mentioned how much she missed sleeping in her own bed. He decided not to disturb her and left for work. Luckily, he would be working inside and would be unhindered by the rain.

CHAPTER TWENTY-ONE

A DRIZZLE OF RAIN CONTINUED THROUGH THE NIGHT and into the morning. Distant thunder rumbled with atmospheric turmoil. Marie woke before Morty and lay on her cot, thinking of what the day would bring. Should she write some stories just to keep him quiet? She had to stall for time. Duke may have noticed that something was wrong when he came home from Amber's. Then again, it was not his custom to check in with her in the morning. More than likely, it wouldn't be until evening that anyone noticed she was missing.

She would have to keep Morty quiet and happy all day. He was explosive and unpredictable. She couldn't afford to take any more chances. The side of her face was still swollen and throbbing with pain.

It was about an hour after she awoke that Morty began to stir. He tossed his head in her direction and noticed that she was fully awake.

"Good morning, my love," he spoke sweetly. "How did you sleep?"

"Fine," she replied with no emotion. "I have to go to the bathroom." And she did.

"I'm sorry," he said apologetically, glowing with a sappy smile. "How thoughtless of me. Now just wait there a second." He casually walked over to the duffel bag and fumbled through it. He pulled out what she had feared. He had a gun. As he approached her, she could see it more clearly. It was her own .357 Magnum that Wil had gotten for her. Morty could see the spark of recognition in her eyes. He untied the ropes that held her wrists and ankles to the cot. He cut her ankles free but kept her hands bound in front.

"You won't need that," she said, nodding in the direction of the gun and trying to act calm. "I promise I'll be good."

The sugary smile quickly vanished from his face, and he became deadly serious. "If you don't mind, you've already proved to me that you're a liar and I can't trust you. Now you've got to earn my trust."

He glanced down at the gun in his hand. "I see you recognize the gun. It's yours all right. I was lucky enough to find it. I wasn't able to pack my own, with all the airport security nowadays." He palmed it back and forth between his hands. "Nice gun," he added.

He walked over to her and unlocked the padlock from her harness. He motioned her toward the door with the gun. Obediently, she stood up. Together, they walked to the outhouse. After looking inside to see if there was anything she could use against him, he allowed her in.

She thought about making a run for it, but with her hands still secured, she wouldn't stand a chance. She really did have to pee badly and didn't think she had the strength to try and be a hero again. She did her business and walked out. Once inside the cabin, she was again secured to the chain. After much pleading and promises of good behavior, she convinced him to free her wrists.

Morty made her a breakfast of cereal and milk. He had done his homework and knew she was a vegetarian. She didn't usually drink milk, but under the circumstances, she didn't complain. Her wrists and ankles were tender, and her muscles were cramping. The injuries in her mouth made it difficult to open it wide enough to get the spoon in. She could tell that both her top and bottom lip had been cut. Each bite brought excruciating pain. Morty observed her difficulty but showed no emotion.

After she had eaten, he cuffed her hands together with felt-lined handcuffs. They looked like they were meant to be sexual toys and not police regulation. She was left to her own devices while he straightened out the cabin and rebuilt the fire. He had measured the chain and arranged the supplies so that they were just out of reach to her. She quickly discovered that she could walk about six-feet out. She could sit at the table or on the floor in front of the fire. That was about it. She chose to sit at the table with her head down. Her nose was stuffed up, and her lips were now pulsating with pain after eating breakfast.

"You need to freshen up." Morty's voice brought her to attention. He set a bowl of water, a bar of soap, and a washcloth in front of her. She let out a sigh of relief as he removed the handcuffs. She could see small cuts and bruises left behind from the tape on her wrists. She washed her hands. Her wrists stung. Morty brought her a toothbrush and hairbrush. She was surprised to notice that they were her own. He had taken them from her bathroom. He set a small mirror in front of her.

It was the first time she had a chance to examine the extent of her injuries. She gasped when she saw herself. Her right cheek was bruised, as was the right side of her nose. Her lips were swollen and split. Dried blood was everywhere. She hardly recognized herself. She rinsed the cloth in the cool water and buried her face in it. Its soothing relief was invigorating.

By the time she finished cleaning up her bruised and battered face, Morty had brought her a glass of fresh drinking water. She brushed her teeth and spat the water into the bowl. She arranged her hair the best she could. Morty, ever observant, took away the toiletries as soon as she was done and set the typewriter and a stack of typing paper in front of her.

"Time to work, Sheila," he commanded.

She sat upright at the typewriter. He sat down next to her. She waited for instructions.

After a minute, he looked at her quizzically and asked, "Why aren't you typing?"

She looked up. "What do you want me to type?"

His face tightened. He butted out his cigarette on the cabin floor and slammed down his fist in fury. "For the third time!" he shouted. "Write a chapter for your new book. Write about our meeting and having hot, torrid sex."

She flinched at the force of his fist on the table and lifted her hands in front of her face, anticipating another slap. To her relief, it didn't come.

"Maybe you need a little inspiration," he said as he stood up. He walked over to one of the duffel bags and reached inside. He pulled out a piece of paper and unfolded it as he walked toward her. He put it down on the top of the typewriter so Marie could read it. "Look familiar? Now write a story around that," he commanded.

On the paper in front of her were the words from the unsigned fan letter she received a few weeks back, the one from the fan who was in love with her with the Detroit postmark. "It was you," she said with surprise.

"It was me," Morty admitted with pride. Then he unzipped his pants. Out came his penis in all its totality. He began stroking it. "Just imagine having this to play with," he said as it began to grow stiff.

She tried to look straight ahead. But he noticed that she wasn't watching, and it angered him. He got closer to her, grabbed the back of her head, and turned it so that his groin was inches from her face. "Look, bitch," he said as he continued stroking his member with his other hand. She had no choice but to take in the ghastly panorama. "Put your hands on it. Grab it," he ordered.

Reluctantly, she grasped the huge manhood and noticed that it pleasured him. He closed his eyes and leaned his head back, enjoying the feeling, but he still held the grip on her hair. "Jerk it," he commanded.

She rubbed her hand up and down the mammoth penis as it got harder. He moaned and sank into the chair next to her. She was thankful when he let go of the back of her head. It was becoming sore from the repeated tight grabs.

After a few minutes, he abruptly backed away and walked over to the corner of the cabin, with his back to her. He continued to jerk himself off with one hand as he reached in his pocket with the other. He pulled out a tissue and ejaculated into it. He put his penis back into his pants and zipped them up. He threw the soiled tissue into the fire and walked back over to the table and sat next to Marie, as if nothing happened. The relief on his face was noticeable.

"Let me give you more inspiration, Sheila. Here are some ideas from my own experience." His mood had become calmer. Now he was relaxed and obliging, almost loving. "You know, you're not the only one who has hot, one-night stands," he said, sounding more at ease. "Maybe later we can act out some of the chapters of your book," he added, looking at her with a twisted smile and giving her a wink.

"He thinks the stories in the book are true," she thought to herself. It was beginning to make sense. Should she try to convince him that they weren't? That Jana was just a made up person? That she didn't write from experience? No, he was too unstable. It would be a waste of time, and it might make him mad again. At least now he was calm. She decided to just let it drop and play along with him. It would buy her some time. She smiled at him.

He looked encouraged and smiled back. He looked up in thought, trying to recall his experiences and tapped his index finger on his cheek. She could see he was relaxing. "Oh," he said with excitement. "I know. You'll love this.

"Once I was at a Nirvana concert, and it was real crowded and everything, you know? We were all pressed together real tight. All of a sudden I feel this tap, tap, tap on my ass. At first I thought it was just someone trying to get a better view, but then it kept up, so I knew someone was doing it on purpose."

He was jabbering like a schoolgirl talking to her friends. "So I turned around and came face-to-face with this guy. He was all grunged out, but he wasn't bad looking. So I says to him, 'Hey, man, you wanna stop tappin' my ass?' And he says, 'Maybe I don't want to. Maybe I like your ass and wanna do more than tap it.' So, I'm intrigued, ya know? The concert was almost over, and I didn't have nothing to do afterward, so I thought I'd play it out. So I reach around and grab this dude's ass and say, 'Wha'd ya have in mind?' So he says, 'Me and my girl are looking for a third in our ménage à trois. You interested?' I look over and see his girlfriend. She's pretty ugly, but she's got nice boobs." Morty looked at Marie's breasts. "Kind of like yours."

He paused for a moment, staring at her chest. He reached out and cupped her breast with his hand. Marie froze in terror but let him have his way. She could see through his pants that he was getting aroused. Thankfully, he shook himself back to reality after a moment of fondling.

"So, I went out to the parking lot with them, and they had this really cool van," he said. "The inside was all customized. It had a bed instead of seats. We smoked a joint and got naked. You can imagine what happened when they saw this baby." He grabbed his bulging crotch area and gave it a shake. "That girl took one look, latched on to it, and started sucking it like it was a Popsicle." A smile came to his face as he remembered the feeling, "M-m-m, she could really give a good blow job. Deep throated it all the way down to the stump. She even gagged on it a couple of times, but I kept pushing her down on it, and she kept going." He smiled sadistically and motioned down with his hand, as if pushing a head downward, and jerked his groin up and down a few times.

Marie was revolted but tried not to show it.

"All this time her boyfriend is fingering her from behind and jerkin' off. Then he starts fuckin' her real hard. She was really enjoying it; I could tell. So just before I blow my wad, she stops suckin' me off and jumps on my face, and the *guy* starts blowin' me. I figure, hey, go with it. So I start eatin' her pussy and shovin' my fingers in her ass. She's squealin' and squirming all over my face. Then the guy stops blowin' me, and she moves down and jumps on my cock and starts humpin' up and down on it."

He paused long enough to unzip his pants and pull out his already-hard dick. He started jerking it again and continued his story.

"Then this guy gets behind her and starts fuckin' her in the ass. So, she's going crazy, and before you know it, she comes like gangbusters and jumps off. Then this guy starts suckin' me off again, and the girl starts suckin' him off. I come in this dude's mouth at the same time he's comin' in hers. Aw, man, it was so cool."

Morty's penis had gown gigantic with his constant fondling. "Hold on a minute," he said as he closed his eyes and jerked himself even harder. His face contorted. He threw his head back and arched his back. He reached for the roll of paper towels on the table and pulled a sheet off. He ejaculated into it as he moaned loudly. For a moment, Marie thought she was going to heave up breakfast, but she managed to keep it down.

He threw the paper towel in the fireplace, and it burst into flame. He looked at her for approval of his story, totally ignoring his sexual display. "So, what do you think? You think you could use that in your new book? You know, like you meet me and we share sex stories together." He was smiling like a child.

She faked a smile and said, "That was a good one all right. It's got possibilities."

He looked pleased with himself. "I knew it," he said. "I've got a lot more stories, too, better ones than that. I like to use toys, and believe me, it can get pretty kinky."

Marie swallowed hard and drew a deep breath. "I'm sure it can," she said reassuringly.

"So let's get started. Start like you do all the others. Describe what Jana puts on after coming out of the shower. Make her wear a white lace bra and panties. I want her to look like a virgin bride the first time I take her."

He knew her stories. All of the chapters of *Dirty Stories of a Rich Girl* began with the main character, Jana, coming out of the shower to get ready for her day's, or night's, outing. They described the color, look, and feel of her lingerie.

"OK," she said quickly, hoping to buy some time and avoid another mood swing and violent outburst. Next time he might want her to do more than just touch it. "Give me a minute to think about it."

He seemed pleased now. He sat back and watched patiently, like a child watching cookies bake in the oven. He looked at her and smiled. "Sheila is accepting her situation now. She's coming around," he thought to himself. "She's much more pliable this morning. I knew she just needed some time." His plan just might work. It had to. He loved her and couldn't bear the thought of living without her.

After what she thought was the longest period of time she dared take, she began to type, very slowly. Her wrists still hurt, and she was unaccustomed to the unforgiving nature of the typewriter. She quickly made errors and had to pause to white them out. Manual typing was clumsy and awkward. She missed the edit features of a computer.

She had gently and politely convinced him that it made her nervous to have him watch over her shoulder while she typed. He consented to sit by the fire while she typed. She was commanded to give him a page at a time as she finished.

She wrote the first paragraphs and handed the paper over to him for review. He approved and told her to write more.

The rest of the morning passed slowly. Sometimes he approved of what she had written. But more times than not, he rejected it. When he disliked it, he would curse and loudly reprimand her for not following his instructions. Sometimes he would grab her by the back of the head and order her to hold his penis for "inspiration."

His violent, extreme mood changes frightened her, exploding at the slightest mistake. His disapproving slaps stung her face. Then, in an instant, he would be applying a cool cloth to her cheek to ease the pain and apologizing for having to do what he had done. He said it was her choice. For more "inspiration," he told her more of his perverted sexual exploits, both with women and men. She cringed at every word. At least when he was talking, he wasn't hitting her.

"Morning, Dad," Duke called as he arrived at the jobsite.

"Morning, Son," Wil replied cheerfully. "Did Marie get in OK yesterday?"

"Yeah, right on time."

"Did she say anything about me?" Wil asked with childlike innocence.

"Yes, Dad," Duke said. "She wanted to know how you were."

"Did she say anything about me coming over tonight?"

"She said she was excited to see you."

"She is?" Wil said with shy pride.

"Of course she is, Dad," Duke explained. "This thing between the two of you has got her all tore up. I think she's as miserable without you as you are without her."

"Do you really think so?" Wil was looking for assurance. This love business still made him feel uneasy.

"I know so," Duke said confidently. "You just better behave yourself tonight."

Wil shook his head in acknowledgement. "Don't you worry, boy. I ain't about to let her slip through my hands again. How did she look this morning?"

"I think she was still sleeping when I left. Her curtains were drawn, and I didn't want to disturb her; I figured she needed the rest."

"Probably right," Wil said, disappointed.

The two worked side by side all day, making jokes and laughing together. Duke was glad of his dad's noticeable mood change. Since the fight with Marie, he had been almost impossible to work with. At about four o'clock, Wil announced that it was time to call it a day. The weather outside had turned from a light, steady rain to a torrential downpour. Loud claps of thunder rumbled the ground and buildings at regular intervals.

"You gonna be around for supper at Marie's?" Wil asked. "Should I get you some Chinese?"

"No thanks, Dad," the boy replied. "You two need some alone time. I told Amber I'd spend the night with her. She's making dinner. I'm going straight there from here. I've been keeping some clothes over there, so I wasn't even planning on going to Marie's after work."

"Sounds good. I'll see ya in the morning. I'm gonna stop and get the food and head home to clean up. Drive careful, Son," Wil said in a paternal tone, patting his son on the shoulder.

"I will, Dad," said the obedient boy. "Don't forget to change your underwear," he joked.

"Thanks for the reminder," Wil answered back. They laughed and went their respective ways.

Wil placed the Chinese food in the refrigerator to keep until he was ready to leave. He had gotten her favorite, mu shu vegetable with plenty of hoisin sauce and a side order of crab Rangoon. He preferred his food hot and spicy and got Szechwan beef with a couple of egg rolls for himself. Marie loved egg rolls, but these had pork in them. He got a small order of vegetable fried rice for the two of them to split. He had also bought her a bouquet of flowers. He thought about the last time he bought her flowers. It was the time she told him about the book. She had left them in the truck, and he'd crushed them in anger. It seemed so long ago, so much time wasted. He intended to make up for it tonight.

He showered, shaved, and put on the Old Spice aftershave that she liked so much. He put on his clean clothes. His hat needed brushing off, and his boots needed polishing, but he was in too much of a hurry to see his honey. Besides, as hard as it was raining outside, his hat was just gonna get wet and his boots muddy. He wondered why he was fussing so much with his clothes. Hell, he hoped they both would be naked soon after dinner. He sure missed that gal. He missed her beautiful, long, dark hair and her striking face, with her dark eyes and long lashes; her skin was so soft and smelled so good. He so wanted to kiss those full lips. And then there was that round ass and those fantastic titties. He thought about the last time he buried his face between her breasts. They were pillow soft and smelled like flowers. He felt himself getting hard and forced himself back to Earth. He was ready to go.

The rain fell on and off all day, and thunder roared across the sky, shaking the cabin to its foundations. Morty was sure the road had completely washed out and was equally as certain that even if they knew where to look, they could not pursue him until the road was clear and dry.

Marie found it nearly impossible to write the more explicit parts of the chapters as Morty described them. She felt self-conscious writing such graphic sexual details in front of someone she found so grotesque. There was nothing sexually attractive about him at all; in fact, he was quite the opposite. He repulsed her. Writing about the "magnificence" of his body and sexual prowess was surely a work of fiction.

"No, no, no, Sheila!" he cried emphatically after reading the new page he was handed. "That's not it at all. I'm getting sick and tired of having to tell you how to write. How did you ever complete the first book? I think you need incentive." With that, he unfastened his belt buckle and pulled his belt out through the loops. "I'm going to punish you every time you have to write it over."

A distant childhood memory surfaced. He could almost feel the hot, searing sting of the paddle on his naked ass—punishment from the nuns at the boarding school. He was paddled for the smallest transgressions. After a while, he began to like it. He was proud of the way he handled the pain. It actually got him off. He thanked the nuns for whetting his appetite for the kinky side of sexuality. He liked to think the nuns got hot and horny when they paddled him, too. After all, they had always made him take his pants down before punishment was administered, and sometimes he'd caught them staring at his huge dick. He smirked at the memory then focused his attention to the task at hand.

The belt was thick black leather. He folded it over in half and snapped it several times to make his point.

Fear crept up Marie's backbone like a river of ice water. She wanted to cry but knew it would have no affect on him. His eyes were dark and sinister, his smile foreboding. He was in a state of insanity that was all consuming.

He slapped the belt down on the table next to her with such force it made her jump. "Now," he commanded. "Rewrite it. This time put in more detail about how attracted Jana is to me. Write about how she noticed the huge bulge in my pants, and it made her hungry for it."

She could do nothing but comply and pray to God that it was what he wanted. By midafternoon, she was exhausted, and her mind was a fuzzy conglomeration of fear and fatigue. The constant smell of cigarettes made her light-headed and nauseous. By now the floor was littered with cigarette butts. She was hungry and tired. She begged him for something to eat. That was when she had her first taste of his black leather strap.

"I can't write anymore," she insisted. "I'm hungry, and I need a break."

Whack! The strap made contact, sending waves of pain across her shoulder and back. She cried out in pain.

"Eat?" he cried incredulously. "You think you deserve to eat? I'll tell you when it's time to eat or take a break. And this ain't the time. All you've handed me is shit." His eyes narrowed. Cruelty oozed out with every word. He had become impatient with her and was reaching a boiling point.

She could see she was talking to deaf ears. She worked diligently for the rest of the afternoon, trying to pacify him with explicit descriptions of sex between Jana and him. Sometimes he seemed pleased, even going so far as to pull out his penis and stoke it as he read. At one point, when she was handing a new sheet of the story to him, she was able to see his watch and noticed that it was six o'clock.

She was hoping against hope that Wil was discovering her absence at this very moment and that he would somehow be able to figure out what happened to her. But the rain had become steady again, and the severity of the storm was washing away her hopes of being rescued, like the rain rinsing the dirt off the windows of the cabin. Morty caught her in her daydream of lost hope.

Whack! Again, the belt hit its mark. He had turned mean again. All kindness had vanished. He gave her no mercy. "Pay attention!" he screamed at her. "Don't be thinking you're gonna get rescued. No one could make it up that mountain tonight. That's providing they know you're gone, and even then, how are those country bumpkins going to figure out where you are?"

But in her heart, she held on to the hope that somehow Wil would find a way. That was what made him different. That was why she loved him. Keeping that thought in her mind, she found the strength to continue.

Wil arrived at Marie's house exactly at six o'clock. He thought it was strange that the curtains were drawn. Duke said they were drawn this morning, too. The hairs on the back of his neck stood up, and he got an uneasy feeling. Marie did not come out to greet him as she had always done before. Did she forget? Should he have called before he came out? He knocked on the door. No answer. He peeked in the garage and saw her car. She had to be home. Maybe she was running late and was in the shower. He knocked again, harder. Still no answer. He decided to let himself in with his key.

He walked around the empty house, calling her name. He noticed several lights were on, and so was the power on the CD player. That wasn't like Marie. Being on alternative energy, she was very consciousence of energy consumption, even going so far as to buy all battery or windup clocks so that it reduced her need for power.

He walked into the bedroom. The bed, though still made, looked as though it had been laid upon. He called out for her again.

No answer. This was totally out of character for her. Something inside him said trouble.

He walked back into the dining room and noticed the pepper spray on the table. Had something frightened her? Was she in danger? He was getting a tense feeling in his gut. He walked back out to his truck and got his rain gear on and grabbed the gun out of the glove box. Where could she be? Maybe she decided to walk the creek. She could be out there, unable to move, helpless.

He walked the creek until it started to get dark. Finding no sign of her, he headed back to the house.

A myriad of thoughts flashed through his mind. He remembered the demonstrations against her he had seen on CNN. Could it be that some of those religious nuts tracked her down? He walked around the outside of the house, looking for signs. The rain had washed away most of anything that could have been there. But by Marie's bedroom window, he hit pay dirt. There he found what looked like the footprints of someone that had lingered long at the window. And then he found the most important clue of all. He found a pile of cigarette butts. They were not domestic butts but the fancy, imported kind in dark brown paper. Could it be?

He had only seen one person smoke that kind of cigarette lately—that strange fella who paid extra for the off-season adventure trip. What was his name? Oh, yeah, Mortimer Jablonski. Wil had detested him from the minute he laid eyes on him. But the extra five hundred bucks was badly needed. And at that time, Wil was looking for any excuse to escape in the mountains for a while.

Wil had constantly had to tell him to quit throwing his butts into the woods. What was it that Marie always said? Smokers think the world is their ashtray. Besides the possibility of starting a forest fire, Wil considered it littering and a sacrilege against Mother Nature.

The guy didn't seem the nature type. In fact, he had insisted on spending a great deal of time at the old stopover cabin; he didn't seem too interested in riding deeper into the mountains. He'd kept asking weird questions, like did anyone ever come up there in the off-season? Could you drive a four-wheeler up the mountain road? How long would that stack of wood last? He'd even wanted to know if there were any shovels, axes, or guns up there. Wil thought nothing of it at the time. He'd thought the guy was just trying to make small talk. He'd tried to distance himself from the creep as much as possible. The guy was too weird. Now it all fit into place. How did this guy know Marie's secret identity?

Was this guy stupid enough to grab Marie and take her up to the cabin? She had been home for less than twenty-four hours. If he had her, he didn't have her for long. Wil walked around the barn for traces of tire tracks. Whoever had her had to have a vehicle. There they were. A high spot next to a tree behind the barn had prevented the rain from washing the tracks away. There were cigarette butts on the ground, brown paper, the same brand. The tire tracks were wide and heavily grooved, like the kind on a four-wheel drive. By the looks of the footprints, it looked like he either took something out or put something in the backseat—Marie.

My God, he had her! Wil was sure of it now. At first, all he could think of was what that creep would do to her. Then he turned angry. "I'll kill the son of a bitch if he hurts one hair on her head," he said out loud as he ran back into the house. He grabbed the phone and dialed Amber's house.

"Hello," a cheery voice said on the other end.

"Amber, it's Wil. I need to talk to Duke. It's an emergency." His heart was pounding, and he was beginning to sweat.

"Dad? What's up?" Duke was puzzled.

"Duke, when you came home this morning, were the curtains on Marie's house drawn?"

"Yeah," Duke replied, puzzled. "That's how I knew she was still sleeping. I told you that this morning. Why? What's the matter? Amber said it was an emergency."

"Marie's gone."

"What do you mean gone?"

"Gone as in kidnapped. And I know who took her."

Duke was at attention. He knew his dad was not an alarmist, and if Wil had surmised that she had met with foul play, you could bet it was true. He didn't question it. "I'm on my way."

"No," Wil said, stopping him short. "I want you to get the police. That asshole I took up in the mountains has got her. His name is Mortimer Jablonski. He's got her up at the stopover cabin."

"Wait for me at Marie's, Dad. I'll get the cops and meet you."

"Bullshit," Wil interrupted. "I'm not gonna stick around here waiting for a bunch of yahoo Keystone cops, so they can come up here and jerk off when that asshole has Marie."

"What are you gonna do, Dad?"

"The roads have got to be washed out with all this rain. No way can we get a vehicle up there. I'm gonna saddle up Pal and take the shortcut. The son of a bitch has a day start on me."

"Be careful, Dad."

Wil hung up the phone and ran out to the barn. He saddled up Pal and loaded him into the trailer.

When he got to the trailhead, he grabbed the .44 Magnum and ammo out of his glove box, unloaded Pal, and headed up the mountain.

The rain was coming down hard. It felt like needles on his face. It was pitch dark. Flashes of lightening gave glimpses of the trail ahead. But Pal and Wil had been on the trail more times than they could count. They knew the way.

"Don't worry, darlin'. I'm comin' to get ya," Wil said out loud

CHAPTER TWENTY-TWO

—⁓—

BY NINE O'CLOCK THE RAIN HAD STOPPED, BUT the wind was blowing. Marie was a weary lump of pain. Nothing she wrote pleased Morty anymore. He had beaten her repeatedly with the belt. She could tell that her back was bleeding. Her blouse was sticky with blood. Her ankles and wrists were swollen and bruised from the previous binding. Even if she were to be freed, she felt too weak to walk.

She handed him another sheet of paper. He looked displeased, and again she felt the burning pain. She began to cry and crumpled to a heap on the floor. She covered her head with her hands for protection, anticipating the beating would continue, but it didn't. After a minute, she looked up. She saw him standing statue still, with his hands in prayer position and eyes closed. He appeared cool and calm. Another minute went by. Suddenly, he opened his eyes and looked straight at her with an ice-cold stare. All emotion drained from his face.

"I guess my prayers to God have gone unanswered," he suggested. "I was afraid of this."

"Afraid of what?" she thought. "What is he going to do?"

"I can see this isn't going to work. Your heart isn't in it. You are too obstinate. You're just like *she* was," he said. He took some granola bars out of a sack and threw them at her. "Eat," he commanded.

"She?" Marie thought. "Who is she?" Marie could tell he was planning something, and she could put money down that it wouldn't be good for her. Whoever "she" was, Marie wanted to find out what happened to her. She grabbed the bars and began to eat them slowly, hoping it would buy her some time.

"Who is the 'she' you mentioned?" Marie sheepishly asked between bites.

He became attentive. "*She* was Linda Grimmes, my first love. I'd have married her by now if those nuns hadn't butted in."

Marie saw her chance to stall for time. "Tell me about her, Morty. It seems like you cared a great deal for her. Tell me what happened."

His eyes narrowed, and he looked at her strangely. "I don't want to talk about her. It has nothing to do with you."

Whoever she was, she was obviously a sore subject. Maybe it was best to let it drop. He remained silent for a minute or two. She could tell he was deep in thought. Suddenly he looked up at her.

"It's no good," he said. "I've tried to be patient with you. It's just no good. I tried to give you good ideas. But you just don't get it. Your passion has died. I can see now that this isn't going to work. You are obviously unworthy and that's why God didn't answer my prayers and make you love me. Well guess what? God has just sent me a new message. I must punish you severely, Sheila. And as totally devoted as I am to you, my first devotion is to God, and I must fulfill his will."

Marie wasn't quite sure what he was talking about but she was sure she didn't like the sound of it. He had that crazy look in his eyes again. His face was totally emotionless. "He's finally snapped," she thought, losing all hope.

He continued. "I thought I could show you that we belong together. We are kindred spirits, but you just refuse to see it. We could have had such a beautiful life together. I've done everything I can. It's up to God now. He will use me as the vehicle to make you pure, so that you are worthy of his grace and goodness in the after-life. I was a fool to think I could make you change. You are defiant and rebellious, Sheila. And you will pay for your wickedness." He was repeating words he had heard many times before from the nuns at school, just before a harsh beating. He had hated it when it was happening, but he knew he had deserved it. Just like Sheila deserved her fate. She didn't love him. Well, if he couldn't have her, no one could. She was no better than Linda Grimmes.

Thoughts of Linda came flooding into his mind. He'd thought *they* would always be together, too. They bonded when they got in trouble in the fifth grade. But after they were caught, her parents made her break it off with him, stupid people.

They were all stupid. But he fixed them. That summer he saw Linda at the corner store and asked her if she still loved him. She said she didn't. It hurt him deeply. But he knew different. Her parents made her say that. That was why he had needed to get her alone and explain it to her. He took her away with him into the woods. She didn't want to come, but he convinced her that he just wanted to talk. Once he got her out there, it was easy to tie her up and build a small lean-to out of fallen trees. He was sure that he could make her fall in love with him again, if he had enough time. But it didn't work. She kept trying to get away. She told him she hated him. He would have to take care of Sheila just like he did Linda.

"Two kids playing with matches," was what the authorities said after Linda's charred body was found in the burnt-down lean-to the next day. "A tragic accident." Morty had convinced them of that with the help of his parents. But his parents knew the real story. They knew he had kidnapped her, beat her, and raped her. But since his dad was a prominent oil executive, he was able to "convince" the police that it was just an accident.

That was when his parents made him start seeing psychiatrists and sent him to that horrible rehab center for the rest of the summer. Right after that, they sent him off to that damn Catholic, all-boys boarding school, where he was cruelly punished by those perverted nuns for even thinking about sex. But the older boys were amazed at the size of his cock and he delighted in showed them what possibilities his big dick had. He was able to indulge in the many pleasures of sex and became obsessed with it. It was easy to sneak out at night and find willing local girls to have sex with, and plenty of classmates who wanted it, too. After high school, his parents had told him that as long as he took his medication and didn't get into any more "trouble," they would give him a hefty allowance every month. He agreed to all of their terms, even the one that said he was not welcome in their home and to stay away.

Well, they would think this was an accident, too, maybe a lightning strike. There would be nothing left but ashes by the time they found her. No one knew that he was in Grants Pass. He paid cash for his airline ticket, and he had been very careful to lay low in town. This place was so remote that he would be back in Michigan before anyone knew what happened. He felt clearheaded and powerful. It was a good feeling.

The wind whipped tree branches against the cabin, punctuating the eerie atmosphere.

Marie was desperate and frenzied. "Morty, what are you going to do?"

"Silence, unclean one," he replied. "I am going to do his bidding."

Grabbing the roll of duct tape, he re-bound her wrists and ankles. Her winces of pain went unnoticed. Then he went about the cabin, furiously gathering up clothes, food, and supplies. He piled them up outside the door.

She saw a glimmer of hope. Maybe he was going to give it all up and take her back home. Then she noticed that he was only gathering his things.

She watched through the open door as he loaded up the Jeep. After completing his task, he walked back into the cabin holding a chain saw and set it down on the cabin floor.

"Morty, can't we talk about this?" She felt that she was pleading for her life.

He looked at her. His hallowed and saint-like look frightened her even more than his disciplinarian guise. He reminded her of a priest during Sunday mass, working on instinct as if being directed from some outer-body source. He calmly walked up to her and began stroking her hair.

"Quiet, my dear," he spoke in soft, wispy tones. "Soon you will see our Lord Jesus. You will be at peace."

Marie knew that he planned to kill her. This might be her last chance to save herself. She had no time to wait for Wil. Morty moved in close to her. So close she could smell his revolting cologne. Leaning over her, he kissed the top of her head. As he was straightening up, she twisted herself so that she faced him. Morty stood motionless watching. In a quick, swift motion she pulled her knees up to her chest and thrust them out as hard as she could. She hit Morty squarely in the chest. He dropped to the floor as he felt the wind get knocked out of him.

Quickly Marie leaned on top of him and tried to remove the hunting knife from his belt. The tape around her wrists dug into her skin as she struggled. She awkwardly flipped the leather cover open and grasped the knife handle.

Suddenly Morty regained his composure and grabbed her hard by the wrists. He threw her off of him. "Naughty, naughty," he said with an evil glare as he wagged his finger at her.

She had failed.

Morty stood up walked over to the door. He grabbed the chain saw and went outside. The buzz of the engine filled the still night air. Then there was the sound of chain against wood. He was cutting down the trees around the cabin. It was then she realized what he was doing. He was going to burn her out.

"Morty, Morty, please, don't do this!" But her cries fell on deaf ears.

Tree after tree came crashing down to the ground with a thud. He came back inside, eyes flaring like a madman. She was crying hysterically, begging him to stop.

He appeared at the door and looked straight at her. "Sheila," he said calmly. "You must trust me. I have been commanded by God to purify you." Then he went back outside. She could see that he had a five-gallon container of gasoline and was spilling it over the trees and splashing it against the cabin. Then there was the sound of combustion, and she could see the orange-and-gold flames encircling the cabin though the windows. Within a few minutes, the wooden fence around the cabin was engulfed in flames.

She was beginning to give up hope—hope of ever seeing Wil again, hope of ever fulfilling their love. Her life was over.

The storm seemed never ending, but Wil and Pal trudged ahead. Pelting sheets of rain cascaded down on the two crusaders. The thought of Marie in danger fueled Wil's resolve to save her. There was no doubt in his mind that Morty had taken her. And he was just as certain that he would find them at the cabin.

Pal bolted when a flash of lightning struck a tree about twenty feet in front of them. It came crashing down to the ground with a thud. Wil stroked the gelding gently and, in a soothing voice, assured him that everything was OK.

The wind made the rain gear ineffective. Wil was soaked to the bone and freezing. His fingers were numbed by their tight grip on the reins. Determination and love drove him on.

By the time they scaled the shortcut, the rain eased up, but the wind whipped its fury on the pair. Tree branches were snapping like toothpicks and falling around them. Wil and Pal stayed the course.

Once back on the old trail, he nudged Pal into a run. By his estimation, they should reach the cabin in about ten or fifteen minutes. Pal ran at full speed. He could hear the mighty beast breathing hard. The horse's eyes were wide, and his nostrils flared, partially from the strain of running, partially from fear. The horse could feel Wil's tension and the overabundance of adrenaline coursing through his veins. Pal was afraid, but he trusted Wil and blindly obeyed every command.

The rain was hardly more than a light, misty drizzle now. Suddenly, off in the distance, Wil detected a golden glow in the direction of the cabin. The wind carried with it a faint scent of smoke. Pal smelled it too, and it made him whinny.

"That crazy son of a bitch," Wil said out loud as he dug his heels into the horse's side, urging him forward even faster. "Come on, boy; time's running out." The flames were growing by the second.

At last, the cabin came into view. The back was engulfed in flames as was a circle of fallen trees around the perimeter's wooden fence. Pal was very nervous now, and Wil had a hard time getting him to move forward. Wil strained to focus on the ball of fire. He searched the grounds for signs of life. He saw the Jeep parked in front of the ring of fire. There he was, that bastard. He could see Morty moving about, admiring his handiwork. He appeared to be dancing and singing.

Wil veered Pal off the trail and found a clearing in the dense forest that was close to the Jeep, but still out of sight, and secured Pal to a tree. He whipped off the rain gear, grabbed a rope and his gun from his saddle, and worked his way to the cabin. He could hear Morty singing. It sounded like a church song. Marie was nowhere in sight, but he thought he heard her muffled voice crying out for help from within the cabin above the roar of the fire and surreal sounds of Morty's chants.

Using the trees and darkness for cover, he worked up close to Morty, checking the ammo and taking the safety off of the .44 Magnum as he walked. The blaze of the trees and cabin lighted the surrounding area, giving it a flickering, ghoulish golden hue. Marie's desperate cries had stopped. Wil stepped into clear view of Morty and shouted. "All right, you piece of shit, turn around!"

Morty jumped in surprise at the sound of a voice. He turned to face Wil and the barrel of the .44. He grinned. "Well, if it isn't Grizzly Adams. Out for an evening stroll?" He seemed undaunted by Wil's sudden appearance.

"What have you done to her?" Wil demanded.

"Done to who?" Morty spoke in complete denial. "I don't know what you're talking about. Just built a little bonfire."

"Marie!" Wil called out toward the cabin.

"What is she to you?" Morty asked, puzzled.

"None of your damn business," Wil replied. "Turn around, and put your hands behind your back." He knew he had to immobilize Morty if he intended to rescue Marie. The blaze was growing bigger and hotter. Wil could feel the heat through his cold, wet clothes. "Marie," he called out again. No answer.

Morty did what he was told without resisting, and Wil quickly tied his hands together with the rope. He secured him to the bumper of the car. "I'll deal with you later, asshole," he promised, sending

Morty a right cross that knocked him to the ground. Morty was motionless. "You just better pray she's still alive," Wil said under his breath.

Wil looked at the Jeep and saw that it was packed with camping supplies. He quickly grabbed a blanket and ran down to the creek to soak it.

He ran up the bank of the creek and attempted to pass through the wall of fire. It was no use. It was too hot, and he couldn't make it over the fallen trees. He needed Pal.

Dropping the blanket, he ran to where Pal was tethered. The horse was prancing nervously. Wil stroked him gently. "Easy boy. We got a job to do." He took a bandanna out of his saddlebag and soaked it with rain from a nearby puddle. He untied Pal and edged him toward the cabin. Pal moved with hesitation but obeyed. Wil stopped and tried to cover Pal's eyes with the soaked bandanna.

Giving his full attention to Marie's rescue, Wil hadn't noticed that Morty had come to and managed to cut the ties of rope with his pocketknife.

Wil was surveying the cabin, trying to figure out the best place to cross. Suddenly, he felt a rope around his neck, and he was being pulled back. He instinctively grabbed at the rope and worked his fingers underneath before it was tightened. "Who's the asshole now?" he heard Morty say.

Morty tightened his grip on Wil's neck. Wil could feel the barrel of a gun jabbing in his side. Pal reared up and bolted away, giving Wil the moment of distraction he needed. With one swift movement, he bent forward, sending Morty over his shoulder.

Morty landed on the ground with a thud. The gun flew off into the woods. Morty stood up quickly and turned to Wil. The two were now face-to-face.

Wil pulled out the .44 from his pants and held it on Morty. Morty's face was already bruising where Wil had punched him. His lip and nose were swollen and bleeding. With the fire behind him, he looked like Satan himself. Morty glanced over toward the woods, where Marie's gun lay, the firelight reflecting off the barrel.

"Go for it, motherfucker," Wil said. "I dare ya."

On the other side of the cabin, a burning tree fell to the ground with a deafening thud. Both men looked in the direction of the noise. Morty took advantage of the moment and leaped toward the gun. He grabbed it and pointed it at Wil. The sound of gunfire filled the air. Morty looked down to see blood gushing out of his chest as he crumpled to the ground.

"You're the asshole," Wil said.

Wil picked up the wet bandanna and succeeded in placing it around Pal's face to cover his eyes. He picked up the wet blanket and mounted his horse. Wrapping the blanket around as cover, he chose a spot to cross and led Pal to it. He gave Pal a kick toward the cabin. The horse charged blindly ahead. When they approached the fallen trees, Wil gave Pal the command to jump. Pal obeyed and jumped with a whine of protest. Keeping the bandanna over the horse's eyes, Wil tied him tightly to the front door. He rushed inside to see Marie lying on the floor near the center pole of the cabin.

"Marie," he called out as he rushed toward her. He took out his knife from his belt and began to cut away at the tape that bound her hands and feet. He could see that she had been beaten, and it tore at his heart. She lay there, motionless. He put his head to her chest and listened for a heartbeat. It was there. She was alive.

It was then he noticed that she was wearing a harness that was chained to the pole. He tried to pull the lock off to no avail. Using his knife again, he cut away at the leather straps. There was a loud crash as another tree fell. This time it landed on the roof. Pieces of the ceiling fell to the floor, exposing the flaming tree. Pal sounded his protest at the front door.

Marie began to regain consciousness. "Marie," Wil said. "Marie, it's Wil."

"Wil," she cried weakly. "Is it really you?"

"Thank God you're alive," he said as he cut the last piece of leather from her harness freeing her.

Marie let out a sigh and winced in pain.

"Let's get the hell out of here," he said as he picked up her frail body and carried her out the door. As they passed the threshold, the roof collapsed, engulfing the room in flames.

"Can you stand for a minute?" he asked as he set her on the ground and leaned her against Pal.

"I think so," she said and pulled herself upright. He tightened the bandanna around Pal's eyes. Then he gently lifted her up into the saddle, grabbed the wet blanket, and quickly mounted up behind Marie, wrapping the blanket around them.

Pulling tightly on the reins, he backed Pal up to give him a running start. Wil held tightly to Marie and gave the steed a swift kick in the side. Pal lurched toward the circle of fallen trees. The flames had grown higher now. Wil once again gave the jump command.

As if jumping through the looking glass, Pal carried his two riders over the trees and through the curtain of flames. Safely on the other side and out of danger, Wil brought Pal to a halt and dismounted. He removed the bandanna that had been covering Pal's eyes. He gently helped Marie down, held her in his arms, and kissed her passionately on the lips.

Setting her to rest against a tree, he returned to his trusted friend. Pal's eyes were wide with confusion; he was breathing heavily, and his nostrils were flaring. "Good boy, Pal," Wil said reassuringly. He cradled the horse's head in one arm and patted him on the neck with the other. Pal was calmer now; he could sense he was out of danger. Besides a little singed hair on his legs and underbelly, he seemed to have made it through with no injuries. "Thanks, Pal. You did it. I knew I could count on you." Pal seemed to understand and nuzzled his head into his master's shoulder.

Wil looked at Marie. His love for her was something he would never again deny. He had to tell her. He walked over to her and sat down. She looked up at him and smiled. He grabbed her by the hand and kissed it.

"I've been a fool, Marie," he said sincerely. "I love you. I don't ever want to lose you again. Will you marry me?"

Marie's heart jumped for joy. "My hero! Of course, I will. I love you, too," she answered.

Wil was overjoyed and embraced her. Marie winced with pain and he released his grip. "We've got to get you home," he said realizing that she needed medical attention. "Do you feel strong enough to ride down the mountain, or do you want to rest?"

She looked behind him at the blazing cabin, by now totally engulfed in flame, and said, "I want to go home."

CHAPTER TWENTY-THREE

—ᴍ—

By the time they got to the beginning of the shortcut, the rain had stopped and turned to fog. Wil dismounted and looked down the steep decline and then back at Marie. She was shaking uncontrollably. "She's going into shock," he thought to himself. He eased her out of the saddle and sat her on a log. She was weak and started sobbing. He retrieved his canteen, a flashlight, and his bedroll blanket from the saddlebag. He lit the flashlight and wedged it into a nearby tree branch, so it gave a soft brightness to the surrounding area. Her hands shook with fear and chill as he gave her the canteen. He cradled his hand around hers as he helped lift it to her lips. It was then that he could see how badly she had been beaten. Hatred for Morty rose like bile in his belly. She noticed the flush and revulsion in his face and looked down.

"I'm sorry," she said apologetically. "I must look a mess."

"No, no. It's not you. You look beautiful to me," he said as he lifted her chin with his hand and looked deep into her dark eyes. He smiled. "You look like an angel."

She shook her head and took another drink as he wrapped the blanket around her shoulders. She flinched in pain, and he noticed the blood on her torn blouse. Even in the dimness, he could see cuts on her back. He could only imagine the horror she must have gone though, and anger burned in his heart. He gently wrapped the blanket around her to warm her.

"You're safe now. I'm here," he whispered in her ear as he embraced her gently, trying hard not to cause any more pain.

"He whipped me," she said in a frail voice.

"I know," he said as he backed off. "I'm glad I killed the bastard."

She looked up at him with relief on her face. She had suspected as much after hearing the gunfire, but now she was sure of it. After a short time, she stopped shaking. She knew she was out of harm's way. The nightmare was over. Wil had come. He had rescued her. His presence and love warmed her.

Wil conducted a quick body check to make sure she had no broken bones. She didn't. How close he had come to losing her. He had missed her. He loved her with all his heart. He always would.

Tenderly, he cradled her chin in his hand and lifted her face to his. "I thought I lost you," he said.

"I thought I lost everything," she responded, looking deep into his eyes. "I prayed that you would find me." She broke down again and sobbed uncontrollably into Wil's shoulder.

"Hey, hey," he comforted. "It's all over. You're going to be fine."

She looked up. Tears had meshed with blood and dirt and streaked her face. He wiped them away gently with the back of his hand, though he felt helpless to ease her pain. She started to calm down and regain her strength.

She shivered from the cold, damp air. He knew he had to get her down the mountain and fast. "You think you're strong enough to go down the shortcut?" he asked. She nodded. He gently helped her back onto Pal then mounted up himself. He led Pal carefully down the narrow trail. But because of the foggy darkness and the steepness of the terrain, most of the time he ended up walking and leading the horse while Marie rode in the saddle. He stopped every so often to make sure she was still OK. It took about three hours to descend from the mountain.

Duke, the sheriff, and an EMS team greeted them about a mile up from the trailhead. It was nearly dawn. The rain had washed out the road, and it was pretty much impassable by vehicle. Just as Wil had feared, it had taken the law hours to mobilize and finally start their pursuit. Duke had filled them in on what happened. So when Wil told them he shot and killed Morty, no one was surprised. He told them the cabin was on fire. A call was put in to the Forest Service to let them know. Marie was rushed to the hospital.

As Wil had already surmised, although beaten, battered, and bruised pretty severely, she had no broken bones and no permanent damage, at least physically. She was treated for her minor injuries and smoke inhalation, and the doctor insisted that she be kept under observation until the next morning.

That evening the sheriff's department took a statement from both of them. It was hard for Marie to relive the experience as she described in graphic detail all that she had been through. It pained Wil to hear it, but he knew it was necessary and also part of the healing process.

She told them that Morty didn't have intercourse with her, but she had been forced to stroke his penis. Bile rose in Wil's throat as Marie told them about the horrific experience. He wished he could kill the bastard all over again. She also said that Morty had mentioned something about a girl named Linda Grimmes. She said she didn't know if was important, but the officer taking the statement said every little detail helped.

Wil's account of what happened was much more cut and dry. There was no question that killing Morty was self-defense.

Marie woke up with a terrible nightmare that first night. Reliving the incident with the sheriff brought everything back and widened mental wounds that had not had time to heal. Wil had camped out on a cot next to her and woke when he heard her scream and cry. She was drenched with sweat and pale as a ghost. He comforted her, hugged her, kissed her forehead, and told her she was safe and that he would never let anything like that happen to her again.

The doctors were satisfied with Marie's condition the next morning, and she was released from the hospital. She was more than ready to go home. As they pulled up next to the house, she noticed a large black cat on the porch. "Is that Spot?" she asked.

"I hope you don't mind," Wil said meekly. "I called Duke from the hospital. Me and Spot moved in today…at least for a couple of weeks until you get back on your feet."

She looked pleased. "I don't mind at all."

Wil helped her get inside and settled her on the recliner in the main room.

She looked around. It felt good to be home. Wil was staring at her, smiling.

"By the way," she said. "Did you really mean what you said back there by the cabin, or did you just blurt that out because you got caught up in the moment?" It was the first time either of them had spoken of the marriage proposal.

"What are you talking about?" he joked. She could see the twinkle in his eye. "I didn't get caught up in the moment. I don't know what you mean."

"Stop it," she chided. "You know very well you asked me to marry you."

"I did?" he said with spurious amazement.

"You most certainly did, and I accepted, in case you didn't hear me."

A huge smile came across his face, the smile that had stolen her heart. His eyes narrowed, and his face softened. She soaked in the view. "Oh, I heard you all right," he said as he reached over and grabbed her hand. He lifted it to his lips and kissed it gently. "And now I'm the luckiest man in the world."

"Then I guess the move is permanent," she said with conviction. "I always wanted a cat." They both laughed.

After making sure that she was OK, Wil decided it was time to lay down the law. He insisted that she cancel any travel plans she had for the next month. She would have to take a nap once a day, and there was to be no discussion about it. After a half hour of unsuccessful attempts to convince him that she was fine, Marie reluctantly agreed to his terms.

With that settled, Wil insisted she take her nap immediately. As much as she hated to admit it, the excitement of the past few days had finally caught up with her, and she found herself physically and mentally exhausted. She did not argue. He escorted her to her room, helped her change into a nightie, and tucked her into bed with a kiss on the forehead. By the time he checked to make sure the slider door was locked and pulled the shades, she was sleeping.

Marie woke suddenly when she felt another body lie on the bed next to her. She turned to see Charles smiling at her. Andy was sleeping next to him on the edge of the bed. She started to talk, and Charles quickly placed his finger across her lips to quiet her.

"I can't stay long," he whispered. He was looking directly into her eyes. She tried to reach out to him but found she couldn't move; she could only listen.

"Andy and I wanted to let you know how proud we are of you. Look what you have done," he said as his hand motioned to encompass her surroundings. "You did good. And you found a good man. He'll treat you well. We want you to be happy."

With that, he leaned forward and kissed her gently on the lips. She felt the pressure of his lips on hers. He pulled back, turned to Andy, and cradled him in his arms. Charles turned to face her once more. "Today is the day, Marie. Remember your promise." She tried to reach out, but their images faded before she could raise her arms.

She thought about the promise, the promise to stop crying for her two lost loves. Then she remembered what Charles had just said about Wil. He said Wil was a good man and that he would treat her right. A liberating feeling came over her, as if a heavy weight had vanished, and she was glowing with happiness. She lay back down on her bed, closed her eyes, and surrendered to the exhilarating pulses surging through her body.

The next time she opened her eyes, it was almost five in the evening. She had been sleeping for four hours. She felt refreshed and alive. She thought about her dream. Was it a dream? It didn't feel like one. Whatever it was, she knew it was really Charles and Andy. She could not deny the new, joyous feeling she had. She intended to keep her promise to Charles. This time it wouldn't be hard.

During her recovery, Wil doted on her, preparing food for her, helping her shower and dress, and insisting that she take her daily nap. She was not used to being treated so specially, but in her condition, she was grateful for it. She rather enjoyed seeing Wil flit around like a mother hen at her beck 'n call.

It was pure torture for him to sleep next to her and not reach over and take her. He was hungry for her but was waiting for her to give him the go-ahead. All he could do was watch her. "Sex can wait," he had said to himself. She needed time to heal.

A few days later, they received a call from the Josephine County Sheriff's Office.

Wil answered the phone.

"Your lady is lucky to be alive," the officer said on the other end.

"I know that," Wil said impatiently. "Tell me something I don't know."

"Well, for starters, Mortimer Jablonski came from a very wealthy Texas family. Seems his daddy is some powerful oilman.

He's wasn't very happy about you killing his boy. He wanted to have you arrested. When we told him why you killed him, he changed his tune. Especially after we told him what we knew about a Miss Linda Grimmes. Seems this isn't the first time Morty has had trouble with women and fire. When he was a teenager, he and Miss Grimmes were playing in the woods, and she died when a lean-to she and Morty had built caught on fire. Official records say it was an accident, but we were able to find out that young Morty had beaten, raped, and killed the girl before he set her and the lean-to on fire—all because she didn't love him.

"Daddy paid a lot of money to keep it quiet. He also used his influence to have his son committed for a summer at some country-club rehab clinic and then sent him off to boarding school, so he could wash his hands him. Psychiatrist put the kid on medication and declared him healthy. Michigan State Police questioned some of Mortimer's friends in Michigan, and it appears that Mortimer has been off of his meds for quite some time now. Actually, ever since he read Miss Trousdale's book, probably explains his bizarre behavior. He told his friends he had been 'reborn and healed.'

"Needless to say, his daddy is trying to keep this off the front page as well. You notice you don't see much about it on the news anymore."

Wil thought about it. The guy was right; the day after it was everywhere, now nothing. It was just as well. He didn't want that kind of attention for Marie anyway. It was bad enough everyone knew who Sheila Exotica was now.

The officer continued. "We've got everything we need from you and Miss Trousdale. We just thought you might want to know what we found out. Did you have any questions?"

"No," Wil answered. "That answers a lot of questions. The guy was crazy." He was still trying to take it all in. "Thanks."

After about two weeks, Marie's bruises had all but faded, and her back had healed nicely. Wil's gentle snoring woke her. She looked at the clock; it was five thirty in the morning, and she had to pee. Trying not to waken him, she gently eased out of bed and into the bathroom. When she came back, he was awake and propped up on his elbows. He watched her as she crawled back in bed. "Are you OK?" he asked. "Can I get you something?"

She told him that she had decided she felt good enough to do things for herself now. The look of relief on Wil's face was priceless when she told him she could resume her duties as chief cook and bottle washer. He laughed and said that was good, because he wasn't cut out for that type of work.

"Don't sell yourself short," she teased. "You did a great job. Look at me; I'm healed and healthy thanks to you."

He blushed. "Shucks ma'am, 't weren't nothin'."

"Well, I think it's something special, and I think I need to give you a proper thanking."

Excitement flashed across his face. He was speechless with anticipation.

She delighted in the sudden change that came over him. She could feel his excitement beginning to rise. "I'm awfully dirty this morning," she said seductively. "Do you think you could help me in the shower one more time?" She could see his pajama pants beginning to rise under his waistband.

"You mean like dirty dirty or nasty dirty?" he asked.

"What do *you* think?" she taunted.

"I'm voting for nasty." He laughed and jumped out of bed. He quickly went over to her side of the bed, scooped her up in his arms, and carried her into the bathroom. He set her down and pulled the flimsy nightgown over her head, revealing her naked body. "At last," he said as he came close. He embraced her and pressed his lips to hers, his hard manhood pushing against her leg.

She pushed him away. "Not yet," she teased as she leaned over and turned the shower on. The shower stall was huge and had two shower heads. She felt the water, and when it was just the right temperature on both sides, she stepped in, closed her eyes, and let the water drench her as she sensuously fondled her breasts and body. Wil stood on the outside of the stall, staring like a love-struck puppy. She opened her eyes, looked deep into his dark eyes, and said, "Now."

With one quick motion, he stripped off his pants and was in the shower, holding her close again. This time when he kissed her, she kissed back, hard and openmouthed. She found his tongue and gently sucked it while running her hands through his wet hair. Euphoric sensations coursed through her as he tenderly made a trail of kisses from her mouth down to her luscious bosoms. He cupped them in his hands and buried his face into their ample, soft mounds. He stopped long enough to look up at her and say, "I love these titties."

"I know you do," she said with a laugh as she pushed him back down on them. After letting Wil have his way with her breasts for a while, she slid down onto her knees and took his now-throbbing manhood into her mouth.

Wil leaned back against the side of the shower and let out a groan; the coolness of the tile against his back contrasted with the heat of their mounting love. He clasped the back of her head with his hands and relinquished control to her. She covered her teeth with her lips and engulfed his long, hard rod again and again with her mouth, flicking her tongue on the end with every repetition. She reached under and cupped him, gently squeezing. The sensation was awesome, and she could tell he was enjoying it, too.

Tenderly, Wil guided her up by her hands and turned her to face the shower wall. He spread her hands apart and held them in place against the shower wall as he pressed up against her from behind and felt the heat of her body next to his. He spread her legs apart as he moved in between them. The shower water pelted them from both sides, trying unsuccessfully to temper their passion. He buried his head in her neck and kissed it lovingly. Slowly, he eased his hard shaft into her. She pushed her firm, round tush out to him, encouraging him to thrust deeper. Willingly, she accepted all of him and met his drives with blissful eagerness. As the room filled with steam, so did the fervor of their lovemaking.

Marie felt the fireworks building inside. It had been too long. She had hungered for his touch, all of him. He was everything she could ever want in a lover, attentive and skilled. She only hoped she met his expectations as well. Her climax burst forth in a flash of crazed delight. Her body contorted with pleasure. Her insides pulsated on his member as the orgasm raced through her body. The feel of her was enough to open the gates of his heated passion, and his orgasm came forth with raging fury.

The two of them stood motionless, spent and satisfied, with shower water raining down on them. He turned her around, cradled her in his arms, and kissed her softly on the lips. "I love you," he said.

"I love you, too," she responded.

CHAPTER TWENTY-FOUR

—ɯ—

Before long, Duke moved back into Wil's house and asked Amber to move in with him. The living quarters in the barn had now become the guesthouse.

The publicity from the incident with Morty spiked Marie's book sales through the roof. A whole new flood of TV interviews and book signings had been requested and scheduled. The book publishers couldn't be more thrilled.

Wil was a little less enthusiastic. He was contracted to build a couple more homes, so he couldn't travel with Marie. He was afraid of copycat weirdos and insisted on hiring two personal bodyguards for her for when she traveled. He made it clear to the two six-foot-plus hulks they hired that they were not to leave her side for one minute, or they would have to deal with him personally. He reminded them what had happened to the last dude who tried to mess with his woman.

Marie thought he was going a bit overboard, but Wil was dead serious. Secretly, it gave her a warm feeling, knowing that he cared that much for her.

After a couple of months, things settled down, and Marie's travel schedule had all but ceased to exist. Frick and Frack, as Wil like to call them, had been let go. Marie's safety was now solely in Wil's hands. Except for the income the book brought in, she was glad the big hoopla had died down. She was able to spend more time with Wil and get caught up on other matters, like their impending marriage.

They decided to fly Marie's parents and Maddy's family to Oregon and have a quiet ceremony at the house. The official wedding was just a formality. It was going to be very low-key. They were already committed, heart and soul, for eternity to each other. The ordeal with Morty had sealed their hearts as one. They decided to get married Thanksgiving weekend. That way it wasn't too hot, and the changing colors of the leaves would add extra romantic ambiance.

Marie decided to call Madelyn and let her know they had set the date.

"Hello."

"Maddy, it's Marie."

"Marie, are you all right?" Her sister was still reeling from the kidnapping and sounded concerned.

"I'm fine. Wil's been taking good care of me." She looked over at Wil and smiled.

"Thank God." Her sister sounded more relaxed. "What's up?"

"What are you doing for Thanksgiving this year?" Marie asked.

Her sister was confused. "I don't know, why?"

"Would you like to have dinner with us and be my matron of honor?"

"Are you kidding?" Her sister was ecstatic. "You actually set the date?"

"Yeah," Marie said. "We want you, Jake, Justin, and Mom and Dad to come out. We're going to have the wedding here at my house. It'll give you a chance to see Oregon."

"Sounds wonderful," Maddy said, half sobbing on the phone. "I can't wait to tell the boys."

The two chatted happily, making plans. Wil saw that as his cue to leave the room. After about an hour, he came back in to check on Marie and saw that the two sisters were still yackin'. Marie looked over at Wil, who pointed to his watch impatiently.

"I better get off the phone," Marie said to her sister. "I'm getting the evil eye from Wil. I'm supposed to help him do some work outside with the horses, and he's ready to go."

"Oh, Marie," Madelyn interrupted. "I forgot to tell you."

"Tell me what?"

"They found Tommy."

"No kidding. Where?"

"They found him face down in the lake. Must have decided to go swimming that night he got drunk. He got tangled in the seaweed, and his body didn't surface until now."

"Wow," Marie said in disbelief. "What happens now?"

"Well, I spoke to Naomi. She said she never legally adopted the girls and didn't feel right raising them, since they really aren't her children, considering the circumstances. She said if I want them, she won't stand in the way of me adopting them."

"That was awfully maternal of her, now wasn't it?" Marie could not hide her disgust. There was a long pause. "Well?" Marie asked.

"They move in this week. So I guess your guest list just grew by two." The two laughed. "Oh, and one more thing."

Marie was aghast. "What else could there possibly be?"

"When they found Tommy, his penis was missing."